HARD AND FAST

erin mccarthy

BERKLEY SENSATION, NEW YORK

THE BERKLEY PUBLISHING GROUP
Published by the Penguin Group
Penguin Group (USA) Inc.
375 Hudson Street, New York, New York 10014, USA
Penguin Group (Canada), 90 Eglinton Avenue East, Suite 700, Toronto, Ontario M4P 2Y3, Canada
(a division of Pearson Penguin Canada Inc.)
Penguin Books Ltd., 80 Strand, London WC2R 0RL, England
Penguin Group Ireland, 25 St. Stephen's Green, Dublin 2, Ireland (a division of Penguin Books Ltd.)
Penguin Group (Australia), 250 Camberwell Road, Camberwell, Victoria 3124, Australia
(a division of Pearson Australia Group Pty. Ltd.)
Penguin Books India Pvt. Ltd., 11 Community Centre, Panchsheel Park, New Delhi—110 017, India
Penguin Group (NZ), 67 Apollo Drive, Rosedale, North Shore 0632, New Zealand
(a division of Pearson New Zealand Ltd.)
Penguin Books (South Africa) (Pty.) Ltd., 24 Sturdee Avenue, Rosebank, Johannesburg 2196,
South Africa

Penguin Books Ltd., Registered Offices: 80 Strand, London WC2R 0RL, England

This book is an original publication of The Berkley Publishing Group.

This is a work of fiction. Names, characters, places, and incidents either are the product of the author's imagination or are used fictitiously, and any resemblance to actual persons, living or dead, business establishments, events, or locales is entirely coincidental. The publisher does not have any control over and does not assume any responsibility for author or third-party websites or their content.

PRINTING HISTORY
Berkley Sensation trade paperback edition / May 2009

Library of Congress Cataloging-in-Publication Data

McCarthy, Erin.
    Hard and fast / Erin McCarthy.—Berkley Sensation trade pbk. ed.
        p. cm.
    ISBN 978-0-425-22847-0 (trade pbk.)
    1. Women sociology students—Fiction.   2. Stock car drivers—Fiction.   3. Stock car racing—Fiction.   I. Title.
    PS3613.C34575H37 2009
    813'.6—dc22

                                                                    2009000372

PRINTED IN THE UNITED STATES OF AMERICA

10   9   8   7   6   5   4

continued . . .

A DATE WITH THE OTHER SIDE

"Ghostly matchmakers add a fun flair to this warmhearted and delightful tale . . . An amusing and sexy charmer sure to bring a smile to your face."　　　　　　　　　　　　　*—Romantic Times*

"Offers readers quite a few chuckles, some face-fanning moments, and one heck of a love story. Surprises await those who expect a 'sophisticated city boy meets country girl' romance. Ms. McCarthy delivers much more."　　　　　　　*—A Romance Review*

"Fascinating."　　　　　　　　　　　　　　　*—Huntress Reviews*

PRAISE FOR THE OTHER NOVELS
OF ERIN McCARTHY

"Will have your toes curling and your pulse racing."　　*—Arabella*

"The sparks fly."　　　　　　　　　　　*—Publishers Weekly*

"Erin McCarthy writes this story with emotion and spirit, as well as humor."　　　　　　　　　　　*—Fallen Angel Reviews*

"Both naughty and nice . . . Sure to charm readers."　　*—Booklist*

Titles by Erin McCarthy

A DATE WITH THE OTHER SIDE
HEIRESS FOR HIRE
FLAT-OUT SEXY
HARD AND FAST

The Vegas Vampires Series

HIGH STAKES
BIT THE JACKPOT
BLED DRY
SUCKER BET

The Seven Deadly Sins Series

MY IMMORTAL
FALLEN

Anthologies

THE NAKED TRUTH
(with Donna Kauffman, Beverly Brandt, Alesia Holliday)

AN ENCHANTED SEASON
(with Maggie Shayne, Nalini Singh, and Jean Johnson)

THE POWER OF LOVE
(with Lori Foster, Toni Blake, Dianne Castell,
Karen Kelley, Rosemary Laurey, Janice Maynard,
LuAnn McLane, Lucy Monroe,
Patricia Sargeant, Kay Stockham, and J. C. Wilder)

FIRST BLOOD
(with Susan Sizemore, Chris Marie Green, and Meljean Brook)

*For all the wives of racing
and your true love stories*

ACKNOWLEDGMENTS

Special thanks to Rhonda Stapleton for suggesting Shakespeare, to Kathy Love for suggesting the name *Imogen*, and to Jamie Denton for suggesting I get out of my own way and just write the book. You all are the best.

CHAPTER
ONE

SLINGSHOT: A maneuver in racing where the car following the leader in a draft steals his good air and takes the lead.

How to Work It: Hang back if your man is interested in another woman. When she proves herself too obnoxious or clingy, move right on past her into the lead.

—From *How to Marry a Race Car Driver in Six Easy Steps*

"OH, my God, run!"

Imogen Wilson had her shoulder nearly dislocated from its socket when her friend Tamara yanked her arm, trying to drag her down the hallway. Stumbling to keep up with Tamara and their other friend Suzanne, Imogen glanced behind her to see why they needed to sprint, worried about a herd of angry race fans, a fire, or a sudden act of terrorism in the speedway.

What she saw was worse.

It was Nikki Borden. Twenty-two years old. Bouncy. Bubbly. Blond. Built like Barbie, thanks to Nikki's campaign of personal starvation and the assistance of breast implants and lip injections. She was definitely a beautiful girl by most male standards, and Imogen knew Nikki worked hard to maintain her appearance. Unfortunately, it seemed to be at the expense of nurturing her mind. The few times Imogen had tried to have a conversation with Nikki, she had been left wondering if there were residual effects of the excessive use of hair dye because there was a whole lot of nothing going on in that girl's head.

None of which would bother Imogen, per se, except that Nikki was dating Ty McCordle, the stock car driver Imogen had an inexplicable attraction to.

"Don't turn around," Tamara said to Imogen, horrified. "She'll see us!"

"Damn," Suzanne said. "Too late."

Nikki was waving to them with a big smile, and Imogen stifled a groan. She did not want to spend her time at the racetrack trying to make small talk with Nikki, and it was her fault they were going to have to do the polite. She should have just run and asked questions later, but that wasn't her personality. She always had to know what was going on, and it was highly likely her curiosity would be the death of her someday. Today it was going to result in fending insults from Nikki, who seemed to think it was her duty in the name of friendship to inform Imogen of all her physical flaws.

"Hi!" Nikki said, making record time over to them despite her high heels. "Where are you guys going? I'll go with you."

"We have passes to sit in the boxes," Suzanne said. "I'm sorry, I'm not sure we can get you into the restricted area."

Suzanne didn't look the least bit sorry, and Imogen almost felt bad for Nikki, who clearly was hanging around the track by herself. Imogen knew what it was like to always be the loner.

"Oh, I have a pass, too," Nikki said, pulling a piece of paper out of her giant purple handbag. She grinned. "I guess having sex with a race car driver ought to get you something, right?"

Ugh. Imogen had known that Nikki was having sex with

Ty—she had to be. It wasn't like Nikki was the kind of girl who could cook a man a meal, discuss politics or racing with him, or even be considered a candidate for bearing his future children. Nikki was a booty call, if Imogen understood the definition of the term correctly. But to know it and to hear it out loud were two different things entirely.

"I guess that I'd rather get an orgasm out of sex than a paper pass, but that's just me," Suzanne said.

Imogen had to concur with that. She would really like to have an orgasm at the hands of a race car driver. *A* race car driver. Ty. Sexy, laid-back, always wearing a grin Ty. Who was instead giving Nikki orgasms and track passes.

It was utterly futile to think she could ever attract the attention of a man like that, and she needed to remember that. Why she even wanted to severely mystified her, but there was something about his joie de vivre, the way he didn't take himself too seriously, that appealed to her. Or at least to the parts of her that resided below the waist.

"Well, let's go sit down," Tamara said. "We're going to miss half of the race and I have a certain rookie driver I need to cheer on."

Tamara was clearly antsy to see her husband Elec driving, already flashing her pass and making her way into the seating area of the boxes. Imogen followed her, wondering if her sunscreen was going to hold up for the duration of the race. She was dark haired and fair skinned, and the North Carolina sun was brutal. Looking around at the crowds, she realized that the straw hat she had brought to shield her face wasn't exactly de rigueur. Everyone else who had on a hat was wearing a ball cap, most advertising their favorite driver. Imogen was aware she wasn't dressed appropriately either. She was wearing a black sundress with a three-quarter-sleeve cardigan and sandals while the majority of the crowd was in shorts and T-shirts.

But considering it was her very first time to the track in Charlotte to watch a live stock car race, she hadn't known the protocol. She had been looking forward to it as a life experience and because she was still fishing around for a thesis project for her graduate degree in sociology. The culture of stock car racing in the South seemed like a great jumping-off point, but she needed to home in on a more specific topic.

Only she hadn't anticipated being stuck sitting next to Nikki. Suzanne had virtually vaulted over the row of seats to get the one farthest from Nikki, and Tamara had already taken the seat next to Suzanne. That left Imogen, then Nikki on the end, who was wiping the seat off with a tissue.

"I don't want to get my white pants dirty," she said in explanation when Imogen stared at her.

"Then why did you wear white pants?" Imogen couldn't help but ask.

"Because they make my butt look good," Nikki said, like this was completely obvious.

"Don't you have other pants that make your butt look good that won't attract dirt?"

Nikki smiled. "Yes. But with white pants you can't wear anything but a thong, and men love that."

Ah. Imogen didn't see the logic in that at all, because wouldn't men generally assume that a woman like Nikki was always wearing a thong? And if they were allowed to actually gain the knowledge of the thong for themselves, she suspected they wouldn't care one way or the other what Nikki had on over them. But there was no point in launching a further discussion with Nikki. Imogen suspected Nikki had made up her mind and that was that.

"Of course." Imogen settled into her own seat and looked out at the track. A pack of cars went whizzing by before she could blink, none of which were identifiable to her by either decal or number. She should have bought a program so she could attempt to educate herself.

Nikki was rustling around in her handbag and Imogen glanced over to see the blonde tearing into a bag of mixed greens. She pulled out a piece of spinach and popped it in her mouth like it was a potato chip.

"Want some?" Nikki held the bag out to Imogen.

Imogen shook her head. "No, thanks." She had zero interest in chewing on greens sans salad dressing. Watching her waistline was as important to her as the next person, but she wasn't about to sacrifice at least some kind of flavor for skinny jeans.

Not that Imogen was really the skinny jeans type. She had probably exited the womb wearing Ann Taylor coordinates. The clean lines and understated harmony of classic clothes made her happy, and she was fortunate to have inherited her mother's naturally thin figure. Of course, the flip side of that was a serious lack of breasts, but it was what it was and she had no interest in buying herself a larger cup size.

"Does that actually satisfy your hunger?" she asked Nikki curiously.

"No. But it keeps me from buying nachos." Nikki had balanced her salad bag in her lap and she was digging a notebook-sized book out of her bag.

"Is that a race program?" Imogen asked. She wanted to look up Tamara's husband Elec, and okay, she could admit it, Ty McCordle, so she could monitor their progress around the track.

"No, it's a book I'm reading."

Imogen gained a whole new respect for Nikki. She was reading at the racetrack. Clearly she was there to show support for her boyfriend, but had brought a book to occupy herself in the long hours alone as the cars did something like five hundred laps.

"Oh, what book is it? Fiction or nonfiction?"

Nikki frowned and pushed her sunglasses up. "I don't know. I can never remember which one means it's real and which one means it's fake."

Huh. "Fiction is a story; nonfiction is based on facts."

"Then I guess this is nonfiction. I think." Nikki held up the book for Imogen to see the cover.

The title was *How to Marry a Race Car Driver in Six Easy Steps*. On the cover was a photograph of a woman kissing a man in a racing uniform with a pair of wedding rings surrounding them.

"Wow, uh, I don't know if that is fiction or nonfiction either." Imogen wasn't sure if the book was intended to be tongue-in-cheek or if someone really thought there was a formula to garner a proposal from a driver. Or if the publisher and author didn't necessarily think so, but knew women like Nikki would buy the book to learn the secret. "What does it say?"

"There are all kinds of tips and rules, plus profiles of the single drivers."

"Are you serious?" That completely piqued the interest of the sociologist in Imogen.

"Yeah. And I broke Rule Seventeen of Step Two by accident. I wasn't supposed to wear high heels to the track, only I didn't read that part until after I was here." Nikki rolled the top of her lettuce bag closed and stuffed it back in her purse. "I hope Ty doesn't notice."

Considering the man was in a car on the track driving at approximately one hundred and eighty-five miles an hour and attempting to pass other cars going an equal speed with only inches of clearance, Imogen highly doubted Ty was concerning himself with Nikki's trackside footwear. "I'm sure it's fine. I don't really see why a driver would care what his girlfriend or wife wears at a race anyway."

Nikki looked horrified. "That kind of attitude will never land you a driver. It's all about image."

"Really?" Imogen glanced over at Tamara and Suzanne. They were both normal, attractive women in their early thirties. Tamara was married to a driver; Suzanne was divorced from a driver. Somehow Imogen doubted either one of them had followed a manual to land her husband. In fact, she would bet her trust fund on it. "Can I look at the book?" she asked.

Nikki clutched the book to her chest for a second, clearly suspicious.

"Don't worry," Imogen said. "I have no interest in following the steps. A stock car driver isn't really my type." Which she would do well to remember. Just because she had a strange and mysterious physical attraction to Ty didn't mean it was anything other than foolish to pursue that. A driver wasn't her type, and she knew beyond a shadow of a doubt she wasn't a driver's type. She was the total antithesis of Nikki.

"Okay." Nikki handed the book over begrudgingly.

Imogen almost laughed. It wasn't like what was in those pages wasn't available to anyone who had twenty bucks and a bookstore at their disposal. She opened the book, and it flipped automatically to the section on your first date with a driver. The "Don'ts for First Date Night" included drinking any alcohol, even a single glass of wine, an explanation of why beer-drinking women weren't at all the thing, and how while a chaste kiss at the door *might* be deemed acceptable, anything beyond that was wrong, wrong, wrong. Girls men wanted to marry did not, repeat did not, have sex with men on the first date.

Feeling like she just might have slid back into 1957 when she wasn't looking, Imogen flipped to a new chapter. It was a list of places to meet drivers, including the stores they might shop at in Charlotte, the bars and restaurants they were known to frequent, and the gym several worked out at.

The wheels in her head started to turn faster and faster as she scanned through half a dozen more pages.

"What are you looking at?" Tamara asked her, leaning toward Imogen to read over her shoulder.

Imogen looked at her friend and sociology professor in satisfaction. "My thesis. I'm looking at my thesis."

The book declared itself an instructional manual on how to marry a race car driver. Which led Imogen to the question that would be the basis of her thesis—did dating rules result in success when altered for a specific occupation?

Imogen was going to follow them and find out.

TY McCordle ducked out of Tammy and Elec's front door and quickly moved to the left on the porch, away from the view of the picture window. He desperately needed a bit of fresh air and a breather from Nikki's constant chattering. It was obvious to him that he had been dating Nikki way past the point of novelty. She got on his nerves just about every minute that he was with her, and had actually brought up the M word—*marriage*. Good God, the thought made him want to chew off his own foot to escape that trap. So he had reached the moment he hated in dating. He had to break things off with Nikki, and that was bound to result in a couple of things from her he had a hard time dealing with—tears and anger.

Truth was, he shouldn't have let things go on nearly as long as they had. He'd known from jump that she wasn't even remotely close to his type for a long-term relationship, but he had been lonely and bored and she had been more than willing to hop into bed with him. But after a time, not even her enthusiasm could make up for the fact that the sound of her voice made every muscle in his body tense with irritation, and now he was dodging her at a damn dinner party.

It was ridiculous, and it made him feel like a pansy-ass wimp. Yet he wasn't going back in there, was he? It was pouring down rain outside, a nice little fall thunderstorm, and the air was clear and crisp, the temperature still balmy. Ty loved the sound of the rain hitting the roof and the ground, and he leaned forward to feel the mist settle over his forearms and hands. Even if she figured out where he was, the rain would keep Nikki in the house. She wasn't big on nature or anything that might ruin her hair, her makeup, or her shoes.

So Ty was going to stand there on the porch and take a breather, then go back into the party, say his good-byes to his friends, collect Nikki, take her home, and break things off with her. In a minute. Or two.

A light appeared in the driveway and Ty glanced over to see what it was. A car door slammed shut and the light went back out. Through the rain Ty saw someone running toward the porch, hands over her head. A thin woman with dark hair and glasses pounded up the steps, then stopped when she achieved shelter, her arms falling to her sides, her breathing heavy.

It was the woman who was some kind of assistant to Tammy at the university, the one who had the name Ty couldn't remember or pronounce. He had seen her inside the house since there were only twenty or so people at the party, but he had avoided her. Something about her intrigued him, made him want to see if the shy and serious woman could open up and laugh, or better still, moan in pleasure, but at the same time, she made him feel stupid with her fancy education, expensive clothes, and complicated name.

At the moment he just felt sorry for her. She was taking deep breaths and almost wheezing, like the shock of having a boat-load full of rain dump on her had just caught up with her. Her hair was plastered to her cheeks and forehead, her jeans were wet clear to the knees, and her black sweater was molded to her chest. For some reason she reminded him of a puppy, startled and forlorn, and he no longer felt so intimidated by her.

"Are you okay?" he asked.

"It's raining harder than I thought," she said, pulling her clinging sweater forward off her stomach. "I think I should have waited a few more minutes. But I had to go put up my car windows, and I got trapped inside the car. I waited, and debated just leaving and going home, but not saying good-bye to anyone would be phenomenally rude, and the rain wasn't letting up, so I went for it. I think, it's safe to say, that was a miscalculation."

It was a hell of an explanation that Ty heard only half of because he was so distracted by the fact that her glasses were covered in rain spots. He liked to see a woman's eyes when he talked to her, and he was curious what color whatshername's were. He was also curious as to how he was going to ask her yet again what her name was without sounding like the total jack-ass that he was. Reaching out, he lifted her frames off her face.

She jerked back with a squeak. "What are you doing?" She

wiped the bridge of her nose dry then followed his hand to re-
trieve her glasses. "I need those."

"I'm drying them off. You can't possibly see anything with
them waterlogged." Ty used the bottom of his T-shirt to polish
them to his satisfaction.

"Oh, thank you."

He lifted them and guided them onto her nose.

"I can—"

Before she could finish her sentence, he had the glasses back
on, frames tucked over each ear.

"Do it myself," she said.

"Too late." He smiled and, using the tip of his pointer finger,
pushed them a little higher on her nose. "And now I know
they're blue."

"What?" Her head tilted slightly to the side. "What's blue?"

"Your eyes. I was wondering." Emma Jean or Imagine or
whatever the hell her name was had eyes that were unaltered by
makeup, and they were big and a deep, rich blue, like denim. She
smelled like rain and shampoo, her soft skin covered in a dewy
sheen. He was standing damn close to her, and he was aware that
he was very much attracted to her and his body knew it. That
was an erection popping out to greet her.

Fortunately, she was looking at his face, not his crotch, so
she didn't know the direction his thoughts were strolling in.

She had a slight frown on her face. "Why would you be wondering what color my eyes are?"

That was a damn good question. He chose not to answer it.
"You need a towel. You're dripping." And shivering.

"I don't want to go in there like this." She glanced at the
front door. "I'll track water all over the hardwood floors."

"I can go get you a towel," he said. Though he would have to dodge Nikki to do it, which might be difficult.

"I'll be fine," she said. "I should probably just go home and call Tamara and apologize."

"You're going to run back through the rain?" he said in disbelief. "I don't think so."

"It's slowed down," she insisted.

But when they looked out at the front yard and the driveway, the wind was whipping torrents of rain down at an angle. "Or not. It's a freaking monsoon out there. You won't have anything dry on you to even clear off your glasses when you get to your car. Can you see to drive without your glasses?"

"No." She sighed, staring toward her car with obvious longing.

"What's under your sweater?"

"Excuse me?" She turned so fast to stare at him that she bumped shoulders with him.

"If you're wearing a shirt underneath, it's probably dry. Just take your sweater off."

"I have a cami on," she said, biting her lip.

Ty didn't know what the hell a cami was, but it sounded promising. "Perfect."

She seemed to debate for a second, then she took off her glasses and handed them to him. "Hold these, please."

"Sure."

Then he didn't even try to look away when she peeled off her sweater to reveal a little white tank top, small breasts clinging to the fabric, her nipples taut. Yeah, he was just full of brilliant ideas. Nothing like telling the woman to strip off clothing when he was standing on his buddy's front porch in full view of a dinner party.

"That's better, right, Emma Jean?" he said as she dropped her sopping wet sweater over the top of the porch railing.

She held her hand out for her glasses and smiled at him. "You do know my name's not Emma Jean, don't you?"

He did know that. He just didn't know what her name really was. He suspected that, aside from the fact he had never heard that particular name prior to meeting her, it was his dyslexia making it difficult for him to retain her name. She had spelled it out loud for him on a previous occasion, but the letters had just jumbled in his head. Which pissed him off severely. But he would cover, make it look intentional. "Yep. But I think Emma Jean suits you."

Laughing, she put her glasses back on. "It does not. As much as I hate to admit it, I am much more of an Imogen than I am an Emma Jean."

Ty had almost caught it that time. The end sounded more like gin, like the alcohol. "Why do you say that?"

"Dark hair, glasses." She pointed to each as she listed them. "Flat chest. Shy. Definitely not an Emma Jean."

Maybe those very things were the reason he found her so fascinating, though after talking to her, he wouldn't call her shy. Quiet, but not shy. He gave her a smile, one that even as he did it, he knew was flirtatious. He shouldn't, not there, not with her, but he couldn't seem to stop himself. "You'll always be Emma Jean to me."

Imogen laughed. "I can't decide if that's a compliment or not."

"It is, but it's a subtle one. But now I'm going to give you an obvious compliment." Even as the words were coming out of his mouth, Ty was telling himself to shut up, to not go there with this woman who was so clearly out of his league, but he didn't listen.

Her eyes widened behind her glasses.

They were standing closer than was necessary for conversation, but Ty noticed neither one of them was backing off. He touched her cheek, amazed at how soft her skin was. "You're very beautiful. Not an original compliment, but it's still true." Ty ran his fingers across her lips. "Pretty women can start to look the same, but you stand out. Your beauty is unique."

Imogen started to think that Ty McCordle had consumed way too much alcohol at the party. He was staring at her like he wanted to eat her, piece by piece, or at the very least kiss her, and he was touching her. He was touching her and she was covered in goose bumps that arguably were from the rain soaking, but more likely were from a sudden surge in her hormone levels, since Ty was the very man that for months she had been fighting a physical attraction to. And now he was staring at her like he was actually attracted to her as well, which was unnerving.

She couldn't explain this turn in events. It couldn't really be possible that Ty was interested in her. More likely it was pure convenience. She was on the porch. So was he. He was a flirt, end of story.

Which didn't explain why he was suddenly stepping back and peeling off his T-shirt to reveal a washboard stomach and a chest that just screamed for her to explore. Oh. My. God. What the hell was he doing?

"What are you doing?" she asked, her voice a full octave higher than normal.

"Your hair is still dripping wet and I never went to get you a towel. Use my shirt."

That was thoughtful and weird, and a personal fantasy of Imogen's sprung to life. And funny how he told her to use his shirt, yet he never let her touch the thing. He was drying her hair himself, squeezing the fabric around the wet hanks of her hair and soaking up some of the moisture. She stood stock-still and just let him, afraid to move, afraid to breathe, afraid to ruin the perfectly beautiful moment that she would never repeat ever again in her very vanilla life.

He smelled like man. There was no other way to put it. He just smelled like a guy, like soap and deodorant and skin, with a hint of aftershave. Imogen had never been so close to what she would classify as a manly man in her entire existence. It was an . . . arousing experience. That was the best way she could describe it. She had the increased breathing, sweaty palms, tight nipples, and warm inner thighs to prove it.

Moving down to her shoulders, Ty continued to dry her with his T-shirt and she continued to want to touch his chest.

"I can warm you up even more," he said.

No way was she actually hearing what she was hearing. It was simply too unbelievable. "How can you do that?" She wanted him to say it out loud, say what she was hoping he was going to say. It was quite possible she had never wanted anything as much as she wanted Ty to kiss her at that moment.

"I can put my arms around you. Heat share." Ty's free hand snaked around her waist. "And I can kiss you."

Wow. Wow. Wow. Imogen's brain completely froze. He'd said it. Now what the hell did she say in return? Even a simple *yes* or *okay* couldn't seem to eek its way past her paralyzed lips.

Light suddenly flooded over them, and Ty swore. He shielded his eyes and turned to the front of the house, though he didn't remove his hand from her waist. Imogen felt an instant blush crawl across her face. Whoever had turned on the light was definitely going to misinterpret what they were seeing.

It was Elec Monroe, Tamara's husband. He had turned on

the porch light and flung open the front door. "Hey, everything okay—"

He stopped talking and a grin spread across his face. "Uh, sorry. Didn't realize you were, um, hanging out together. Tamara was just wondering where Imogen went."

"I got caught in the rain," Imogen said, torn between wanting to stay standing with Ty's hand on her waist and wanting to put distance between them so Elec didn't get a negative impression of her. She stayed still, big shocker. "Ty was just—"

Elec held up his hand. "It's cool. I'll tell Tamara you're fine. And Ty, just an FYI, your friend is looking for you."

Imogen suddenly remembered that Ty had come to the party with Nikki.

That was enough to send her stepping back three feet and grabbing her wet sweater off the railing to use as a shield. How could she have forgotten for one minute that Nikki Borden intended to follow the six steps to marrying a race car driver and that her target was Ty?

Nikki and Ty were dating.

And he was playing with Imogen.

Elec went back into the house and Imogen turned toward the front steps, rain be damned. She needed to go home and take a hot shower.

"Where are you going?" Ty grabbed her elbow.

Feeling mildly insulted and majorly disappointed in both herself and the fact that she was not going to get to experience a kiss, Imogen paused on the top step, still under the porch overhang. "I'm going home. Please give my apologies to Tamara and Elec for leaving early, and to Nikki for monopolizing your time."

"It's not what you think, Emma Jean. I had every intention

of breaking up with Nikki after we left tonight. I should have done it two months ago."

Imogen frowned. Now that had the same ring to it as male statements like "I am going to leave my wife, I promise," and, "You feel so good with a condom, I just want to feel you without one."

She may not have a lot of experience dating men like Ty McCordle—okay, she had none—but apparently a man was a man and they were all just full of it.

"Okay," she said.

Now he frowned, still gripping his T-shirt in his hand. "Okay? What the hell does that mean?"

"It means okay. Break up with Nikki or don't. It's irrelevant to me."

With a deep breath and a wince, Imogen rushed down the steps in the pounding rain and left Ty standing on the porch.

CHAPTER
TWO

EXCEPT that Ty had followed her. Imogen couldn't believe it. After running through the rain, beeping her car doors open, and sliding in, wet and miserable, she had barely gotten her own door shut before the passenger side opened and Ty climbed in.

He was sitting in her car.

"What are you doing?" she asked in disbelief.

"I'm dripping, that's what I'm doing." He shook his head and ran his fingers through his shaggy wet hair. "Damn, that's a lot of rain."

And he was still shirtless.

Ty was sitting in her car wet and bare-chested.

"Why are you in my car?" Hadn't she made it completely clear that she was leaving the party to go home?

Yet he looked at her like she was the one overlooking the obvious. "So we can talk."

"About what?" Imogen considered herself a fairly bright woman, but she was having troubling following Ty's train of thought.

Without answering her, Ty pulled his T-shirt out of the interior crotch of his jeans. He saw her staring at him with what she was sure was an expression of total horror. He winked. "Kept it dry down there."

As he dragged the wrinkled shirt on over his head, Imogen tried not to succumb to the physical attraction she felt for him. Too late. Her hormones were alive and well and doing a sexy samba. She was undeniably aroused by him, despite the fact that he had a girlfriend, which she found incredibly distressing. It seemed that her intellect should be able to instruct her animal nature that Ty was not a viable candidate for mating.

Well, it was instructing, but most of her wasn't listening. So she was going to have to be careful. She could not complicate her thesis by flirting with a man she actually did find attractive. She had to use Nikki's marriage Bible only on race car drivers she had no interest in so that she could stay in control and objective.

"Why did you run through the rain?" she asked, still having a little trouble with that.

"Because I wasn't done talking to you before you cut out on me."

"I didn't cut out on you. It was an appropriate time to exit the conversation." They'd been interrupted. He had a girlfriend. It had definitely been time to leave.

"Exit the conversation? That's a polite way to say you ran away."

Maybe. But she had done what was necessary.

Ty turned slightly in his seat, his T-shirt sporting wet spots in random locations from where he had dried her hair, his own light brown hair dark and disheveled from the soaking he'd taken. He shifted his knee so his legs had more room, then glanced down at the floor. "Damn, I'm sorry. I knocked your bag over and spilled your stuff."

Imogen knew what was in that bag—half a dozen dating manuals and the incriminating *How to Marry a Race Car Driver in Six Easy Steps*. Feeling a blush steal over her cheeks, she frantically reached over between his legs and tried to feel around for the books to shove them back out of sight. If he spotted the titles and thought she was reading them in an attempt to snag a husband, she would be mortified, and she had no intention of explaining her thesis to him because she had a feeling he would mock it.

"Whoa." Ty lifted his arms out of the way. "I could have just put them back, but I like this better."

That made her freeze. She was effectively draped across him, her face by his kneecap, her breasts perilously close to his thigh. "Sorry they were in your way," she said, then realized she actually had nothing to apologize for. He was the one who had entered her car without an invitation.

"It's not a big deal. In fact, I'm enjoying this," he drawled.

God, that Southern accent did outrageous things to her neutrality. Imogen was determined to follow the dating rules only for the purpose of her thesis—she was not supposed to allow herself interest in any of the men of stock car racing she intended to flirt with. Least of all Ty. She had intended to leave him out of the equation altogether when embarking on this bit of unscientific research to jump-start her thesis.

So how exactly she had wound up groping around between his legs while his voice raised goose bumps on her spine was beyond her.

She crammed the last book back in the bag and sat straight up. "Not everything needs to be turned into a sexual innuendo."

"Well, of course everything doesn't *need* to be about sex. But it's much more fun when it is."

"This conversation isn't about sex."

"It isn't? Well, that sucks the fun right out of my night."

Hers had been sucked out the minute she had realized that she was nothing more than a game for him—a time filler while he avoided his girlfriend at a dinner party. She was probably quite simply the challenge of a different type of woman than Ty was used to dating.

"So leave, then. That's what I'm trying to do." She looked pointedly at him and then the passenger door.

"It's early still. You don't want to leave. And I have a few questions for you."

"I don't have any answers for you." That she could say with total honesty.

He continued like he hadn't heard her. "Do all women want to get married? Do *you* want to get married?" His expression was curious and maybe mildly puzzled.

Imogen was confident he was actually asking a genuine question, because he had asked her that once before, at Tamara and Elec's wedding. Clearly the issue of marriage and why women wanted it was weighing on him. Maybe it was the age. Men and women reached thirty and everyone around them seemed to think they either should be married or should be trying to get married. Imogen wasn't opposed to marriage, per se, but she definitely wanted to hold out for her version of Mr. Right, so Ty's question immediately brought to mind Beatrice in Shakespeare's *Much Ado About Nothing*.

" 'Not till God make men of some other metal than earth,' " she quoted to Ty.

Ty looked at her blankly. "What?"

Imogen had always loved Beatrice's witty replies to prying and often insulting questions, so she continued to use her words, getting into the monologue, despite the clear incomprehension on Ty's face. " 'Would it not grieve a woman to be overmastered with a piece of valiant dust? To make an account of her life to a clod of wayward marl? No, uncle, I'll none.' "

"It sounds pretty when you say it, but I have no clue what the hell you're talking about."

"It's Shakespeare," she said.

"Well, I was pretty sure it wasn't Kenny Chesney. Still doesn't tell me what it means, though."

Imogen shifted in her seat, her damp sweater and hair uncomfortable, her attraction to Ty McCordle even more so. He didn't look annoyed with her, just bewildered and, maybe, a little amused. She really didn't understand what he was doing sitting in her car, but since he was there, she figured she might as well enjoy the picture of manly perfection he presented, even if he had put his shirt back on.

"Beatrice is telling her uncle she will get married only when God makes men out of something other than dirt." A little harsh perhaps, but having briefly tried online dating, Imogen could see where she was coming from.

"Ah. A man hater."

That took Imogen aback. "Man hater? I don't think that's entirely true."

"Of course it is. She is lumping all men together, calling them all dirt, not giving any guy a chance. And probably walking around with a sour look on her face all the time and a big old chip on her shoulder, so she gets negative attention from men, which in turn pisses her off more and convinces her that her theory is right." Ty nodded. "Man hater."

Imogen was speechless for a second, horrified at the realization that while Ty's explanation was simplifying the situation, he might actually have a point. Beatrice had a wicked tongue and was almost always on the attack.

"I think you've just shattered my entire perception of *Much Ado About Nothing*."

"I wasn't trying to shatter anything. But it's pretty obvious the chick is bitter because guys aren't knocking down her door."

"How do you know they aren't knocking down her door?"

Ty gave her a long look of disbelief. "Come on. If they were, she wouldn't be so bitchy. Am I right? She's spending Saturday night with her BFF instead of getting some action, right?"

"Well, it's usually her cousin, actually. And you have to consider the context. A woman at the time couldn't just sleep around without serious consequences."

He scoffed. "Yeah, like that ever stopped anybody. Just ask any senator."

Imogen laughed. "True." Then since she was curious and he didn't appear to be leaving her car at any time, she asked, "But why are you asking about marriage in the first place? Are you thinking of proposing to Nikki?"

His reaction was so extreme it was comical. His face went into a series of contortions and his hand came out. "No. No, no, no. She brought it up, which means she is way more into this relationship than I thought, which means I have to break up with her, which I hate to do, because I don't like hurting anyone's feelings. But the truth is, Nikki and I have nothing in common. Except for one thing, really."

"Sex?"

Ty grinned. "Yeah. I love that you just threw it straight out there."

Well, it didn't take a rocket scientist to figure that one out, and Imogen, while considering herself shy, had always been curious enough to be direct with people. She got more information that way and, most of the time, was unable to resist the urge to pry a little in her quest to understand the people around her.

"It seemed logical to me that sexual attraction was what drew you to each other."

He shot her a funny look, like he was trying to read her expression and couldn't. "Yeah, that always seemed to work out pretty well for us. As for conversation or hanging out together, well, we were always stumbling a bit there, you know? So why the hell she thinks she wants to be stuck with me day in, day out in a marriage is beyond me."

Imogen thought it was damn obvious. Nikki wanted the prestige and money of being a race car driver's wife. But it seemed incredibly rude to point that out to Ty, especially if he hadn't figured it out on his own already. "Maybe she's in love with you."

Ty gave a laugh and stuck his index finger out at her. "Now that's funny. That girl has more genuine affection for her shoes than for me."

She couldn't tell if he was just stating a fact, or if it bothered him that Nikki wasn't emotionally invested in him. So she made light of it. "Good shoes are really hard to find."

"Look at you, calling up your inner smart-ass." Ty grinned at her. "I like that from you."

"Well, it's true." Imogen smiled back at him. "When you're shoe shopping, there are all these choices but it's so hard to find the perfect pair. They don't match your outfit right, or they're too casual or too dressy, or they're out of your price range. The store is out of your size, or they pinch your toes or rub your heels or give you blisters or make your feet sweat. The heel is too high or too low, or they make your ankles look fat."

"You're scaring me," he said. "This only goes to show that women spend far too much time worrying about a whole lot of nothing."

She wanted to laugh, but she wasn't finished making her point, so she added, "It's important because shoes affect the way a woman feels when she steps out of her house. No single pair of shoes covers the gamut of outfits in your closet. Not even close. So you need at least a half-dozen pairs to cover most of what you wear on a daily basis. Which makes me wonder if women should do the same with men. Have a different one for each of her moods."

The laugh that Ty gave was full and genuine and made Imogen smile back at him.

"Now there's an idea," he said. "So what mood would I be? Casual Friday?"

No, he would be for the days when she wanted to play porn star, but she wasn't about to say that out loud. "I imagine it depends on the woman who might want to wear you."

She didn't mean that to be suggestive, but the moment the words left her lips, she knew it would sound that way, and it did. Ty's eyes darkened and his eyebrow went up.

Imogen spoke again before he could because she wasn't sure she was prepared to hear what might come out of his mouth. "I think that for Nikki, you would be her high heels. What she wants to wear when she wants attention and to feel good about herself."

Maybe that wasn't true. After all, what did she really know about Nikki and her true emotions and motivations? But given what Imogen had seen and heard from the girl, she thought she was fairly accurate in her assessment. Nikki was using Ty for fame and fortune. Imogen wanted him to recognize that at the same time she didn't want him to suffer hurt feelings.

"I can see that," he said slowly. "I know exactly why Nikki is involved with me. It's for my money and her share of the racing spotlight. It doesn't exactly bother me because I know it is what it is, and I am not in any danger of falling in love with her." His knee bumped Imogen's when he shifted in his seat. "But the truth is, I want to be some woman's work boots, not her high heels."

"Work boots?" What was sexy about that? And did women have work boots?

"Yeah. You know, the boots she pulls out when she wants to get down and dirty, hiking or gardening or boating or painting the kitchen. The ones she relies on and trusts and lives her life hard and good and on her terms in. Her favorites."

Oh, my God. Imogen was having a little trouble swallowing. That was the weirdest and sexiest description of a man's role in a relationship that she had ever heard, and it suited Ty. He was weird in that she didn't really understand him and he was damn sexy, and she was mentally reminding herself that he was in fact still involved with Nikki and she absolutely could not molest him in her car in Tamara's driveway.

"But a woman doesn't feel sexy in work boots. Don't you want to make her feel sexy?"

"Of course she does. In her favorite shoes, playing or working hard, she feels strong. And feeling strong makes a woman feel sexy."

Ty touched Imogen's knee and pulled her legs slightly apart, sending a hot rush of warmth to her inner thighs.

"What shoes do you have on, Emma Jean?" He leaned over and checked out her footwear.

"Black ballet flats," she said, her voice a little raspy.

"Do you feel sexy in them?"

His hand was still on her knee, his thumb making little circles on her jeans, and it was driving her to distraction. "I feel reasonably cute when I wear them," she admitted.

Ty gave a soft laugh. "You look more than reasonably cute in them."

She knew she should tell him to leave. That they were weaving into dangerous territory when he was still technically with Nikki. It was totally inappropriate and she was going to tell him that. Immediately.

No words left her mouth and they sat in her warm car, the heater cranked, the windows fogged, and the wipers rushing back and forth combating the driving rain.

"Thanks," she said, then jumped when something slammed into the hood of her car, causing the whole vehicle to rock slightly. "What the hell was that?"

Ty could honestly say he didn't give a rat's ass if a meteor had dropped onto Imogen's car, but he looked anyway. Maybe the distraction was a good thing, because he was damn close to kissing the woman sitting next to him and he knew she didn't want him to. Well, she *wanted* him to. That wasn't arrogance on his part, just the truth. He could read the desire in her eyes. But she didn't think he should because of Nikki. Big difference. And she was right. Just because he had made the decision to break things off with Nikki didn't mean Nikki knew that.

So he looked out the windshield and commanded his erection to disappear.

It did when he realized that the thump on the hood of Imogen's car had been made by Nikki.

As her skinny ass had been slammed onto the car by a man whose face wasn't visible because it was buried in Nikki's ample chest.

"What . . ." Imogen's sentence died out as they both stared in shock.

At least Ty was shocked. Maybe Imogen wasn't, but hell, he was. Nikki had just dropped the M word on him an hour earlier, had pursued him relentlessly the entire four months they'd been dating, and now here she was, making out in a goddamn downpour with some random guy?

Nikki didn't like the rain. She hated the rain because it messed up her hair. Yet she was perched on the car hood, thighs spread, arms around the dude's back as he nuzzled her breasts, her head thrown back in ecstasy, normally meticulous hair sopping wet. Didn't seem to be a major concern for her at the moment.

Ty tilted his head, still not sure who the guy was. Nikki was blocking most of him from view. Not that it mattered, really, unless it was one of his good friends, which would piss him off on principle.

Whoever he was, he was into it. The guy pushed Nikki back in a fit of passion, their hands and lips everywhere on each other, her moans of excitement so loud they could hear them in the car over the rain. Wow. Here he'd been thinking the sex with Nikki had been alright, but he could honestly say she'd never shown that much enthusiasm with him. Her back and head rested on the hood, and rain pummeled her as her friend pulled down the neck of her shirt and suckled the tops of her breasts.

"Why . . ." Imogen started to say, then stopped.

"Why are they doing this in a fucking downpour? Yeah, I

was wondering the same thing." God, he was as horny as the next guy, but when it was raining so hard it hurt your skin and you couldn't even see what you were kissing and where, it was time to get a room.

"I'm so sorry," Imogen said, glancing at him in sympathy.

Was he sorry? A little disturbed, but not really sorry. Especially when the guy raised his head to wipe his face off and Ty saw it was Jonas Strickland, a rookie driver in his first cup series season. Ty didn't know Jonas all that well, and he would throw down a hundred-buck wager that the kid had no idea Nikki was dating anyone. He was a good kid—God, when had Ty started thinking of rookies as a lifetime younger than him?—and a methodical driver, but he didn't strike Ty as all that socially savvy off the track.

'Course, he seemed to be doing alright for himself at the moment.

Nikki was going to drown if she didn't close her mouth. In that position, with her head tipped back and repeated exclamations of "Yes!" coming out of her open mouth, he figured it was only a matter of time before the rain had her full-out choking. Unnerved by the fact that Nikki and Jonas were actually only a few feet away from them and he and Imogen could get a bigger eyeful than either of them cared for if Jonas's pants came off, Ty wondered how he should go about alerting the little love bugs to his presence.

It might just take a bomb to get their attention, given that Nikki's hair was now caught in the windshield wipers, whipping back and forth, and she didn't seem to notice.

Imogen reached forward in the driver's seat and silently turned off the wipers.

CHAPTER
THREE

FOR some reason, Imogen's quietly killing the wipers made Ty burst out laughing. The whole thing was just damn ridiculous.

Here he and Imogen were clearly fighting their attraction to each other so that Ty could do the respectable and decent thing and break up with Nikki first, when Nikki was indulging in a downpour fantasy with a guy Ty didn't think she'd even met before that night.

"Do you really think it's funny or are you laughing out of defense?" Imogen asked him, giving him a concerned look, tucking a stray hair behind her ear.

"I really think it's funny," he assured her. "I think I'm staring at a little life lesson—two people shouldn't be together just for convenience's sake. It only ends in sex on the hood of the car. And not with each other."

"True." Imogen made a sound of distress. "Oh, my God. He's actually undoing his pants."

Before Ty could react, Imogen laid on the car horn. They heard Nikki shriek and catapult forward into Jonas's arms, who stumbled backward, unzipped. It was raining too hard to see their expressions, which was a little disappointing. Ty thought it might be amusing to see guilty blushes.

Instead, Nikki stomped over and knocked on the driver's side window. "Who is in there?" she screamed.

"You don't have to answer that," Ty told Imogen, annoyed that Nikki hadn't just slunk off the way most people would.

Jonas was hovering awkwardly behind her, like he didn't know what he was supposed to do.

Imogen glanced over at Ty. "Do you want me to get rid of her or do you want to talk to her?"

"Oh, we can talk to her." Why prolong the stupidity?

Imogen cracked her window slightly. "It's Imogen. And Ty."

There was a pause, then Nikki shrieked, "Ty? That bastard is in there?"

Excuse me? What the hell had he done to deserve that title? Ty leaned across Imogen to try to see Nikki. "Since I'm a bastard and you're swapping spit with Strickland, I think we can call our relationship over."

"Unlock this car," Nikki demanded.

"Why?" Imogen asked even as she did it.

Nikki opened the back door and climbed in. "Because it's raining cats and dogs out there and I don't want to have this conversation standing in that mess."

"It didn't seem to bother you a minute ago," Ty remarked, watching Nikki slide across the backseat until she was directly behind him.

She made a *tsk* sound, then yelled, "Jonas! Get in the car."

The idiot did, which made Ty grin. "Nikki, I don't really think we have anything further to talk about."

"I suppose you're mad at me," Nikki said, frowning at him.

"No, not really. A little surprised maybe, but you're entitled to screw whoever you want. It just might have been nice if you'd let me know we were breaking up first. You know, just maybe."

"I wouldn't have had to if you had been reasonable."

"What exactly was I unreasonable about?" And how soon could he get her out of the car? He was getting a crick in his neck from looking into the backseat, and he was feeling bad for poor Imogen stuck watching the Nikki train wreck roll. He had to admit he was feeling the sting of embarrassment that Imogen was seeing what was clearly his poor judgment in living form.

"You don't want to marry me." Nikki was pouting, her plump lip shoved out.

Oh, Lord.

Jonas frowned. "Wait a minute. Are you two dating?" His finger went back and forth between Ty and Nikki.

"Not anymore. It's all good, man," Ty assured him.

But the poor guy's frown got deeper. "You didn't tell me you were seeing anyone." He looked at Ty. "Dude, I'm sorry."

"It's cool." Ty turned to Nikki. "No, I don't want to marry you."

"Why not?" Nikki wailed, her hands coming up to her face as she sobbed.

"Wait a minute," Imogen said, sounding totally exasperated. "Nikki, be honest, are you in love with Ty?"

Nikki's sob cut out. She frowned. "No."

"Then why do you want to marry him?"

"Because I'm already twenty-two. I should be married."

Ty winced. Was Nikki honestly only twenty-two? He probably had known that in theory but hearing it out loud was a second wake-up call. At thirty-three, he suddenly felt too old to be dating a woman that young. It was no wonder they never had anything to talk about.

He was about to say something, he wasn't sure what, but it would probably involve swear words. Fortunately Imogen beat him to it.

"I'm twenty-eight years old and I'm not married and I'm not in the least bit stressed out about that. Being ready to commit yourself to one man for the rest of your life takes serious thought and self-awareness, not to mention a healthy dose of love and passion. You can't rush that or force that or compromise on that."

Exactly. Took the words right out of his mouth.

"Whatever," Nikki said, rolling her eyes.

"I think I need to leave," Jonas said, looking like he would give his right nut to be anywhere but where he was.

"I'm going with you," Nikki said. She stared hard at Ty for a second while he tried to imagine what exactly was going to come out of her mouth. She said, "I hope you understand the mistake you've made."

Oh, hell, yeah, he did. No more twenty-two-year-olds. No more dating women who wanted his status and money more than him. And no more casual sex for a while. It was time to step back and wait for a woman he could really connect with.

"I do," he assured her. "And I'm sorry things didn't work out. I hope you and Strickland have fun tonight."

Nikki's face brightened. "We will. Thanks."

Then she nudged Jonas to get out of the car, which he did with a speed and dexterity that defied his rather bulky frame, and Nikki followed.

Suddenly Ty was alone again in the car with Imogen, who was frowning.

"God, I'm sorry about that," he said, feeling downright sheepish.

She just waved her hand like it was irrelevant. "It's okay. But I find it incredibly curious that Nikki would want to marry you."

Ty laughed, at the same time he hoped she hadn't meant that exactly how it had sounded. "Wow. Way to stroke my ego there."

The corner of her mouth turned up. "That's not what I meant. It just surprises me that in this day and age young women still think they need to be married to feel a sense of completion."

"I don't get it either," he told her with all honesty. He truly didn't understand why some women seemed to feel their self-worth was tied to being with a man. Especially one like him. He was always on the go, restless, inclined to make a joke when it wasn't appropriate, and not exactly what anyone could call an emotional anchor for a woman.

Which was why he had thought that casually dating Nikki made sense.

Only now he knew that wasn't what he wanted, yet was he really ready for a real, committed, mature relationship?

He didn't know, and wasn't even sure why he was asking himself that question. It wasn't like it was an option at the moment anyway.

"And that they're willing to just latch on to the first guy who shows interest in them whether he's a total loser or not, it just baffles me."

"You know," Ty said to Imogen as he wondered how many more slams he could be expected to take in one conversation. "It really sounds like you're insulting me."

And he was having one crazy-ass kind of day. He hadn't seen any of this going down when he'd crawled out of bed that morning, that was for certain.

But she just looked at him. "I'm not insulting you. I'm speaking theoretically, not about you specifically. I'm sure you have many qualities that make you an excellent candidate for a serious relationship, but it doesn't take a genius to see that your cup doesn't exactly overflow with love for Nikki."

She pushed up her glasses to emphasize her point, and at the same time Ty thought he'd never heard any woman speak quite as strangely as Imogen did, he found her incredibly cute. Like, so adorable that he wanted to kiss the tip of her nose.

He didn't actually do it. He just grinned wryly. "No, it wasn't love flowing out of my cup, that's for sure."

"Is that a sexual innuendo?" she asked, looking curious.

"Do you want it to be one?" He couldn't tell from her expression at all.

"It's not a matter of whether I want it to be or not. I am just curious as to the exact intent of your words."

Ty thought about being a smart-ass, but then again, he was intrigued by a woman wanting to understand exactly what he had meant. Being dyslexic and unable to read at a functional level, Ty was always conscious of the meaning and mystery of words. He was addicted to audiobooks and found the flow of language in novels fascinating and wished he could see and read them for himself. That Imogen was looking at him and wanting to hear the true intent behind his words gave him pause.

So he answered her truthfully. "I'm uncomfortable with this whole situation. So it was meant to be a crack at myself, that no, it wasn't love leaving my body whenever I was with Nikki but something else entirely." And beyond that, he wasn't spelling it out. He had a few gentlemanly tendencies instilled by his Southern mother, and he wasn't saying "ejaculation" to a woman he barely knew.

"That's what I thought," she said. "But I wanted to confirm it."

Ty laughed. "Why?"

Now she blushed. "Because I'm just incredibly curious all the time. I want to know everything about everything. I like clarity and I ask endless questions. I know it's annoying. I'm sorry."

"You don't have anything to apologize for. And I see curiosity as a sign of intelligence."

She looked at him in surprise. "I think it is, too." Then she blushed deeper. "Not that I'm calling myself intelligent. I mean, I'm not stupid but I'm no Einstein, that's for sure."

"I think you probably do alright," he told her. "Given that you're getting a graduate degree." A thought had just occurred to him. "And you're clearly smarter than me, because not only did the girlfriend I was planning to break up with make out with another guy in front of me, but she also left me stranded here." For the first time since he'd ditched Nikki and escaped onto the porch, he felt real annoyance.

"What do you mean?"

"I don't have my car here. Nikki picked me up, and she drove because she lives in the opposite direction from my place to here. So now I've got no way to get home."

"I can drive you."

"You don't have to do that." He didn't want her to feel obligated, but he really did want her to. Not to mention he wanted to kiss her, dipping his tongue inside his mouth and running his hands all over her petite body. "I can get a cab."

"Where do you live?"

"Mooresville."

"Well, that's on my way, then. It's not a problem at all for me to drop you off."

"Okay, thanks, Emma Jean. I appreciate it." Ty smiled at her, slowly, enjoying the way her cheeks went pink and she broke eye contact. She was just as attracted to him as he was to her, and he was going to get his kiss before the night was over. A simple kiss wouldn't break his newfound conviction to steer clear of casual sex for a while.

"Should we tell Tamara and Elec that we're leaving? I hate to be rude."

"Does it really matter?" he asked, thinking he didn't really give a shit. He'd call Elec or text him on the way home.

"I just feel so terrible. Here I've been missing half the night . . . Elec knows I was outside with you. I'd hate for any rumors to get started. That's not fair to you."

Now he *really* didn't give a shit if anyone thought he was making a move on Imogen because the God's honest truth was that he was. But it clearly was worrying her, so he said, "It's still pouring outside. I'll run back in and tell them we're leaving. You wait here."

"No, I'll go with you."

"What is the sense in both of us getting soaked all over again?"

"I don't mind getting wet."

"There are all kinds of wet, and some are better than others," Ty told her, unable to resist.

Her eyes went wide behind her glasses and she dug her fingernails into her thighs. "That was a sexual innuendo."

"Yep. Sorry, I couldn't resist. And you tell me which wet is more fun . . . getting nailed by rain or just getting nailed?"

He should shut up. Quit tweaking her. But it was warm and humid in her small car, and she was so close to him that he could smell the dampness of her skin, see the way her hair was drying in tiny wisps above her ear, hear the catch of her breath behind her teeth. Ty was intrigued by her in a way he hadn't been by a woman in a long, long time. He wasn't sure what he expected her to say, but he was almost certain he would enjoy her answer.

"Well, I think, inarguably, unless someone is suffering from a sexual dysfunction, that most people would prefer the wetness of arousal to the wetness of a cold rain."

Ty laughed. Yep, he liked that answer. "Which do you prefer?" he teased her.

Imogen didn't stop to think about the ramifications of her words. She just spoke honestly, "Oh, arousal. Undoubtedly."

The look on his face told her she was playing with fire. He wasn't just having a casual conversation where they were making sociological observations. He was flirting with her and she had known it all along. From the minute he'd spoken to her on the porch.

Now they were alone in her car, he was suddenly single, she had offered to drive him home from Tamara's, and they were discussing sexual lubrication.

Often throughout her twenty-eight years, her mother had told her that her curiosity and innate honesty were going to get her in trouble, and if winding up naked in bed with Ty McCordle was trouble, Imogen had the feeling that was precisely where she was headed. Interesting that she didn't seem to be running from said trouble, but was actually leaning closer to the source.

"Should we test your theory?" he asked, his hand snaking over and resting on her knee, his thumb caressing in a small circle. "Get you wet both ways and see which one you enjoy more?"

Imogen swallowed. She was no sexual novice. In fact, in college she'd had quite a hot and heavy affair with a grad student, and considered herself fairly well versed in male mating techniques—aka pickup lines—but she'd never had anyone throw it out there in such an obvious way as Ty did. At least she thought it was obvious. It occurred to her she should verify that before she misinterpreted, given her lack of experience with men like him.

"Are you suggesting that we have sex?"

He grinned. "Well, I'm not talking about a dunk in the lake, that's for sure."

"This seems a bit impulsive."

"Sex usually is."

Ty's hand had slid farther up on her thigh, and while her intellect might be hesitating, her body certainly wasn't. Imogen felt a jab of desire low in her womb, and her heart rate had kicked up a notch or two or three. She tried to ignore it. "But you're just coming out of a bad breakup, and I don't know how I feel about being a one-night stand you indulge in on the rebound."

His hand paused in its northward trek up her leg, and he made a sound of impatience. "It wasn't a bad breakup. I am relieved, do you understand? Totally relieved to be done with Nikki. And who says it has to be a one-night stand?"

"Because in most cases when two people who don't know each other very well get naked and have sex impulsively, if they try to continue seeing each other, they struggle to define the parameters of their relationship afterwards. It very rarely works to engage in extreme intimacy before you have some working knowledge of each other's personality and how you interrelate."

Ty snorted. "Ask a hundred married couples how many of them waited more than a minute before getting horizontal. I don't see the sense in waiting if you want someone."

Damn, his hand was trekking upward again and Imogen was struggling to concentrate on her point. She was no longer even sure why this particular point was important, and why she couldn't just dive into bed with Ty. Yet even under a haze of desire, her sense of logic warred with her curiosity. She wanted to see, to feel, what it would be like to have sex with Ty, but her logical side said she absolutely did need to know why he wanted to get intimate with her, and what they would do about it after the moment passed and tomorrow rolled around.

"It's not a good idea."

Curses on her need for control, to always know the answers ahead of time. She could see the irritation growing on his face.

"Look, I'm not going to talk you into it, Emma Jean. I want a woman who wants me with zero hesitation. But if you change your mind, you know where to find me."

Imogen frowned. "No, I don't. I don't know where you live or your phone number."

Ty laughed. "God, you can't stop your brain, can you? It's always working things out."

It struck a chord with her. She knew that sometimes her logic, her need to analyze and assess and study from every angle, was a huge detriment to just enjoying moments in life. It was something she struggled with, constantly being the observer instead of the participant, and it caused a twinge of shame that Ty had seen straight through her to what she considered her one true flaw.

"There's nothing wrong with using my brain," she said defensively. "If more people did, maybe we wouldn't have a society on the brink of a complete breakdown, its social and moral structure decimated. Maybe if women were in charge instead of men, we—"

Imogen squeaked and forgot what she was saying when Ty's hand slid under her legs and started to lift her up off her seat. "What are you doing?" she asked in a panic, reaching for the steering wheel, off balance in more ways than one.

"Get your sexy ass over here, Beatrice," he said, dragging her across the gearshift until she was in his lap. "So I can kiss you until you've forgotten all your logical arguments why I shouldn't kiss you."

"But . . ." She had no idea what she was going to say because her mind went utterly and completely blank. She was sitting on Ty's lap. His hard thighs were beneath her butt, his strong arms wrapped around her, and his mouth was inches from hers. She could smell him, a mixture of rain and aftershave, see the even whiteness of his teeth in the dark. He had lovely teeth.

And he had called her Beatrice. He had understood the conversation they'd had, given it back as good as she'd given it, even if he had never read Shakespeare.

Did she really want to be Beatrice? Alone, arguably bitter, holding firm to her principles? Or did she want to enjoy the moment? After all, Beatrice had met her match in Benedick in the end.

"Stop thinking," Ty told her. "Stop worrying, analyzing, debating."

"I can't," she whispered. "I tried. It worked for a second, then it all started again."

He shifted her legs so that she was firmly on his lap sideways. His hand settled on her waist, and she was startled by how big it was, how much of the small of her back he covered with his spread fingers.

"I can make it so you can't think at all."

"I have no doubt of that," she agreed.

He made a small sound, almost like a growl, and held her more firmly. "Say no now and I won't do this," he said.

Every nerve ending in her body was firing in anticipation and desire. She had the urge to both dig her fingers into his hair and wiggle her backside on his lap. Was she going to say no?

Yeah, right.

She'd worry about the awkwardness later. She'd stress about her thesis tomorrow. She'd examine why he was capable of creating such a total lack of control in her at some point down the road.

Right now she wanted him to kiss her.

"You're not saying no." His thumb was on the waistband of her jeans and dipping down into the gap between the denim and her panties.

"No, I'm not saying no."

"So you're saying yes?"

Imogen would have thought that was obvious, but she appreciated that he gave her time to change her mind, that he wanted to make completely sure she was on board with what was about to happen.

She was.

"Yes, I'm saying yes."

Ty smiled, not a grin, but a slow, satisfied smile, as his amber-colored eyes darkened considerably to a rich chocolate brown. "Gentlemen, start your engines."

Imogen paused. What did that mean, precisely? That she had the potential to start his metaphorical engine? That this was the beginning of a race? Or the beginning of a relationship? That . . .

She forgot to think the second his lips touched hers. Oh. My.

He didn't hesitate, nor did he test the waters. He kissed her, and he kissed her with confidence and aggression. With fire.

It was the kind of kiss that had her mouth opening immediately, and her fingers clawing into his hair, and her ass pressing down into his lap. It was the kind of contact that stole the breath right out of her, made her inner thighs ache, and her head swim with a heady elixir of pheromones and excitement.

He swept his tongue across hers, and Imogen would have groaned if she could have gotten a breath. Instead, she just held on to his shoulders and gave it back. She didn't think that in general she was uptight or reserved, but she was fairly certain she had never attacked a man so thoroughly during a first kiss as she was doing with Ty. She was pressing her chest against his, destroying his hair, sliding her tongue across his, and bumping her backside against his erection.

His hands were on the move, too, caressing her back, brushing against the sides of her breasts, heading under her sweater at the small of her back as his kisses got more urgent and demanding.

Imogen broke away to suck in some air and stare at him in wonder. How could he do that? How could he make her so damn hot with just a few kisses?

Ty shifted underneath her, dumping her onto the seat. "That's it. Time to go back to my place."

"Really?"

"Really. After that look you just gave me, I could pretty much eat you right here in the car and that's probably not a good idea."

Well. "Okay."

"Shit, sorry. I kicked your books again." Ty, half-sprawled across the gearshift and her lap, reached down and picked up a book.

Damn. It was the marriage manual. Imogen winced and fought the urge to rip it out of his hands, which would probably only result in calling attention to it. He did glance at the cover, but he didn't say anything, so she didn't think he had bothered to read it, given the angle he was at. He just stuffed it in the general direction of the bag and continued to crawl across the gearshift into the driver's seat, his tight butt in her face. Unable to resist, she tentatively touched him, sliding her hands over the worn denim.

"Hey, now," he said, his voice rough. "Save that for when I can do something about it."

"What are you doing anyway?" she asked. "This is my car."

"But I know where we're going." Ty settled upright into the seat and turned her wipers back on. He shot her a grin. "Besides, I like to drive."

She had no doubt of that.

Imogen swallowed hard and wondered what exactly she had gotten herself into.

CHAPTER

FOUR

SO much for swearing off casual sex.

Ty had meant to stick to that conviction.

It wasn't his fault that Imogen had tested his resolve a mere five minutes after he had made his decision.

She was definitely worth breaking the vow for, and somehow he just couldn't think of her in the same category as Nikki or any woman he had randomly hooked up with in the past. Imogen was more than that.

It wasn't just her physical appearance he was attracted to; it was her personality, her intelligence.

The way her mind worked fascinated him, and he liked her openness, her innate honesty. Whatever was going on in her head came out of her mouth, and that was a damn refreshing change. She was a logical little thing and didn't seem prone to emotional outbursts. When was the last time he had dated a woman like that?

Never.

Ty looked behind him, put Imogen's car in reverse, and shot out of the driveway way faster than he needed to, causing her tires to screech.

"Ack!" she said, grabbing on to the dashboard with one hand and reaching for her seat belt with the other. "Was that really necessary?"

"No. But I like speed as much as I like to drive."

"Save it for the track, Mr. Checkered Flag. My car will self-destruct if you push it too hard."

Ty grinned over at her. "Did you really just call me Mr. Checkered Flag?"

"Yes," she said grudgingly. "I couldn't think of anything better. But I'm serious. This car can't go over sixty-five or it will start to rattle and vibrate. It's old and cranky and seems to have some digestive issues."

"I bet I could coax it to some speed, Miss Victory Lap."

The ridiculous name he called her in return made her laugh, but she shook her head. "Don't try it."

"Watch me. We'll skip the highway and take the back roads to my place."

"It's raining. The roads are slick."

"You think I can't handle a little slick blacktop at a puny hundred miles an hour?" Ty shifted gears hard and opened the car up a little as they turned out of Tamara and Elec's suburban neighborhood onto the rural route heading south.

"The real question is how you'll handle my hands around your neck throttling you if you don't listen to me."

He laughed so hard at her unexpected words he started

coughing. Swallowing hard, he said, "Them's fighting words, Emma Jean."

Damn, it was a refreshing change to have a woman tell him exactly what she thought. Nikki had been a pouter, not a protester, which was annoying. Pouting from a woman made him feel irritated and guilty. Imogen's firm no-nonsense approach amused him and had him obeying. He eased up on the gas pedal.

"Thank you," she said in acknowledgment of his decreased speed.

"You're welcome. But for the record, you're too small to throttle me with any success."

"Do you want to test the theory?" she asked, pushing her glasses up on her nose.

"No, ma'am." He shot her a look. "I can think of a lot better things you could be doing to me with those hands."

"Part of me assumes that what you are saying is so obviously sexually charged, you don't actually mean anything specific. It was just meant to be a sort of verbal foreplay. So I shouldn't bother to ask the inevitable 'like what?' question. But the other part of me wants to know if there is actually something you would like me to do to you in bed. You know, if you have a particular fantasy or position that you've been contemplating."

Ty almost groaned. He did shift in his seat to try for a more comfortable angle since his jeans were suddenly cutting into him from the erection that had sprung up at her words. There was something so unbelievably hot about Imogen's bold curiosity. She didn't say anything to be coy, but to satisfy her own curiosity and to make sure that she was in full awareness of all the facts.

He'd never tried the academic approach to sex before and it was doing a number on him.

There hadn't been any particular action he'd been thinking of when he'd spoken. He had just wanted to keep her aroused and focused on sex until he could get her back to his condo. But now that she had asked, he had a whole slideshow of positions clicking through his head. He didn't think he could pick just one.

"Let me think about it and I'll let you know."

"Okay." She bit her lip. "But just so you know in advance, I'm not having anal sex with you."

Ty almost drove off the road. He could not believe she had just said that. Trying desperately not to laugh, he nodded carefully. "Okay. I'll make note of that. Though that ruins all my plans for the night. Guess I'll have to reorganize and come up with a new strategy."

"Really?" She sounded a little unnerved.

"No." He tossed a grin at her.

It was hard to tell in the dark, but he thought she might have blushed. "I didn't need to announce that, did I?"

"Probably not, but I can appreciate you wanting to make that clear. Anything else I should know?" It was more than likely a bad idea to ask Imogen to list her sexual taboos, because God only knew what would come out of her mouth, but he wanted to reassure her.

"Well, I suppose there are but it occurs to me that normally those likes and dislikes, off-limit areas, and an agreement on a mutual level of kink are revealed in the bedroom together with a combination of hands-on and verbal discovery, not ahead of time in casual conversation."

He wasn't sure he had understood a damn word she'd said. He had pretty much lost all his blood from his brain to his erection when Imogen used the word *kink*. "Doesn't matter, babe.

We can forge our own path. You want to talk about it now, I'm on board with that."

Ty pulled onto his street and opened up the engine a little bit. It would disappoint his neighbors if he didn't fly into his driveway at sixty miles per hour.

Imogen grabbed the dashboard again and held on. "I don't think I do want to talk about it."

Glancing over, he saw she was biting her lip. "What's the matter?"

"I've sucked the spontaneity out of this, and I'm annoyed with myself."

She did look upset. "No, you haven't. We can go on in and be totally spontaneous. Like whose shirt will come off first? That's still a mystery at this point."

Now she was actually chewing her bottom lip with her teeth, frown lines etching into her forehead as they sat in the idling car in his driveway. "That's not spontaneity. That's simply variances of an already established intent."

Say what? "Speak English, babe." He gestured to himself with his thumb. "Dumb driver here."

"You're not dumb. That's ludicrous. You're obviously quite intelligent."

That made him feel oddly humble and flattered. He thought of himself as fairly street smart, but in no way was he book smart, yet it felt good to hear Imogen say she didn't see him as a box of rocks. "Well, I can't balance my bank account, but I do alright, I guess."

"And the reason you can't understand me is because I'm not making any sense."

That seemed fair enough to him, but he wasn't about to point that out. He had learned enough in his lifetime to know that you didn't point out to a female that she was making no sense. "We're here," he said, turning off the car. "Come inside and let's see if we can make sense of it together."

"Okay," she said, but she still looked worried.

Ty was starting to wonder if this was a bad idea. He was looking at Imogen's face and seeing tomorrow's regrets written on it.

She opened her mouth like she was going to speak again, then shut it.

He waited, but she didn't say anything so he prompted her. "What are you thinking, babe?"

"That I'm keyed up, and you're going to be disappointed."

Now he knew this was a bad idea. If Imogen went into sex with that mind-set, she was going to be nervous and inhibited. No matter what he did, it had the potential to wind up awkward and unsatisfying for her.

Damn it. He should have driven faster.

"I can guarantee that I will not be disappointed." Ty turned and brushed her still-damp hair off her cheek. "I find you fascinating. And I don't want this to be a one-night stand that leaves you feeling like you can't even look me in the eye next time we see each other."

She opened her mouth, but Ty leaned over and gave her a soft kiss to stave off any protests. "So I'm going to get out of the car now, and I will call you tomorrow and hope like hell that you'll agree to go to dinner with me."

"You're going in and I'm supposed to go home?" she asked. "Is that what you're saying?"

"Yep. I don't want to screw this up, Emma Jean. So I think we need to call it a night right here and pick up where we left off another day." He saw things going nowhere but south if he tried to get her naked. As nervous and agitated as she looked, she just wasn't going to enjoy herself.

"I see."

Ty waited for her to expound on that statement, since Imogen seemed fond of using seventeen words to his one, but she didn't. She just got out of the passenger side and walked around to his side. The rain had stopped and the glow from his garage lights turned her face a pale pearl white.

"Good night," she said with a smile that was anything but genuine.

Shit. He knew that look and it wasn't a good one. "I'll call you tomorrow," he said.

"Fine."

That was it? Ty sat in the car and stared up at her, trying to read her expression. She looked irritated. Maybe even veering toward angry. Determined not to leave it on that note, Ty reached over and pulled out the first book in her bag he could get a grip on. "Can I borrow this?" he asked.

She gave him a funny look.

Ty wondered what the book was, given the incredulous expression on her face. All he could tell was that it was the one with a couple on the front of it, but he couldn't read the title. Great, it was probably a romance novel. But he had been thinking he would take it, have his assistant order it on audio, then he could discuss the book with her. Show Imogen he could participate at her level, have a decent conversation.

So he just brazened through. "I've been wanting to read this," he drawled.

"Really?" Her voice dripped with doubt.

"Uh-huh."

"Okay. Enjoy."

She actually opened the door then, so he had no choice but to climb out of the car. Ty brushed his legs against hers when he stood up, but she moved backward out of the way. He handed her the car keys and kissed her forehead. "I'll give it back to you in a couple of days."

"Sure."

"Good night." He gave her a smile, hoping for one in return, but she just blinked up at him behind her glasses.

Ty turned and started up his driveway, envisioning a night spent in the shower with a glob of conditioner and his hand to ease some of the tension he was feeling. It was a poor substitute for Imogen in his bed, but sending her home was the right thing to do. Painful, but necessary. Like a root canal. Definitely the right thing to do.

Her voice came calm and even behind him. "You do realize that in us attempting to avoid post-sex awkwardness all we have achieved is pre-sex awkwardness?"

Or not. Wincing, he stopped and turned, but Imogen was already in the car and slamming the door shut. In another ten seconds she was peeling out of his driveway like a circuit pro, and he was feeling a little deflated in more ways than one.

CHAPTER

FIVE

"*OH,* my God, I'm sweating like a pig eating soup," Suzanne said to Imogen as she did a near jog on the treadmill.

Despite her doubts that pigs actually ingested soup, Imogen sympathized. She was sporting wet circles under the armpits of her T-shirt, and she was having serious trouble breathing as she tried to keep up with the pace of her own machine. "I . . . am . . . really out of shape," she told Suzanne, sucking in air to her oxygen-deprived lungs. "I used to walk all the time living in New York and now I just sit at my desk or in my car."

"I've never been in shape," Suzanne said. "I've just always had naturally good genes so I looked decent even if my lung capacity sucked. But since I turned thirty, it's all starting to head south, and I don't mean Florida, honey."

"I don't think anything is shifting on me, per se, but I suspect there are small children with greater muscle strength than me."

Imogen tried to ignore the burning in the backs of her legs as she walked. Jogging was completely out of the question. "You know it's sad to say, but I wouldn't even be here if it wasn't for the book. It says in order to be date ready for the man of your dreams, you have to exercise, drink water, and have a balanced diet."

"I can't believe you're actually going to follow those steps. It all sounds silly to me."

"Yeah, well, that is the point. To determine if it's possible to follow guidelines in order to meet and marry a driver, or if it is simply left to the vagaries of human beings. Are there truly dos and don'ts in relationships? Or can anyone fall in love and marry for any reason at any time, essentially breaking the rules?" Imogen wheezed and tried to slow down her walking pace. That had been too many words to manage while her body was under severe strain.

"Well, I think there are definitely nos to dating. I mean, you can't pick your nose when you meet a man and expect that he'll fall head over heels for you."

"True."

"But as for a more rigid set of rules, I don't know. I'm going to have to read this book—which needs a nickname, by the way. I can't keep calling it *How to Marry a Race Car Driver in Six Easy Steps*. I think we should just call it the *Man Manual*. Or *Six Steps*." Suzanne wiped her dewy forehead. "Let me borrow it so I can help you with your thesis. I know a ton of drivers. I can introduce you."

Imogen sighed. "I can't let you borrow it. Ty borrowed it from me last night."

"What?" Suzanne squawked. "Why the hell would he borrow a manual on snagging a man?"

"I don't know," she admitted. "I think he was doing it to be funny, but I'm not really sure. This was after, uh, he decided we shouldn't have sex, and I think he was trying to lighten the mood."

Imogen had lain in bed for two hours staring at her ceiling trying to figure out exactly why Ty had come on so strong, then changed his mind. Had he really been telling the truth that he didn't want her to feel awkward, or had he lost interest in the face of her prying questions and blanket statements about sex? Either way, it was just mortifying, and despite her best efforts to feel otherwise, she felt rejected. Intellectually, she knew it didn't matter, that it had been for the best, frankly, because she had been something of a wreck just anticipating how she might disappoint him. She could only imagine how disastrous it would have been if they had actually gotten to the point of removing clothing, but she still couldn't help but feel, well, rejected.

"Come again?" Suzanne asked, gripping the sides of her treadmill as she stared at Imogen. "What do you mean Ty decided you shouldn't have sex? What the hell happened? I didn't even know you were with him last night."

"Well, he needed a ride after he and Nikki broke up. We were talking and he kissed me and we decided to have sex." When she said it out loud, it all sounded rather dubious. "Then he drove my car to his place and said we shouldn't have sex. Then he borrowed the book and I left." Imogen looked around the gym to make sure no one had heard what she had just said. The gym they were at was a haven for race car drivers, and one of them could be wandering by at any given moment. It was originally why she had chosen it, at Suzanne's recommendation, but now she was thinking it wasn't all that wise.

"Wow. That's weird. Just weird. How was the kiss? Did he suck or something? Maybe he was embarrassed."

"He didn't suck." Not in the slightest. She had been completely prepared to have her mind blown in bed, given what a sampling of his kisses had done to her. "And I don't really think that he has confidence issues. I just think he realized that I'm not his usual type and that he's not really attracted to me."

Which she found more than mildly distressing.

"Oh, that's horse pucky," Suzanne said. "If the man wasn't attracted to you, he wouldn't have been cramming his tongue down your throat in the first place."

"I believe it's universally accepted that men frequently engage in sexual acts with women they do not find attractive. Hence the origin of the alcohol-related one-night stand and the term *beer goggles*."

"Well, he wasn't drunk and he's not a teenager. Not to mention he may have a thing for young and dumb, but Ty is a good man. He would only have sex with a woman if he was attracted to her. I'm sure of it. And if he was certain she was attracted to him."

Suzanne's hand shot out and grabbed Imogen's wrist. "Oh, my Lawd, what if he thought you weren't attracted to *him*? That would explain why he pulled the plug."

Imogen was struggling on her machine to find a rhythm, so Suzanne's unexpected contact caused her to lose her balance. Grabbing the handles of her treadmill, Imogen slowed down her pace and tried to recover. "I don't know. I suppose it's possible, but it seems a little unlikely. I think I am just a bit too much of a freak for him."

Suzanne's eyebrow lifted. "You're a freak? Like freaky deaky in bed? Did you tell him that?"

Imogen's already pink cheeks burned from more than exertion. "No, I'm not a freak in bed! I meant, I'm odd in that I'm nothing like the women he usually dates. But it doesn't matter anyway. I need to let it go."

Maybe if she kept telling herself that, it would actually be possible. "I need to focus on my thesis. I'm supposed to be in prime physical condition so I can go hiking and dirt biking and jet skiing, since drivers are inclined to participate in aggressive and physical hobbies. I need to watch my diet, drink lots of water, and educate myself on the history of the sport."

Just thinking about it made her wonder why this had seemed like a good idea. She was a bookworm, not a dirt biker. She had an innate fear of anything that might result in every bone in her body being broken. And judging by the way she was feeling light-headed and on the verge of severe muscle spasms in her thighs, she was not in prime physical condition by any stretch of the imagination.

"That sounds like a lot of work. It seems to me that a man and a woman should just meet, decide they like each other, and call it good."

"The point is to increase your odds that he will meet you and actually like you."

Suzanne made a disparaging noise. "And I can't believe we're working out at seven in the morning. This is an ungodly hour of the day to be sweating. If I'm working this hard in the morning, I'd prefer it be because my man has woken me up with an eight-inch nudge."

That was a reminder she didn't need. That could have been Imogen that morning if she hadn't somehow scared Ty off the night before.

"I don't mind the early hour." Imogen grabbed her water bottle and sucked some down. She was starting to think she wasn't going to survive to the thirty-minute mark.

"Alright, so we have to sweat our asses off and eat salads and shit and then what?"

"You don't have to do this with me, you know."

"It will be fun, and it will piss Ryder off to see me flirting with other drivers." Suzanne shot her a grin. "And getting on my ex-husband's nerves is worth the torture of this treadmill. Besides, I have the insider track on who you should target to flirt with and who you shouldn't."

"Sounds good, but only if you're sure. This has the potential to be fairly awful."

"Since when is flirting with hot men awful?"

"I was born without the flirt gene. It's truly awful for me." That was no exaggeration. "I mean, look at how I screwed up last night with Ty. He was flirting and tossing off sexual innuendos, and I just looked at him and said I would not have anal sex with him."

"You *what*?" Suzanne shrieked so loud that Imogen saw half a dozen other fitness patrons swivel their heads to look at them. "Did he ask you to? At the party?"

"No, of course not." Which was what made it all the more ridiculous. "We were in the car and he was hinting about positions, what was to come, etc., and I just blurted out that I wasn't doing that with him."

"Girl . . ." was Suzanne's thought on the matter, her expression one of total horror. "Do not bring up the back door unless he's knocking on it."

Imogen was about to agree that was the wise thing to do when she glanced toward the front door and completely lost her rhythm on the treadmill. Ty was standing in the doorway with a gym bag in one hand, a cell phone in the other. "Oh, damn," she managed to say before her feet lost the fight to stay ahead of the machine and she went flying backward on the belt.

In a split second she was on the floor on her backside, stunned from the impact, and totally mortified. Before she could even think to force her uncoordinated limbs to jump to her feet, hands were under her armpits hauling her to her feet. A glance over her shoulder showed a guy Imogen found vaguely familiar pulling her up.

"Are you okay?" he asked.

"Yes. Just embarrassed."

He gave her a grin. "Don't worry about it. Happens to the best of us. I sneezed once and wound up with free weights on my chest. That didn't feel too good."

"I imagine not." Imogen tried to focus on the man in front of her and not glance over to see if Ty had noticed her graceless spill onto the gym floor. "Have we met?" she asked him as she took in his caramel hair, broad shoulders, and crooked smile. He looked very familiar. "Are you a driver?"

His friendly expression went wary and she realized her mistake. He was going to assume she had known all along he was a driver and that she had taken a dive on the treadmill right when he walked past in order to get his attention. But she was actually positive she had met him before, she just couldn't place his face. And not that he would know it, but she couldn't imagine herself ever taking a fall just to get someone's attention. It went against everything in her to risk personal injury or to start a relationship on a false pretense.

"Yeah, I'm a driver. Evan Monroe." He was moving back from her, clearly intending to leave before she could trap him for the next half hour gushing over him, or whatever he thought she was intending.

But Imogen smiled. "Oh, duh, of course you're Evan. I can't believe I didn't recognize you right away as Elec's brother. I'm Imogen Wilson, Tamara's colleague at the university. I met you at Elec and Tamara's wedding."

His face cleared. "Oh, sure. Good to see you again. Did you just join this gym, or do we just never work out at the same time?"

"I just joined in a vain attempt to improve my overall physical condition. I have zero coordination, as I just demonstrated for you."

"You look in pretty good shape to me." Evan smiled.

Imogen shifted in her gym shoes. She recognized that smile. It was interest.

This was an unexpected turn of events.

"And there's something different about you," he added. "You got new glasses since the wedding, didn't you?"

She had.

Wow. Falling off the treadmill might have just handed her the perfect opportunity to flirt per the rules.

Of course, she was supposed to exercise to get in shape, not to fly off the machinery and land at the feet of a driver. But whatever worked.

"I did get new glasses." She smiled back. "I can't believe you noticed."

"I'm very perceptive," he replied, leaning forward slightly. "Especially when it comes to beautiful women."

It was a perfectly nice and flirty thing to say, and Imogen knew she should be excited at the opportunity being handed to her, but she still found herself glancing over at the doorway to see if Ty was still there even as she answered Evan.

"Thanks," she murmured, suddenly disappointed.

Ty was gone.

TY figured he could squeeze in a workout before heading to the office and suffering at the merciless hands of his assistant, Toni Bodine. Mondays and Tuesdays were his days to play catch-up, and while he had put in a full day doing appearances and autographing merchandise the day before, Toni wasn't about to let him slide in late on a Tuesday, and it was already past eight.

He had been walking in the door to the gym when she had called him.

"Any chance you're going to grace me with your presence today?" was her greeting.

Ty had to admit, he wasn't a business-savvy kind of guy. He liked to drive; he liked to win. Plain and simple. Toni, who was in her fifties and a formidable force with a spreadsheet, kept him organized and where he was supposed to be. But he didn't shirk his responsibilities, ever, and Toni knew that. She just liked to annoy him, and he liked to grumble and grouse. It was the way their relationship worked.

"Maybe if you beg."

"No chance of that. But I imagine your sponsor might be less than thrilled if you aren't at Wal-Mart at five P.M. to sign autographs."

Pacing back and forth in front of the doorway, Ty said, "Have I ever missed a single appearance?" Those he actually liked doing. He enjoyed talking to the fans and having his picture taken. It was press conferences and cocktail parties he couldn't always hang with.

"There was that one time at Talladega."

"I had the stomach flu!" And they had had this argument a hundred times. Toni was never going to let him live down a virus he'd had no control over.

"So?"

"I was a public health risk."

"Wimp."

"And you're a nag. But a gorgeous one."

She snorted.

"Hey, did you order that book on audio that I left on my desk?" Toni was just about the only person who was privy to the fact that Ty was dyslexic, and she frequently ordered books on audio for him, and helped him sort through all his paperwork.

"Yes. Though I'm not sure why you want to know how to win yourself the heart of a race car driver."

"Huh? What do you mean?" Ty frowned.

"It's a dating manual on how to win a race car driver in six easy steps. The end goal is marriage."

"Are you freaking kidding me?" Ty was shocked. What the hell did that mean? Why would Imogen have a book like that?

"I am not kidding you. Where did you get it from anyway?"

"From a friend."

"A female friend? Was it Nikki? Because that would not surprise me in the least."

"No, not Nikki. We're done. It was someone else, a sort of new friend."

"Well, it looks like your, ahem, friend is on the prowl for a driver. Careful, Ty."

"I don't think she is." That seemed nothing like Imogen,

frankly, and hadn't they talked about marriage after the disaster with Nikki? Imogen wasn't the type to try to hook a man based on a dating book. He was sure of that.

"I've been flipping through it. It's interesting. The first step is all about eating healthy, exercising, and learning about stock car racing. So if you spot her at the gym, look out."

There was a startled yelp from across the gym and Ty glanced up, distracted.

What he saw made his jaw drop. It was Imogen, flying backward off a treadmill and landing on her ass on the gym floor.

"Oh, now you've really got to be freaking kidding me," he repeated, absolutely appalled. It had to be coincidence. It had to be. Right?

"No, I'm not kidding you," Toni said. "Are you sure you want me to buy this thing for you? I can probably still cancel the order before it ships."

"Yes." Ty watched as Evan Monroe helped Imogen up off the floor. "In fact, I might not want to wait until the audio arrives. I might just have you read out loud to me, sweetheart."

Normally, he hated to have Toni read things out loud to him, but watching Imogen fuss with her hair and her glasses and move around on the balls of her feet as she chatted to Evan, Ty had a sudden burning desire to know exactly what the hell was in the book he had borrowed from Imogen.

And why she had it.

"Oh, goodie. That sounds like fun for both of us," Toni said, her voice dry.

Yeah. Fun. That's exactly what he was having.

Feeling the undeniable sensation of jealousy crawling up his spine and settling in his gut and temples and fists as he watched Evan lean closer to Imogen, Ty took a deep breath.

Then got the hell out of there before he did something stupider than what he'd done the night before.

BY six o'clock Ty had fulfilled all of his business obligations for the day and had forced Toni to read him Chapter One of the book he had borrowed from Imogen. Not only did it have advice to the would-be bride on maintaining a healthy and attractive appearance, what to wear, and how to research stock car racing, it listed the gym he worked out at as a possible place to spot drivers.

Toni looked up at him, her reading glasses sliding down her nose, her lips in a smirk. "Did you see any new girls at the gym today? Like maybe your new friend?"

"Of course not," he lied, not willing to admit the truth. It was just too embarrassing and too confusing to make any sense of it all yet, and he didn't need Toni's ribbing.

He crossed his arms across his chest, rubbing the cotton of his T-shirt in distraction as he tried to sort it all out. What was Imogen doing?

If their roles were reversed, he had no doubt Imogen would just ask him straight out, but Ty wasn't sure he wanted to do that. What if he hated the answer? What if she said she wanted to marry a driver, any driver, and was willing to follow a book to get that result?

He just couldn't believe it.

"Does it suggest anywhere in there that you should have sex with a driver right after you meet him?"

Toni's dark eyebrow shot up, but she didn't say anything. She just licked the tip of her finger and turned the page. After a few minutes of flipping through the book, she said, "Actually, it says you shouldn't have sex until a commitment is firmly established. The whole 'don't give it away for free' adage." Her brown eyes pinned him. "Why?"

"No reason. Just curious." It was strangely satisfying to know that Imogen had fully intended to sleep with him, despite what that book said and why she might have it.

He suddenly felt the irrational regret that he should have taken her to bed. That he should have stripped her naked, licked and touched and sucked every inch of her, until she could no longer think, and she was his. All his. Only his.

"Alright, that's good, thanks, Toni. I'm going to make a phone call."

"You're done learning how to win a race car driver? Who knows what little gems might be in Chapter Two."

Rolling his eyes at her, Ty said, "It's so nice to have an assistant who is a comedienne."

With that, he stood up and went into the interior office that was his personal space. It was actually smaller than Toni's office, because he had no paperwork, no calendar, no computer. He had long ago perfected the art of memorization, and once Toni told him his schedule verbally, he remembered it. He programmed alerts onto his phone as an added reminder, eternally grateful that technology had gone the route of using picture icons for menus.

Mostly his office was a place for him to relax between doing whatever Toni told him to do, and he had a minifridge and a TV with video games in there. He had no desk, just a couch and an easy chair, and he flopped down on it now and dialed Imogen's number. He wasn't really sure what her schedule was like, but he knew she was a grad student, so hopefully her classes were done for the day.

She answered on the third ring, but her hello was wary.

Sinking back in the chair, he said, "Hello, Emma Jean. How are you doing today?"

There was a slight pause. "Fine. How are you, Ty?"

"Full of regrets."

"About what?"

No sense in beating around the bush. "About you getting upset last night. I was just trying to do the right thing. Make sure you didn't have any regrets this morning. But it seems like we both do."

"I'm sure you were right," she said carefully.

"Maybe I should have trusted you to know what was right for you and we should have gone forward with it and had wild, boot-stomping sex." He hadn't intended to say anything like that, but the very idea of Imogen trolling the gym for other drivers, following some goddamn manual to win a man, had his skin tight and his gut twisted in knots.

"Maybe we should have," she said with the honesty he appreciated in her. "But it's irrelevant at this point. I think, unfortunately, when two people rush the traditional mating process, it results in awkwardness whether there was any extreme physical relationship or not. I don't see where we could go forward in any capacity now that there is confusion and reservations on both our parts."

Damn, her logic turned him on. Every time Imogen started in on one of her declarations of how it had to be, he got hard as a rock, and determined to prove her wrong.

"I don't have any reservations. I still want to peel your clothes off and make love to you all night long, just like I did yesterday."

She cleared her throat and Ty grinned.

"Can you give me a brief overview of the history of stock car racing and how the season works?"

He blinked. That wasn't quite the response he'd been hoping for. "Come again?"

"I'm trying to learn about the sport, and I assume you're a reliable source."

So she could woo some other driver with her knowledge about his job? Ty felt the muscle in his jaw twitch.

"Why, of course, gorgeous. Why don't you meet me at my house for a drink, and I'll teach you anything you want to know."

He may not have a fancy degree from some university but there were two things he considered himself an expert in—stock car racing and sex.

And she was going to get both from him.

CHAPTER SIX

IMOGEN didn't know what in the world she was doing driving over to Ty's house in her ancient and temperamental car. But she hadn't been able to say no.

It had surprised her when he had called. For some reason, she had thought, regardless of what he'd said the night before, that they were done. He wasn't going to want to see her again. That she had bungled the situation too badly and he was going to decide she was more work than was worth it.

Understanding his motives and intent was more than a little challenging. So her curiosity had gotten the best of her yet again, and she had agreed to come over in person to question him on the ins and outs of racing. No doubt she could have asked him anything over the phone, but he wanted to see her, and she wanted to see his reaction to her in person. She also wanted to ask for her dating manual back and see if she could ferret out why he had actually taken it in the first place.

As she pulled into his driveway, checking the house number against the one he had given her and she'd scribbled onto a piece of scrap paper, she tucked her hair behind her ear and sighed.

She was really the worst student the graduate program had ever seen. Instead of focusing on her thesis, she was playing some kind of inexplicable game with Ty McCordle. She should be setting up interviews with drivers and their wives to determine how they had met and fallen in love. She should be following the *Six Steps* on a sampling of drivers to record their effectiveness.

Yet somehow she was justifying being at Ty's house under the flimsy guise of having him instruct her on the intricacies of stock car racing. Which she could just as readily learn from books, the Internet, and her friends Tamara and Suzanne.

The truth was, and she strove to be entirely honest with herself and everyone around her at all times, that she wanted to see Ty just because she wanted to see him. Because he made her laugh and caused her heart to race. He also made her feel sexy, and it was safe to say that, while she always felt reasonably attractive, fairly intelligent, in control, and self-aware, she had never really felt sexy. Not in the "men want to rip my clothes off" kind of way.

Ty made her feel that way, and she was drawn to it. Wanted to explore it.

The garage door went up, and Ty strode into the driveway. He was clearly visible under the coach lights, and as usual, just the sight of him made Imogen swallow a mouthful of spit. God, he was just gorgeous. It really wasn't right that any man should be entitled to claim that much masculinity, yet still retain such an easy prettiness. He had fine features and a narrow face, soft hair, and an even softer chin stubble, yet he was so confident, so toned and defined, so inclined to swagger, that he was all man and then some. It was a combination she was struggling to resist, with little success.

Especially when he grinned that naughty little smile, which he was doing at the moment.

Yeah, that would be her jeans going up in flames.

Opening the door, she was intending to get out and meet him in the driveway, but he waved her back in.

"We're going to switch cars. Back out so I can pull out, then you can park in the drive. We'll take my car."

Imogen stared up at him. He had moved out of the light and she couldn't really see his face all that well anymore. Damn daylight savings. It was only quarter to seven and it was pitch-black outside.

"Why? Where are we going?"

"To the garage. That's the best place to learn about stock cars."

Right. Stock car research. That was precisely why she was there. Not because she was an undersexed woman, he was a highly sexed male, and their bodies would fit together like a couple of click-and-lock puzzle pieces.

"Oh, wow, that would be great." If she were capable of concentrating on anything other than him. "Isn't it rather late though?"

"Nah. Someone will be around."

"Okay. Great."

They did a quick car switch, and then Imogen was back in the passenger seat with Ty peeling out of his driveway, an odd reverse of the night before. Only his car was a tricked-out sports car, and he was singing along to a country song on the radio, looking more cheerful than sexual. Damn it.

After enduring his off-key singing of lyrics that involved a man declaring his undying love for a woman, Imogen felt compelled to interrupt. "So when can I expect my book back?"

"In a day or two," he said, cutting her a sideways glance. "Are you one of those people who guard your books like gold? Don't worry, I won't break the spine or spill beer on it."

"I wasn't implying that. It's just that . . ." Imogen trailed off. She couldn't say she *needed* the book. That would sound calculating.

"What? Look, if you need the book that badly, I can return it to you when we get back to my place. I wasn't trying to inconvenience you."

Great. Now she sounded thoroughly ungenerous. "No, of course not. I agreed to let you borrow it, so you can absolutely keep it for a few days. But I am curious as to why you wanted to read it."

"I thought I might learn a thing or two." He glanced over at her and winked.

Now what did that mean, exactly?

Never one to beat around the bush, Imogen said, "What does that mean exactly?"

"Why women want certain men, and if my worth to the opposite sex is truly just based on what I do on Sundays."

"You doubt why women want you?" she asked incredulously.

"Well, there's a couple of reasons why they want me. I don't doubt that. But after Nikki, I'm feeling a little gun-shy. Like maybe while I've been so busy avoiding getting to know a woman too closely, they've all been doing the same. Like maybe I'm just a target for attention seekers and gold diggers."

"Of course women enjoy the prestige of a driver, and there will always be attention seekers and gold diggers, but if Suzanne and Tamara are any example, they would have loved their husbands regardless of their occupations. Of course there is a woman out there who will value you as a human being as opposed to a commercial commodity." The very thought irritated her in multiple ways. One, that he would doubt that. Two, that there were women who would try to use him, like Nikki. Three, that he might find the woman who wouldn't, fall in love with her, marry, and have little McCordles. And that woman wouldn't be Imogen.

"Maybe Ryder and Elec got the only two who will." His voice had more of a teasing quality than concern.

Imogen snorted. "I imagine some other wives in the sport might dispute that."

"Of course. What else are they going to say? Admit to greed?" He took a hard left turn. "But no, I'm not really serious. I know most of the guys who are married are all sorts of happy and so are their wives. Maybe I'm just starting to wonder what's out there for me, for real."

It clearly wasn't her, for more reasons than she had fingers to count. Obviously he felt the same way or he wouldn't be discussing it with her. That just wasn't something you did with someone you felt might be a potential candidate. Imogen knew all of that in reality. It wasn't like she had completely lost her senses and thought that she and Ty could actually have any sort of long-term relationship—they couldn't even manage to have sex—yet it still stung. Just a little.

"You'll find the right woman for you. And I imagine she'll be a lot like Suzanne."

"Suzanne?" Ty's upper lip curled. "No, thanks. Women like

Suzanne are not my type. Too uneven, all those ups and downs of their temper. It would give me an ulcer, all that trying to guess their mood, and wondering what the hell I'd done wrong. No, I want me a nice even-tempered woman. Someone who says what she means, but without the sting."

Imogen's throat was tight. "I'm sure you'll find her."

"When I least expect it? Isn't that what people always say?"

"I have heard that." The same held true for attraction. Imogen had never dreamed she would find herself consumed by lust for a race car driver. But it was safe to say, given the cottony feeling in her mouth and the ever-present dampness between her thighs when she was with Ty, that she was head over heels in lust.

"So why do you have that book, Imogen? You looking to marry a race car driver?"

Damn. Imogen's mouth went hot and she dug her fingernails into her thigh. She had been hoping that her own inquiries regarding his reading the book would not be turned around onto her. That had clearly been underestimating his curiosity.

"I believe we discussed my opinions on marriage once before," she said vaguely, not wanting him to believe she was that mercenary or calculating, but also not wanting to explain her thesis. For some reason, she had the feeling he would not appreciate her admission to intentionally flirting with his coworkers for educational purposes.

"Yeah, we did. Which doesn't explain why you're hauling around that book." Ty glanced over at her. "You got secrets, Emma Jean? You have a crush on some driver and you're hoping to up the odds with that dating guide?"

If only it were that simple. But somehow she couldn't imagine that anything in the *Six Steps* would help her wade through her attraction to Ty McCordle. "No, that is not why I have the book."

Ty pulled into a parking lot going way too fast, and the force bounced Imogen around on her seat. She grabbed the door handle for leverage when he hit the brakes hard so he could swipe a security card in the gate kiosk.

"You sure?" he asked, his voice sounding casual. "Maybe it's Evan Monroe. He's a good-looking guy."

Uh-oh. Warning bells went off in Imogen's head. She was observant enough and well versed enough in human nature to know the edge of jealous anger when she heard it. Ty must have seen her at the gym talking to Evan. And considering she had actually given Evan Monroe her phone number, for future research only, of course, she could feel the stain of a guilty blush covering her checks.

Screw the consequences, she was incapable of sustaining a lie of that magnitude. She just couldn't pretend that she was genuinely interested in Evan, nor did she want Ty to think that she was, therefore, off-limits to him. It was ludicrous, but she did not want to close any doors regarding Ty. Especially the bedroom door.

"I have the book for research. I'm working on my thesis."

That seemed to take him aback. "Come again?"

"I am trying to determine if dating rules specific to stock car racing result in a higher percentage of successful relationships or if there is no correlation between following a set of rules and marriage."

"Oh." Ty pulled into a parking spot and shifted gears hard. "So wait a minute. Let me see if I have this right. You're trying to see if dating rules work? How are you going to do that?"

Imogen hedged. "I have a few test subjects." If a reluctant

Suzanne and a wild card like Nikki could be considered test subjects. "And I intend to interview married couples to see how they met and started dating." She tacked that on to throw him off her first statement, but he just frowned.

"Are you using these stupid rules on me?"

Somehow she had never actually expected him to reach that conclusion since it had never been her intent to use the rules on him. The opposite, in fact. But she could admit it was a logical conclusion for him to reach, even if it absolutely, thoroughly, one hundred percent mortified her. Actually, though, when she thought about it, it wasn't logical at all.

"No, of course not!" Imogen pushed her glasses up on her nose. "When have I ever hit on you or thrust myself into your path? If you recall, we met up by accident on the porch last night. I could not have predicted you would step outside at the very moment I was rolling my windows up. Nor could I have predicted that Nikki would be in the arms of another man, thus effectively ending your relationship with her." Her cheeks grew hotter at the thought that he would actually think she was systematically pursuing him based on a book. Yuck. Yuck. Yuck. It made her feel pathetic and more than a bit ridiculous.

She continued before he could respond. "And just for your information, the book says that a woman should not have sex with the driver she is interested in until they have been dating for quite some time and a level of commitment and intimacy is clearly established. So obviously I wasn't following these rules because I was more than ready to have sex with you last night and we barely know each other."

So there.

At the end of Imogen's speech, Ty just stared at her for a second while his brain processed exactly what she had just said.

Then he broke into a huge grin, thoroughly amused by her yet again. He absolutely loved that Imogen played no games. She told him exactly what she thought and felt.

"Well, that's a good point you make," he said, his car in park and idling. Sliding his hand down the leg of her jeans, he rested it on her kneecap. "You were more than willing to have sex with me. And I was more than willing to have sex with you."

"So why didn't we?" she asked, licking her bottom lip in an unconscious gesture that made Ty shift on his seat.

The only illumination was from the lot lights, and he couldn't see her eyes, but he could practically *smell* the attraction between them. Her body had tensed, and so had his, and he glanced into the backseat, wondering for a split second if it would work for a quick tussle. But when he took Imogen to bed, which he was going to, sooner or later, he didn't want it to be quick and awkward, with a gearshift up his ass. Awkward was why he had pulled the plug the night before.

"We didn't because we started thinking too much. Worrying." He squeezed her knee. "And you're right. I'm sorry, it was stupid to think that you had somehow planned to target me based on that book. That sounded insulting and I didn't mean it to. It's just that I got to thinking that maybe you weren't really interested in me."

She could be honest, so could he. Even if admitting his momentary insecurity made his skin crawl and a sweat break out down his back.

"Of course I didn't target you. Especially considering the way your profile reads." Imogen flashed him the first smile he'd seen from her all night.

He would have enjoyed it except he got stuck on her words. "My profile? What profile?"

"Didn't you read Chapter Two? There are profiles of all the single drivers. Yours says you were voted least likely to commit by other drivers' wives."

"Excuse me?" Ty was both shocked and offended. "That's in a *book*?"

"It is. It also mentioned your astrological sign is Taurus, giving you a propensity for stubbornness."

Imogen looked amused.

Ty was not.

"What the hell? I can't believe they're using that 'what's your sign?' crap to put character flaws on me. In print. God, that just makes me look like an asshole. And I can so commit." He yanked the keys out of the ignition more aggressively than was necessary. "I was engaged once. I would have married her. She was the one who dumped me."

Imogen's grin disappeared. "Oh, I'm sorry. What happened?"

Ty rubbed his chin, instantly sorry he'd brought the subject up. "I was only twenty years old and scraping along doing local races and I was in love with her. She cared about me, I guess, initially, but then she went off to college and reassessed her options. She decided she wanted someone with a little more earning potential. Someone smarter than me."

"Intelligence isn't equal to the credentials you can hang on a wall. There are all kinds of intelligence, and clearly she was lacking in some if she missed your good qualities."

"Like that I'm stubborn?" Ty said stubbornly, not wanting to accept Imogen's sympathy.

"No, like your honesty, your tenacity, your quick wit. Your loyalty, your focus."

Ty found himself stupidly touched by Imogen's assessment of his character. But hearing he was profiled as a commitment-phobe and bringing up his ex-fiancée had him feeling tight in the chest and edgy. He didn't want to get emotional, lose control of the situation. So he tamped that all down and hid his feelings, giving her a slow grin.

"You see all those things in me yet you still didn't target me? Damn, I'm offended."

"I can't target you, because I am trying to objectively follow the rules of the dating manual to see what level of success I achieve with them. Therefore, I need to stay uninvolved and un-biased in regard to the men I flirt with, and I cannot achieve that with you."

Ty didn't think he could be more shocked by anything Imo-gen said, but she always managed to find a way to do just that. "Wait a goddamn minute. So you *are* planning to use the dating rules to hook a man? Just not me?"

"No, of course not. I don't actually want to catch a man. I just want to see if the initial chapters regarding preparation, meeting, and flirtation have any level of success as part of my research for my thesis. I only intend to flirt a little with some of the drivers and see what reaction I get."

Ty was feeling his blood pressure rise with each ridiculous word she spoke. "I can tell you exactly what's going to happen! You're going to have drivers crawling all over you, hoping to get a piece of your classy ass."

She frowned. "Don't be ridiculous."

"Me? I'm being ridiculous? You're the one flirting for your thesis. What the hell kind of degree is that anyway? A doctorate of dick tease?"

It was a petty thing to say and he knew it, but what exactly was her objection to flirting with *him*?

Imogen gasped. "I beg your pardon?"

"It doesn't sound like science to me, babe. But what do I know? I'm just a stubborn driver who has commitment issues."

"I'm a sociologist. I study and observe the patterns of behavior of humans. And your behavior right now is irrational."

Ty felt a tic start in his eye. He wasn't sure how they had gotten there, but he was going to finish the conversation because he couldn't contain his frustration much longer. She hadn't even gotten a tiny peek at irrational yet. "Just one more reason why you can flirt with everything that walks but I'm leprosy."

This would be the point where every female he had every dated either (a) threw something at him or (b) started screaming expletives.

Imogen did neither. She turned in her seat, looked him straight in the eye, and said, tightly but calmly, "You are missing the point. The reason I cannot flirt with you is because I am attracted to you. I am invested in the outcome of my actions towards you. I want you to be attracted to me in return. In short, I like you. Therefore, I cannot remain detached if I try to follow any sort of rules with you. In fact, I think it is safe to say, I wouldn't be able to follow any rules where you are concerned."

Ty felt a grin threatening. "You like me?"

And Imogen surprised him yet again by making a face and saying, "Well, *duh*."

Alright, then. He laughed. "I like you, too, Emma Jean."

"I suspected, but I appreciate your confirmation."

There was his prim-and-proper Imogen again. "So what are we going to do about it?"

"We're not going to do anything about it at the moment. We're going to be friends and get to know each other. You're going to help me learn about stock car racing, and steer me in the direction of who I might interview for my research. I'm going to focus on my thesis, and then when all that is done, we can reassess our relationship."

He wasn't liking the sound of any of that. "You're telling me I'm just supposed to sit back and pretend I don't want you naked all while I'm watching you hit on my coworkers?"

"I had to watch you with Nikki on several occasions," she pointed out. "Hardly my idea of a good time."

Ouch. "Fair enough. But I didn't really know you then and I really didn't know you were interested in me. This is going to mess with my head."

"I'm sure you'll manage. Look, what does a month matter? If we're still interested in each other, then we'll only have the added benefit of having gotten to know each other better. It's a win-win situation."

Not for his dick.

"Maybe you can live that logically but I can't. You've already figured out I'm stubborn and irrational and determined. I am not hanging with this." He wasn't. It was stupid and he wasn't doing it.

Her dark eyes blinked up at him behind her glasses and if he wasn't mistaken, her bottom lip jutted out slightly. "Please? I really, really need your help, Ty. Teach me about racing."

Shit. All those goddamn girl tricks weren't fair. Soft voice, big eyes, pouty lip . . . he couldn't resist them. "Fine," he growled. "Get out of the car and into the garage before I say something I will seriously regret."

Or before he hauled her into his backseat and showed her that sometimes logic had no business between a man and a woman, but that pleasure always did.

CHAPTER

SEVEN

NOT sure exactly what they had established between them,
other than the fact that they wanted to have sex, which they already knew, Imogen climbed out of Ty's car warily. This had all
the makings of a bad idea. "So where are we exactly?"

"This is the garage and offices of Hinder Motors, the team I
race for."

"What does driving for a team mean?" She was really struggling to understand the ins and outs of racing.

Ty gestured for her to follow him across the parking lot. "It's
too expensive for individual drivers to have their own car and
crew. A car and engine alone can cost a hundred and fifty grand,
so there is a car owner who handles all the expenses associated
with racing, including securing sponsors. The driver benefits from
all that money and the expertise of quality staff, and he gives a

piece of his purse to the team in exchange for them paying all his expenses. A lot of car owners have multiple cars today, and that's why we call it a team. The Monroe brothers and Ryder and I all race for Hinder Motors, so it's to our advantage to help each other even as we compete with each other. If the team is doing well, the corporate sponsor dollars coming in to Hinder Motors on the whole will be better."

What amazed Imogen was that Ty berated his personal intelligence. He sounded pretty damn savvy to her. "Wow. I knew it was complex, but I had no idea."

"It's really not, once you understand it. And having multiple cars on one team gives us the ability to info share on pre-race tests at tracks. Each car is only allowed four single-day test sessions of your car, but if you have four cars racing, you can share any data you learn from all those runs with each other."

Imogen was wishing she had brought a notepad to jot things down on. "But doesn't that make you all sort of even when you start a race?"

"Cars are close to even. It's the skill of the driver and how the lady in black treats you that day that determines the winner."

"The lady in black? Who is she?" Imogen frowned up at Ty as he flashed his ID for a security guard and they entered the building. If there was another Nikki in Ty's life, she was going to be profoundly irritated.

Ty grinned at her. "The track, sweetheart. The lady in black is the track." He strode down the hallway, but he shot her an indecipherable look over his shoulder. "And did your dating manual tell you that you should be prepared to share the man you snag with the lady in black? No point in getting jealous because drivers are in love with her and she's a huge part of our lives."

She had read the entire book, and there was nothing that Imogen would classify as a warning or a word of caution. It was all full steam ahead until you had achieved your goal of marriage to a driver and lived happily ever after. But she could see Ty's point. Any woman looking to live with a race car driver had to accept that his career consumed a large majority of his time. You either had to accept it or be miserable, and jealousy and unhappiness over it could destroy your relationship.

Truthfully, she didn't know how she would feel about that herself. She didn't think she was needy, and her own aspirations consumed a lot of time, but maybe the inflexibility of it would eventually wear on her.

Ty pushed open a door and Imogen followed him into a garage. There were several cars in various stages of construction, some just raw frames, others looking ready to roll onto the track with all their decals in place. The room was cool and smelled like tires, and Imogen was surprised to see that while there weren't a lot of people working, it wasn't empty either. One car was a flurry of activity with at least eight men moving around it, talking, drilling, or screwing, or whatever it was they did to prep cars.

"Whose car is that?" she asked. "What are they doing to it?"

"The fifty-six car is Elec Monroe's."

Of course, she should have known that. Tamara had her husband's car number tattooed on the interior of her wrist, in a gesture that had impressed Imogen. She wasn't sure she could handle being jabbed repeatedly with a needle and permanently discolor her skin to prove her love. Needles made her light-headed and she'd probably faint during the procedure, knocking the tattoo artist over and winding up with an indistinguishable blob.

But Tamara seemed happy with hers.

"Why are they working on it so late?"

"There must be something they're tweaking. That car should already be on the hauler ready to go to Martinsville in the morning. The rest of our cars for this weekend are already loaded."

"Then what are all these cars I'm looking at?"

"Cars for Texas, two weeks out."

"You don't drive the same car every week?"

"No. Have you seen a race, babe? We beat the hell out of them. They need some work done after a race."

That was true, but she had never thought about the implication of such abuse.

"And every driver needs an immediate backup car, in case his is wrecked in pre-race testing or qualifying."

"Where is your car?"

"The sixty car, over there. Looks like they finished the paint job. I got saddled with green this year, which is just about my least favorite color. But for a ten-million-per-week sponsorship deal, I'll suck up the fact that I'm driving around looking like a moving golf course."

Ty started walking toward his car, so Imogen followed him, drinking in the sight of all the cars in various stages of construction around her. It looked so intricate, so complex.

A few guys waved and greeted Ty from their industrious labors over Elec's car. One even asked, "Who's your girl there, McCordle?"

"This is Emma Jean," Ty told them. "She's a research student at the university."

Despite the fact that he refused to use her real name, Imogen was pleased by his description. He could have easily dubbed her the lunatic who wanted to have sex with him, but only after she conducted research on a thesis that was rapidly turning into the educational equivalent of quicksand.

"Whatcha researchin'?" a young guy in his early twenties asked curiously.

"I'm getting my doctorate in sociology." Unlike a doctorate of dick tease, as someone had rudely phrased it. "I'm studying the dating and mating techniques of stock car drivers."

The young gawky guy's eyebrows shot up and he looked overwhelmed by the very thought. Another man, older and rounder, glanced up from the tire he was fussing over and snorted. "That makes it sounds like one of them animal shows on Discovery Channel. I'm guessing that's about the right of it, though. Most men are animals."

"Speak for yourself," Ty said.

There was another snort followed by a grin. "Hell, I think I am speaking more for you than for me. I'm a happily married man. No dating and mating for me these days. But you're doing enough for you and me both."

"Hardly," Ty said loudly, clearly annoyed with the conversation. "I'm showing her around so you all need to behave while she's here."

Ty took her hand, which startled her, and led her away from the crew. "It was nice to meet you," she said over her shoulder.

They all grinned and waved.

"Sorry," Ty said.

"Why? They didn't say anything rude to me." And now she was way too distracted by the fact that he was still holding her hand to think about anything else. He had a strong grip, yet he was tender with her, his hand in hers just warm and stable and . . . right.

Oy. That was a scary thought.

Could two people actually be any different than she and Ty?

There was no way she should let her thoughts go there. Ever.

But his hand did feel good.

"Alright," Ty said, clearly unaware of the ridiculous direction her thoughts were going in. "Stock Car 101. We're putting you in the car and I'm going to tell you what everything is."

Imogen eyed the very vibrant green car in front of her dubiously. It didn't look dangerous. It wasn't on. So regardless of what she saw the vehicle doing on Sundays, it wasn't going to spontaneously start itself parked in the garage. She didn't think.

"Okay," she said nervously and reached for the door when he let go of her hand. "Where's the door handle?"

"There's no door handle. The door doesn't open. You have to climb in the window."

Was he serious? Imogen looked at him and frowned. Ty was giving her a very calm and reassuring look.

"No big deal," he told her. "Just one leg over, then the other, and you slide on into the seat. Go on, it will give you a real feel of what it's like to be in the driver's seat."

That did intrigue her, she had to admit.

"So this is like a *Dukes of Hazzard* thing? I just climb in?"

"Exactly. Go for it, Emma Jean."

Although an Emma Jean undoubtedly could just hop right into a race car, an Imogen was destined to have issues.

Imogen lifted one leg up, ruing the fact that she had thrown on tight skinny jeans with flats at the last minute in an effort to look somewhat cute when meeting Ty. It was kind of hard to haul her leg past her knee when the denim was restricting her movement. She actually lost her balance and wobbled, grabbing on to the car frame above the open window.

"Do you need a lift?" he asked.

"No, no." Yes. Imogen tried again, swinging her leg as high as she could and managing to hook it over the opening. But she couldn't seem to shift her weight to the left leg and was standing there, one leg up, one down, hands clinging to the car.

"I can help you."

"No, I'm fine." There had to be a more logical way to do this. She wasn't strong enough to haul herself up, and in the meantime she was potentially doing internal damage to her reproductive organs perched on the doorframe the way she was.

Retreating back out of the car and down onto the concrete floor, Imogen peeled off her black pin-striped blazer and set it on the hood of the car. Pushing up the sleeves of her white button-up shirt, Imogen grabbed on to the window and jumped, her belly landing on the frame. Her head was in, but nothing else, so she wiggled and tried to pull herself up and forward.

Suddenly Ty's hands were on her waist and she stopped moving.

His voice rippled over her. "And you say I'm stubborn? You go in like this, you're going to land on your head and splatter those brilliant brains all over my seat."

"I have it under control," she said, breathless both from the activity and from his touch.

"Oh, really?" he asked, laughter in his voice. "But just so you understand, this position you're in is not helping me stick to your no-flirting rule."

Imogen felt her cheeks grow hot. She could only imagine what her bum looked like from his perspective. Not as good as Nikki's, she could guarantee that, given she didn't have a taste for plain lettuce and couldn't handle more than fifteen minutes on the treadmill. Even if her butt could be toned to the point of Nikki's, Imogen wouldn't know what to do with it because she had been born without the sex kitten gene.

"I'm sorry. I wasn't trying to—"

"I know you weren't. That's part of what makes it so damn hot. You're not being calculating, just naturally sexy."

Imogen wished she could see his face instead of staring at the black interior of the car. He couldn't possibly be serious. "There is nothing sexy about me, Ty. It's not in my DNA to intentionally entice men."

"Intentional or not, it's there, honey. You are smoking-hot sexy."

Flopped over the doorframe like a human teeter-totter, Imogen wondered if Ty had forgotten to wear his helmet a time or two. She was not sexy. If she could have rested her hand under her chin in that position, she would have. Instead she just hung there and felt suspended both literally and figuratively.

She squawked when Ty lifted her up and back out of the car, her shirt riding up and exposing her belly. He turned her around and she stared up at him, yanking her shirt back into place.

He had that look in his eye she was starting to recognize. It was lust and it was flaming red-hot at the moment. Which was sincerely puzzling to her. Since when did dangling in a car window entirely clueless as to what she was doing constitute sexy?

"Let me help you," he said, leaning closer and closer to her.

There was a split second before he kissed her that Imogen could have used to move away, protest, stop him. She didn't.

As a matter of fact, when his lips touched hers, Imogen forgot everything—her thesis, their differences, where they were—and put her arms around his neck and kissed him back.

He had such a nice mouth, and he used it so well, warming her from head to toe with a few presses of his lips. Each kiss had her gripping him harder, which had him kissing her harder, until they were melded together, breathing heavily and taking and sharing passion. When his tongue invaded her mouth, Imogen felt an eager tug between her thighs, and she rocked forward in her flats, losing her balance.

Ty buried his hands in her hair and worshipped her with his mouth over and over again. Her glasses were in the way, but she didn't give a damn, and clearly neither did Ty, since he showed no signs of slowing down for the next hour or two.

They might have stayed that way indefinitely if they hadn't heard a man's voice say, "Damn, somebody needs a room."

They both pulled away and Imogen could feel her cheeks burning as she peeked around Ty to see who had caught them. It was a man in a golf shirt and khaki pants, very trim and toned, an attractive man in his fifties.

"Shit," Ty muttered under his breath. Then louder, "Hey, Carl, how are you this evening?"

"Not as good as you, clearly." The man gave Ty a half smile. It wasn't full-blown, but it looked genuine, and there was nothing leering or suggestive about the way he glanced at Imogen, which reassured her.

Ty turned back to her, and shifted her so she was next to him, his hand in hers. "This is Imogen Wilson, a friend of mine. She's a grad student in sociology who is very interested in the culture of stock car racing."

Amused that Ty chose now to prove he did in fact know how to pronounce her name, Imogen smiled. No one needed to know that she was mostly interested in the dating and mating habits of one particular driver.

"Imogen, this is Carl Hinder, the owner of Hinder Motors and the man responsible for my career being where it is."

Oh, Lord. Given that Ty had just explained a car owner's role, she knew the importance of this man in front of her. And he had caught them making out against Ty's kelly green car. She was certainly creating a new definition of classy.

"It's a pleasure to meet you, Mr. Hinder," Imogen said.

"Likewise, Imogen. And that's a lovely name you have. Shakespeare?"

"Yes." She smiled openly at him now. "My mother was a fanatic about her William."

"Where are you from? I don't hear any North Carolina in your voice."

"I'm from New York, born and raised there. I just moved to Charlotte last year and I'm enjoying it immensely. The people are lovely."

"Well, don't let this joker monopolize your time," Carl said with a nod and a grin in Ty's direction. "Charlotte has more to offer than punk drivers."

"Hey," Ty protested. "The lady likes punk drivers."

Carl laughed. "They always do, especially on Sundays. Good night, y'all. Pleasure meeting you, Imogen."

"You, too."

When Carl walked away, Ty leaned against his car and picked at his T-shirt. "Lord, that man scares me."

"Why? He seems very friendly."

"Don't let him fool you. He's sharp as a tack and a killer businessman. I don't think I'm afraid of anything for the most part. Not losing, not failure, not death, not snakes or spiders. But that man makes me sweat."

"What could he do to you?" Imogen asked, amazed to see that for the first time she'd been in Ty's presence, he did look genuinely uncomfortable.

"Fire me."

"For what?"

"I don't know. Anything. Then that's it. Who am I if I'm not driving?"

Wow. Imogen would have never guessed Ty had insecurities in any way, shape, or form. She was about to reassure him that he wouldn't be fired unless he did something catastrophic and that, even if he was, he could find another team to drive for, but Ty cut her a grin.

"Never mind," he said before she could speak. "Just wasn't expecting to see him, that's all. Now, let's get you into this car."

Imogen bit down on a shriek when he scooped her up in his arms and turned her so her legs slid into the car. One minute his hand was on her butt, her weight supported by his lean but powerful muscles, the next she was sitting in the driver's seat of a race car.

Ty watched Imogen sitting stiffly, her hands up in the air like she was afraid to touch anything for fear of what it might to do to her, and he felt immeasurably better. God, what had he been thinking, blurting out that crap about being afraid of being fired and being nothing more than a washed-up loser driver? He didn't say things like that to anyone. He didn't let anyone know at any time that the only thing he was really afraid of was being cut off from the one thing he loved and the one thing he was good at. If he couldn't drive, there was no backup plan for a guy who couldn't make sense of the words on a piece of paper or on a computer screen.

How did he explain that to someone as brilliant as Imogen? He couldn't. Of course, neither should he be spending time with her, and he wasn't planning to stop that anytime soon. She just made him laugh, made him feel good.

Turned him on.

Really, really turned him on. It was the way she blinked up at him with those big blue eyes behind her glasses, all curious and aroused, that made him lose focus on everything except getting her into his bed. Wiggling her cute little ass in front of him hadn't hurt the cause either.

"Just relax, Emma Jean. The car doesn't bite. Unlike me." He winked at her as he leaned in the window.

"I don't want to destroy anything," she replied, not even responding to his innuendo.

"Babe, this car can hit the wall and still be salvageable. You can't do anything to hurt it."

"You're positive?"

"Trust me. You're fine. So here's the history—stock car racing got its start from guys taking a car they could buy from any dealer, tricking out the engine, then racing it on the beach initially, then on the track. So it was a 'stock' car in that it was the same as the family car when they acquired it. Now only the body of the car is the same as a passenger car, and even that has some modifications, but we still use the name *stock*. But if you look around, you can see there isn't much that reminds you of your personal vehicle."

"Well, my car isn't exactly the latest model to roll off the assembly line, but I see what you mean. There are no other seats and I don't recognize any of these gauges."

"No seats other than the driver's, no key ignition, no windows, no speedometer, no locks, no horn, and quite a few other things. Though I wouldn't mind a horn. Sometimes I feel like hitting one to tell another car to get the hell out of my way."

"Somehow I don't think that would have them moving gracefully out of your way."

"Probably not. So a car is built for speed and safety. It's aerodynamic, with a powerful engine with 750 horsepower. There are gauges for oil and water temperature, oil and fuel pressure, and a few other things. A brake, an accelerator, and a clutch. A cooling system to keep my ass from burning to the seat or me passing out, and a roll cage in case my car flips."

"This looks like a regular gearshift." Imogen put her hand on it.

"Don't touch that!" Ty said, then laughed when Imogen snatched her hand away. "Just kidding."

She shot him a look of annoyance. "That was not funny."

"Yes, it was."

Her lips formed a little moue of disgust. "This isn't a very comfortable seat."

"Well, it's custom fit for my body so I don't move around too much, and it's made of aluminum for safety. Head and neck restraints are mandatory, and no, it isn't very comfortable. But this isn't a lazy drive in the country. I'm going over a hundred and eighty miles per hour." Ty couldn't quite keep the pride out of his voice. He loved his job, loved the thrill of racing, the satisfaction of making a car that his crew had worked so hard on perform well for them.

"In golf course green."

He grinned. "Yes, smart-ass."

"How do you control the car?" She was leaning over and peering at the gauges, the floor, the pedals.

"Skill, honey. That's all."

"I can't imagine going that fast."

"I bet you would like it." Ty couldn't resist the urge to reach out and stroke her silky dark hair as it trailed over her shoulder. "Bet you like it hard and fast."

Her head snapped up. "That was an innuendo."

"Sort of." He shrugged. "Okay, hell, yeah, it was. I admit it."

He was a guy, he couldn't help himself. Almost everything reminded him of sex and how much he wanted to get her naked. "But I do think you'd like riding along on the track with me. We should do that sometime, they have special events for that. You can have the thrill of the speed without having to be the driver."

"I would like that." Imogen stared up at him, and the tip of her tongue came out and slid across her bottom lip. "I would like that a lot."

Since she had stripped off her conservative yet very hip blazer, Imogen was wearing only a long-sleeved button-up shirt that was currently gaping at her cleavage. She didn't have large breasts at all, but what Ty could see—and okay, what he had liberally felt up the night before—was that they were firm and pert. He could see her nipples through the fabric, and it was so obvious to him that she wanted him. Why the hell had he sent her home the night before? It had made sense at the time in that he had wanted to do the right thing, but who was he to tell her they should wait if she didn't want to?

Seriously, what guy was stupid enough to do that?

Apparently him.

But that was last night. Today he was going to take what her eyes and her lips were offering.

Ty leaned into the window and kissed her quickly, rougher than he intended, but he was on the edge. She didn't seem to mind, given that she stared up at him and gave a soft moan of pleasure. Damn, he loved the way she gave in to him, the way she let him lead.

He could see the question in her eyes, knew she wasn't going to ask it. Not that he could blame her. She felt like he had turned her offer down the night before, and she wasn't going to put herself out there a second time and risk rejection. But that had never been his intention, not at all. He wanted her in the way he hadn't wanted a woman in so long, maybe ever. This was urgent, a burning, biting need to take Imogen and make her his.

Brushing his finger across her bottom lip, he said, "Come home with me. Spend the night with me. Please."

Ty leaned against the side of his car, muscles tense, mouth hot, waiting for her answer. He wouldn't blame her if she said no, but he would probably cry.

But Imogen just looked up at him and said, "Get me out of this car and take me to bed."

That was not going to be a problem.

CHAPTER

EIGHT

IMOGEN figured she was the one who should be embarrassed given the way she had just blurted out that Ty should take her to bed, but as they drove back to his place, he was the one who was rambling, indicating that he was nervous and felt the need to fill the silent void with inane conversation. She had never been one to babble when she was nervous, leaning more toward retreating into that silence, but a lot of people had their anxious energy burst forth in rapid speech, and clearly Ty was one of them.

"Do you like football?" he asked her, then shook his head. "Of course you don't like football. What the hell am I talking about? Nothing about you says pigskin. And I mean that in the best way. Though it would be very cool if you were smart, beautiful, *and* liked sports. But somehow I can't ever see you throwing on a jersey and cursing at the referee. What about camping?"

It intrigued her to think that he might be invested enough in the outcome of what they were about to do to actually be nervous, and she tried to follow his rapid conversation.

"Camping? What about it?"

"Do you like it?"

"I've never been camping."

"You've never been camping?" Ty sounded shocked, like she had confessed to being a twenty-eight-year-old virgin. "Not even as a kid?"

That amused Imogen. "No. I grew up on the Upper East Side of Manhattan. My mother runs an art gallery and my father is an investment banker. When they wanted to escape the city, we went to the Hamptons and stayed in my grandparents' beach house. Aside from those trips to the beach, the closest I ever got to nature was watering the potted plants on the terrace of our apartment."

"Wow, I never thought about it, but yeah, I guess why would you go camping? I should take you, you'll love it."

Imogen felt a fair amount of alarm. "No, no, you don't need to do that. I suspect I actually won't like it at all. I don't feel like my life is lacking because I haven't been camping. I mean, I've walked in Central Park hundreds of times and that's very bucolic."

Ty scoffed. "That is not the same as going deep into the woods, lying down on a sleeping bag, and listening to nothing but the sounds of nature."

"I'm a sociologist, not a botanist." Plants were green, end of story. She didn't feel the need to submerge herself in them.

He cut her a look that told her he wasn't amused. "No arguments, I'm taking you. This is the stubborn Taurus talking."

That irritated her in return. "You can't make me go. And we're not even supposed to be dating."

Now he really shot her a look that told her he did not appreciate that little reminder. "Okay, here's the deal. Everyone should be open to new experiences, right? So you agree to go camping, and I'll agree to do something you want me to try. You can drag me to an art gallery or something, whatever you want."

They had just pulled into Ty's driveway and he put the car in park as Imogen watched him. He was serious about his offer, and it intrigued her. What would she like Ty to experience? And was she willing to venture into the woods for a weekend of bug bites, misery, and uncertain hygiene to introduce Ty to something from her world?

Without hesitation, she realized she was. Because it occurred to her that both she and Ty had lived very narrow lives and could only benefit from a little broadening of experience. Plus she knew that he underestimated his own intelligence, and she wanted him to appreciate and understand that he was a very bright guy.

"Okay. I will go camping if you read *Much Ado About Nothing* in its entirety."

Something flickered in his eyes, but he only hesitated a second before saying, "It's a deal. I'll pick me up a copy in the next few days. And you look at your calendar and see when you have a Monday and a Tuesday free and we'll hit the woods."

"Oh, that's going to be tricky," she said, seeing an out for herself immediately. "I have class."

"Don't you have any days off? Veterans Day is next week, don't you get that off?"

"I don't know," she lied. Then because she never lied and wasn't comfortable with it, she immediately admitted the truth. Her mother had always said she didn't need to confront Imogen about her lies, she just needed to wait thirty seconds and Imogen would confess. It was clearly still true because she said, "Yes, we have the day off."

"So we'll go then. We can leave first thing Monday morning and come back Tuesday. Just one night. I'll clear those two days with my assistant Toni and find a campsite." He smiled at her. "We'll have a great time."

That she seriously doubted. "You're going to regret taking me out into nature. I am confident I'm going to complain the majority of the time."

But Ty just said, "You can't complain if your lips are busy doing other things."

"Like what?" she said, even though she knew full well what he was talking about.

"Come inside and I'll show you."

He didn't need to ask her twice. In fact, he'd only needed to ask her once—she'd been ready the night before. Of course, she had been a nervous wreck about the whole thing and probably wouldn't have enjoyed herself as much as she could have. She couldn't say why precisely, but it was only twenty-four hours later and she was experiencing none of the anxiety she'd had the night before. It wasn't logical but she decided not to question it and just accept it for what it was.

This was her fantasy. This was her opportunity to step outside of the academic dating pool of men in ill-fitting sweaters and experience sex with a very masculine race car driver. A man she had been attracted to from the first moment she had laid eyes on him, even as she had known having any kind of relationship with him was sheer lunacy. She had never even thought that Ty would be attracted to her in return, she had never expected to be given the opportunity to share a bed with him, and she wanted to take advantage of it. She wanted to discover if he was as aggressive and fun and sexy in bed as he was out.

"Lead the way," she said, and even as she spoke the words, she had a sexual epiphany. Every man she had dated had been confident in his intelligence and his career, but not necessarily sexually. She had been forced to be more dominant than she would have chosen, and that was part of the appeal of Ty—she wanted a man to take the reins while she sat back and enjoyed. Or laid back as the case may be.

The very thought of Ty taking and giving, in total control of her pleasure, sent a rush of liquid warmth between her thighs.

She was aware that her voice had gotten husky and it was clear Ty was aware of it, too. They stared at each other in the shadowy dark of the car for a long, drawn-out minute, each second of his eyes on her working as effectively as if they were his fingers stroking over her bare flesh, causing her nipples to harden, abdomen to tighten, legs to shift slightly apart.

"Oh, fuck," Ty said, shaking his head slightly. "You are so hot."

"I'm not doing anything," Imogen said, bewildered.

"Yes, you are. You're devouring me with your eyes. And God, you have the deepest, most intelligent eyes I've ever seen. I can see the complexity of your brain in your eyes and it turns me on."

"And here I was just thinking I would love to run my hands all over your chest and squeeze your butt."

Ty gave a soft laugh. "You're more than welcome to any-time. Now I'm going to get out of this car before I take you right here. Which has its merits but might upset the neighbors."

Imogen didn't even have time to answer before Ty was out of the car, so she opened the passenger door and bent over to snag her purse off the floor. When she looked up, she was startled to find Ty in the doorway, his crotch almost eye level to her. Not sure what he was doing, she dragged her gaze off his promising erection and up to his face.

"What are you doing?" she asked.

"Just giving you a hand." Ty reached out to help her out of the car.

For some stupid reason, that touched her. It was a basic courtesy, yet it melted her very vulnerable heart. Other men could do the same and she would think nothing of it, except that they were decent human beings who had been raised well, but there was something about Ty that had always affected her differently, from the very first time she'd met him.

She wasn't sure whether she liked it or hated it.

"Thanks." Taking his hand, she got out of the car, expecting he would let go of her the minute she was vertical. He didn't. He just held her hand and led her into the garage and through the back door into his kitchen, flicking on lights as they went.

Imogen wasn't sure what she had expected his house to look like, but immediately she realized it suited Ty. The kitchen cabinets were Shaker style, light wood with simple lines, of a high quality with furniture like detailing. He had a farmhouse sink and soapstone countertops, and the walls were a rich, deep red. She only caught a glimpse of the family room, but it had a stone fireplace that went from hearth to ceiling and big plush furniture in warm caramel and suede tones. If she wasn't mistaken, there was also a giant deer head hanging on the wall, which wasn't unusual for a man who loved the outdoors, but she was still grateful it was too dark to see those glassy eyes staring down at her.

The only thing she had ever hunted down were bargains at Saks and elusive research documents.

When they stepped into his bedroom, Ty turned on the light, which was an iron chandelier dead center over the very big, very masculine bed. It was made up, with a plethora of red throw pillows on the faux suede duvet, and the whole room was tidy and clean. She was impressed.

Ty dropped her hand and left her standing on the plush beige carpet, feeling incredibly aroused and terribly awkward. He dug into his nightstand and emerged with a lighter that he used to light several candles placed around the room. His nervous dialogue seemed to have disappeared and she longed for it to return, because with each second of silence, her anxiety increased, which irritated her.

She was a grown woman and she wanted to do this. A lot.

Which was ironically why she was so nervous. She was vested in the outcome. She wanted to please him and was aware of her shortcomings. No one had ever put the words *bimbo* and *Imogen* in the same sentence. Or *badass*. Or *seductive*. Any of what she had to assume were the typical male fantasies. Her approach had always been enthusiasm rather than technique, and what if that wasn't good enough for Ty?

She was giving herself a mental lecture when he dimmed the overhead light and turned to her with a smile that immediately disappeared when he caught sight of her. "What's wrong?"

"Nothing."

"Liar." He came over to her and took her hand again, stroking her skin with his thumb.

Imogen sighed. "I suck."

"Well, that's promising."

That made her smile despite her best intentions to look worried. "I'm just thinking too much."

"I can tell. And you need to stop it." He slipped his arm around her waist and pulled her to him. "I'm going to make you stop it. I'm going to kiss you and suck you and lick you until there isn't a single thought in your head except amazement that you are coming *again*."

Wow. Yes, if the state of her damp panties was any indication, she responded well to alpha male domination. "Again? I haven't had an orgasm yet."

"Give me five minutes." Ty stepped back and yanked off his T-shirt. He took her hands and put them on his chest. "Touch me," he demanded.

She could do that. His skin was warm and firm, and she slid her greedy fingers all over it while he bent down and kissed her. His mouth always did fabulous things to her insides, pushing aside those pesky doubts with each desperate press, each thrust of his tongue into her.

"I'm going to unbutton your shirt and taste your nipples," he said, moving down her neck with hot kisses, his fingers already working at her buttons.

Cool air hit her overheated flesh when he undid the first button, his breath raising goose bumps on her where he had left damp spots from his tongue trailing down to the dip between her breasts. He was still working on the second button when without preamble he shoved the fabric of her bra to the side and took her nipple into his mouth.

"Oh!" Imogen squeezed her nails into his chest in shock, her head falling back at the jolt of pleasure that shot through her.

He lifted his head and murmured into her chest as he finished off the second button. "Your nipple is perfect. Like a little raspberry, tart and rosy."

She could honestly say no man had ever said that to her before. Kind of liking the idea of being tart and rosy, Imogen said, "Thank you. I have two."

Ty gave a soft laugh. "I know. Is the other one jealous?" He blew on the nipple he had dampened with his tongue, causing her to shiver in delight, then covered it back up and bared the other one.

Instead of covering it with his mouth, he slid his tongue around it, over and over, his lips brushing the tip but never giving it his full attention. Imogen bit her own lip to prevent a groan from slipping out, and shifted, trying to force contact. He ignored her and continued to lick everywhere on her breast except her nipple, giving a teasing little flick now and again but for the most part torturing her by getting close but never giving her the satisfaction of pulling her tight nipple into his mouth and sucking. Imogen moved her hands restlessly on his chest, shifted in her shoes uneasily, tried to maneuver to anticipate his movement and have him land on the aching bud, but he evaded her.

"Ty," she said, a little desperate, grabbing the back of his head and trying to force the issue that way.

But he stopped altogether and pulled her hands off his head. "Put your hands in your back pockets," he told her.

"Why?" she asked, a little jolt of desire hitting her between the thighs. She wasn't sure why he wanted her to do that, but it sounded mildly kinky and she liked that.

He was already sliding her hands down into her back pockets, his own hands cupping hers, applying pressure so that together they were caressing and feeling her backside, her elbows bent and half-bare chest jutting toward him.

"Because you are so sexy, and I want to give you pleasure all night."

Okay, then. She was good with that.

His hands retreated, leaving hers in place. "Don't move them," he told her, his eyes dark with desire.

It was an odd position, a strange, erotic feeling to be standing there, not knowing what he was going to do, but anticipating it, waiting with bated breath for the next touch. Slowly, he undid the rest of her buttons and pulled open her shirt.

"Where is your jacket?" he asked. "Did you leave it at the garage?"

Disoriented by the way his thumbs were skimming across her bare belly, she said, "No, I grabbed it. I think I left it in your car."

"Good. It looked expensive. I'd hate to think it was lost."

That was oddly touching and considerate, but she couldn't care less about her blazer at the moment, especially when he popped the button on her jeans, but did nothing else, moving back up to lift her bra out of his way. Moving quickly, his mouth was suddenly on her, sucking her nipple hard.

Imogen let a moan go ahead and escape this time, then hitched in a breath when he gently bit her before abandoning her again. His hand cupped her breast, and he rubbed his thumb across her swollen and damp nipple, while his mouth migrated to the other tip, his tongue laving it in rhythm with his thumb, until Imogen was fighting for breath, her head lolling back.

She tried to pull her hands out to grip his hair for balance, but he sensed the movement and said, "Leave them." Since it also resulted in his thumb descending to hold her hands in place in her pockets, Imogen went still. He went back to licking her nipple, still cupping the weight of her, but now his free hand gripped her backside, his fingers shifting down along the seam of her jeans, down, then up, down, then up, so that the friction heated her, and the tease of where he almost reached, then always retreated, had slick moisture easing down into her panties.

"Ty," she said, not sure what she was asking for, her thoughts jumbled and erratic.

"What? You want your shirt all the way off, don't you?" He stood up and leaned against her, his firm chest brushing against her swollen nipples. "Here, pull them out for two seconds." He shifted her hands up out of her pockets, then before she could blink, he had her shirt yanked down her arms and onto the floor. The bra followed and she was totally naked from the waist up.

She was about to wrap her arms around him and scrape her nails across his broad back, but he forced her hands back in the jeans pockets.

"No," she protested.

"Yes." Ty stepped back. "Let me look at you."

Imogen felt a pang of self-consciousness, her shoulders slumping slightly forward.

But then Ty said, "Oh, baby, look at how gorgeous you are." His jaw was clenched, his erection clearly visible in his jeans. "Such creamy, soft skin." His finger floated up her arm, barely skimming the flesh. "Silky hair . . . so dark, so sexy."

He flicked the end of her hair, causing it to slide across her shoulder and chest, and Imogen forgot to be self-conscious. She licked her lips, aware that she was breathing hard, her fingers digging into her own flesh to give her something to hold on to.

Ty gave a soft moan. "Do that again."

"What?"

"Lick your lips. I bet you can do amazing things with that tongue, knowing what it does in my mouth."

Imogen straightened and did it again, dragging her tongue

slowly across her bottom lip, enjoying the way his eyes darkened, the way he stared at her mouth in dark fascination.

"Do you leave your glasses on or take them off when you're having sex?" he asked, his voice low and rough.

They weren't sliding down her nose at the moment, so Imogen wasn't bothered by them. She shrugged. "I don't know. It depends. Why?"

"Because things are about to get down and dirty, and I don't want to knock them off your face by accident."

Down and dirty. She liked the sound of that, though she couldn't picture anything they would do that would send her glasses sailing off her face. "It doesn't matter."

"Can you see without them?" Ty played with the stems, lifting the frames up and down on her nose.

"I certainly can't see when you do that."

He grinned and let them go. "Sorry."

"Things are a little blurry without them but I can manage. But I need my hands to take them off."

Ty leaned forward and kissed her long and tenderly, his mouth open as it took hers over and over. "Okay. I can take the glasses off for you, but I'll let you have your hands back. For now."

He reached behind her and extracted her hands from her jeans and pulled them to her thighs and slowly let her go. Imogen took off her glasses and closed the stems neatly. Ty took them from her and leaned back and set the glasses on his dresser. Then he stepped in front of her again, close, invading her space and making her so damn glad she was half-naked. She could feel the heat radiating off him, and she loved the way he was bigger than her, the way he could surround her. Without her glasses, he was a little fuzzy, but he was close enough that it was mild, and because of the soft candlelight of the room, she couldn't see every detail of his face anyway. But she could delineate his basic form, his shoulders, his muscular chest, the small shock of hair that rose above his waistband, the shadow of his pelvis where his jeans hung low. She could see his expression clearly enough to read that it was mischievous, bold, confident.

Funny now that her hands were loose, she didn't know what to do with them, and she knew that she was waiting for him to direct their seduction. She wanted that, craved that, was completely and totally aroused by the fact that she didn't have to be in charge, that there was no fragile ego here to bolster.

Ty wanted to take and she wanted to be taken.

"After all your fussing and complaining, your hands are free," Ty said, teasing her as he brushed his lips over the corner of her mouth, shifting so that his chest moved against hers. "So why did you want them out so bad? What do you want to touch?"

Ty could practically see the wheels turning in Imogen's head. She wouldn't answer impulsively and she wouldn't avoid his question with a vague answer. Imogen would tell him precisely what she wanted, he had no doubt.

She said, "I don't know. I want to touch everything and I'm debating where to start."

He would pretty much give his bank account to have her go down on her knees and take his cock into her mouth, but he wanted her to take that kind of action on her own, not because he asked. "Well, while you're deciding, I'm going to touch you again. I want to suck your sweet nipples again."

Imogen made a delightful little sound of anticipation, her eyes wide, no lenses to obscure their deep, endless blue color from him. Ty kissed her, loving the softness of her lips, the honey-eyed tang of her tongue and mouth, his hands on her waist. She was thin and toned, but still soft, with small, perky breasts that fit nicely into his palms. He could spend all night running his lips over her neck, across her shoulders, down into the cleft between her breasts. Ty nuzzled her flesh, tasting the pureness of her skin, appreciating that she didn't wear heavy lotion or perfume. Imogen just tasted like sweet woman, and she had the most amazing nipples.

Playing with one with his tongue, he rolled it around before sucking gently, his eyes half-closed. He was rewarded by a soft sigh and Imogen reaching a decision on where to put her hands. They started on his back, stroking softly, lithe and small and gentle, then as he got more aggressive, sucking her harder, her touch migrated down to his ass and she squeezed. It was a simple touch, but one that made Ty's erection throb.

He wanted all of her. He wanted it slow, yet fast. He wanted her to scream, to orgasm over and over at the same time he wanted to just pound himself into her and let himself come in a hard, hot burst. Still playing and licking, he shifted his hand to her jeans and undid the zipper. Slipping his hand inside, he cupped the outside of her panties, feeling her heat soak into him. He started to move his middle finger, bending it so it slid up and down on her mound, the satin of her panties making a smooth, easy surface to glide across.

Imogen moaned very softly into his ear, her hands abandoning his ass and hurrying up his back to grip his shoulders for balance. The way she clung to him, the way she trusted him to give her pleasure, thrilled Ty. He wanted to give her ecstasy like she'd never known before, and he wanted to have the total satisfaction of watching her shatter beneath his touch.

Moving inside her panties, Ty gave his own groan of approval when the pad of his finger hit slick moisture immediately. The farther he moved down, the wetter she was, and their breathing matched, a steady pant, pant, as Ty dipped inside her then drew back to swirl the hot fluid around her swollen clitoris.

"Oh, Ty," she murmured.

"What, honey?" He buried his mouth in her hair as he worked her with his finger, aroused by the feel of her tightness, the way her body gave to welcome him when he thrust inside her, the way she gripped his shoulders convulsively each time his finger went deep.

"I . . . I . . ."

"Yeah?" Ty nuzzled her ear, dipping his tongue inside.

Imogen groaned and swayed back on her feet, inadvertently pulling away from his finger.

Ty took his hand out of her panties completely and urged her back, his hands on her waist.

"What?" she asked. "Why did you stop? Where do you want me to go?"

"Just back up," he said. "I want you against the wall." He wanted help in keeping her still while he fucked her with his fingers, then his tongue, then his cock.

"The wall?" she asked, curious excitement in her voice as she walked tentatively backward.

"Yep. Almost there," he said, putting his hand behind her head when she reached it so she wouldn't conk her skull. "Now all you have to do is stand there."

Ty returned his finger to its previous position, only this time he added a companion so he had two fingers moving in and out of her hot, tight hole. Imogen stiffened and her eyes and mouth shot wide-open. Her hand grabbed his wrist and held it while he fingered her, pulling all the way out to flick across her clit with each stroke. When her breathing got erratic and her back arched,

Ty knew another minute or two would have her at an orgasm, so he slowly withdrew and bent down.

"Why did you stop again?" she asked, disappointment in her voice.

"I'm taking your shoes off," he said, going down on one knee, lifting her foot and doing just that. "Then I'm taking your pants off."

"Right. Of course," she said, obediently lifting her other foot so he could slip off her flat black shoes.

"How many times do you come, Emma Jean?" Ty asked, as he stood back up and moved his hands inside the back of her jeans and panties, cupping the smooth flesh of her tight little ass.

"What do you mean?" She leaned into him, her eyes half-closed.

"In one sex session, do you usually come once, twice, three times . . . five?"

Her forehead creased with her frown. "Usually just once. But it's a good one. Why?"

"Just strategizing how soon I'm going to let you come." He nipped her bottom lip. "It sounds like we're going to have to draw it out."

"We don't *have* to," she said. "It's not like I don't continue to enjoy myself post-coital, because I do. So don't feel that you need to cease and desist once I have."

"But the buildup is always better." Ty shoved her jeans and panties down and lifted her leg so he could remove them, brushing his lips over her soft, ivory thigh. "Don't worry. I'll make sure you enjoy it."

With her pants and panties half off and his mouth on her thigh, he was inches from her sex. He could feel the warmth of her inner thighs, he could smell the tang of her arousal. Ty turned his head and breathed in her scent deeply.

"What are you doing?" she asked.

"Smelling you."

"Why?" She sounded more curious than horrified, which would probably be the reaction of a lot of women.

"Because you smell good. Like a woman who is very turned on and that turns me on."

"I am turned on."

"I know." Ty shifted a little closer and lavished his tongue on her clit, using his fingers to spread her so that he could have a clear view and taste of her swollen pink flesh.

"Oh, God," she said, the words low and drawn out. "*Ty.*"

His name tearing off her lips like that made his own body clench and tighten and he jerked back. She gave a cry of disappointment, but he ignored it and made fast work of pulling her pants down her other leg and tossing them somewhere behind him. Ty stood up and with one hand slipped his finger inside her again to keep her hot and wet and eye-rolling eager, while he dug in his pocket with his free hand for a condom.

Holding the packet in his mouth, he undid his jeans and shoved them and his boxer briefs down one-handed. They got to about his knees and he figured they would fall on their own after that. Using his teeth, he opened the condom and managed to get it rolled on his erection all while still stroking inside Imogen. Pleased with his multitasking skills, Ty finished securing the condom then took Imogen's hands, which had been fluttering around by his waist, and gripped them together. He raised her arms up over her head, wrists together, flat against the wall.

When she would have protested, he swallowed her words with a kiss, one that tasted of her arousal. He loved to kiss a woman after his mouth had been between her thighs. He loved to give her a taste of her own desire, loved the woman who took it, enjoyed it, appreciated it. Imogen clearly did, her tongue slipping into his mouth, kissing him feverishly and eagerly. Ty nudged her legs a little apart with his feet, stepping out of his jeans as he did, enjoying the feel of her hips arching to bump against his, her nipples taut and thrust forward for his attention.

"Go up on your toes, Emma Jean."

He knew she wouldn't protest, that she would do it. But she would ask why, and she did.

"Why?" she asked, even as she obeyed and raised herself up on her toes, providing him with a gorgeous view, her arms up, her breasts heaving with her rapid breathing, her hips and legs long and sensual.

"It makes the angle better." Ty brought his erection between her legs and moved it slowly up and down over her folds. "Open yourself for me."

"Are you really going to penetrate me while I'm standing against this wall?"

"Yes. For a minute or two."

"I find that exciting."

"Me, too. Now open yourself for me," he demanded, rougher this time. He wanted inside her and it was sheer torture to feel her slickness over his head, lubricating the condom and teasing him with all the warmth she would provide.

"You don't really have to, you know," she said, eyes half-closed. "You just push it in and that usually works just fine. A rather clever design, actually, that it remains closed until in use, but no complicated system is required to—"

Imogen yelped when Ty bit her nipple.

"I want you," he said carefully, "to take your right hand, slide it down between us, and open yourself for my cock. Now. Not because you have to, but I want to see your fingers on yourself, because I want to feel you pulling yourself apart for me to thrust into you and fuck you. Do you understand?"

She stared at him in shock, completely still except for the rise and fall of her chest. Ty knew he was being demanding and a little impatient, but he was aching to take her and he wanted her acquiescence, her very obvious acceptance of him into her body. And she liked it. He could tell. She was shocked, yes, but most of what he saw in her eyes was excitement. Lust.

Which made him harder than he would have ever thought possible. The thought of taking Imogen to a place where she no longer analyzed every action, where she just felt and did, made him ache with red-hot desire. He was going to do that, give that to her.

"My goodness, you're bossy," she said.

"And you didn't answer the question. Do you understand?" Ty started to move his cock away from her.

She quickly nodded. "Yes, I understand."

"Then do it." He moved back into position.

Imogen sucked in a breath and tentatively moved her left hand down. She abruptly stopped herself and switched them. "Wait, you said right."

Ty bit back a groan. He should have known she would follow him to the letter. "Yes. Good girl."

Her fingers snaked down between their bodies and she closed her eyes as she found her hot, wet core. Ty watched her accidentally brush against her clit, then linger there for a second, rolling her thumb over the tight button before she redirected, sliding her first two fingers down over her folds, then opening them in a V. Opening herself for him.

Raising his right hand, Ty enclosed it over Imogen's left hand still above her head against the wall. He gripped her for leverage and for the connection, gave her temple a soft kiss, then thrust himself into her. They both moaned, his loud and raw, hers tapering off into a whimper.

"Damn, you feel good," he said, resting in place for a second, savoring the snugness of her enclosing him, the way their thighs were pressing together.

Her reply was another soft moan, followed by, "I feel really . . . full in this position."

"Is that a good thing?" Ty pulled back slowly and thrust back into her, biting back a curse.

"Oh, yes," she said, nodding, her hair puffing up above her head in a funny little cone that bobbed as she moved her head enthusiastically. "It's incredibly good. Indescribable. De—"

She stopped speaking when he thrust into her again.

"—lightful," she finished.

Ty would have laughed under any other circumstances, but nothing about burying himself in Imogen against his bedroom wall made him want to laugh. He picked up speed, found a rhythm that had her groans coming in regular staccato bursts, one for each time he drove deep, no matter how fast he set the pace. It was hot as freaking hell and Ty rested his head against his arm, closing his eyes as he squeezed her hand beneath hers and just moved inside her, taking in the sound of her pleasure, enjoying the feel of her slick, welcoming body.

He sensed again when she was treading too close to an orgasm. Her breathing changed, her head started to shift back and forth, and she went up higher on her toes, like she was trying to escape the intensity of his thrusts.

If Imogen said she usually came only once, Ty wasn't going to argue with that, or think he could somehow manage to drag more than one from her. Not their first time together. He would learn how to make her come repeatedly with knowledge of her body and her likes and dislikes, and that would take familiarity. He would act on the assumption she was only going to have one orgasm tonight, and if that was the case, he damn well wanted to have done everything he could to her before it happened.

He wanted her desperate, clinging, screaming, insensible, incoherent with pleasure, groaning and squirming and so turned on that she would agree to anything and would be hard-pressed to remember her own goddamn name.

Then, and only then, would he let her have the biggest, hottest, loudest orgasm of her entire life, where she scratched and clawed and begged and lost every thought she'd ever had from her logical little brain.

So Ty pulled completely out of her and stepped back, panting as she dropped onto the balls of her feet and stared at him in shock and disappointment. He was holding her hand against the wall, but she still sagged down a little.

"Why did you stop?" she asked, dropping her eyes to his erection. "You didn't come. Did you?"

"No. No one is coming yet. I'm just getting started with you."

CHAPTER
NINE

THE man was trying to kill her.

There was no other explanation for taking her to the edge like that—twice, Imogen might add—and then just *stopping*. But she had no ability to protest, because it was clear from his words and the look on his face that he was dead serious. He was not finished with her, and she suspected she was going to get a lesson in drawing out pleasure as long as humanly possible.

He had already excited her more in half an hour than other men had in six months, so she just slumped against the wall and waited for him to take his next course of action. For a fleeting second, she thought she should contribute something, maybe suggest a position or two, but she dropped the thought immediately. He had a plan, or at least liked taking control, and she was perfectly content to be on the receiving end.

Maybe next time she could be more aggressive.

Of course, if there was a next time. There were no guarantees.

All the more reason to just enjoy the attention he was lavishing on her.

Ty squatted down in front of her. She shivered in anticipation, knowing precisely what that meant. He was going to do those amazing things to her with his tongue.

"Keep your hands above your head, but reach over and grab the doorframe," he told her. "You're going to need the leverage."

Hello. Leverage for what? She did as he instructed, amazed at how easily he could get her excited, how a shiver of delight rippled through her body when he moved in front of her.

"Look at that," he said. "You are so fucking wet it's on your thighs. That is so sexy."

Then he raked his finger across that moisture, raised his finger to his mouth, and sucked, his eyes trained on her. Imogen felt an answering kick of desire deep in her womb, her vagina still tender and aching from his thrusts. She actually ached everywhere, was aware of every single inch of her entire body, her skin sensitive, every muscle, every nerve ending tight and poised for pleasure.

"I like that you get nice and wet," he said. "It's very satisfying to see it, to feel it, to taste it. It means you want me."

"I do want you."

"Slide down the wall," he said. "Still holding the doorframe. Just slide down, nice and sexy, and spread your knees apart while you do."

She realized then part of the appeal of Ty's directives. Imogen had never felt particularly sexy, had never known how to use her body to visual advantage, had never felt comfortable posing and displaying herself. Ty was teaching her, probably without even realizing it, how to do just that. How to take advantage of both the tactile and the visual appeal of her feminine shape and intimate places to drive a man deeper into desire.

So she followed his instructions and bent her legs so that her bare bottom and back slid down the cool wall, holding on to the door for balance. When she was down about halfway, she took a deep breath and opened her knees, exposing herself fully to his view, watching to see his reaction.

It was a good one.

His eyes darkened and he rubbed his bottom lip with his thumb as he drank her in, not looking at her face, but between her legs. He put his hands lightly on her knees and gazed up at her with a look so intense, so hot, that she sucked in her breath.

"I hope you're flexible."

Wondering what he had in mind for her, fairly certain she would like it, Imogen still had to admit, "Probably not."

"We'll work it out." Ty lifted one of her legs. "Hold on." He placed it over his shoulder so that her knee hooked him.

The shift shot her butt up in the air and threw off her balance. "I'm going to fall," she said, grappling at the doorframe.

"No, you're not. I'm too close to the wall for you to fall. Stop wiggling and relax."

"I'm not . . . ahhh." Imogen forgot what she had been about to say when he bent forward and deftly inserted his tongue inside her. "Oh, my God."

He moved in and out, quick, swordlike thrusts that had her making sounds she hadn't even known she was capable of. The soft moistness of his tongue, coupled with its width, tripped off shudders of ecstasy with each stroke. She could feel him so acutely inside her, his nose bumping against her clitoris.

Ty lifted her other leg up, so they were both on his shoulders.

His hands were on the small of her back, and somehow between the wall and his grip, she didn't seem to be in any danger of slipping down and smacking her head on the floor. Not that she really cared, because it was the hottest, most erotic position she had ever been in. It was kind of like riding on someone's shoulders in reverse. The only way she could be more fully enveloping his face would be if she were sitting on it, and that would not have the added bonus of knowing it was his strength holding her up. Imogen turned her head side to side, held on, and let him do the most delicious things to her with his mouth while she regressed to a time before language, expressing her pleasure through whimpers and guttural groans.

There was no time, no awareness of the room, cold or hot, dark or light, just the feel of him and her taut, overstimulated body. There was just him, just his mouth, his hands, his breathing, his ability to strip away all her thoughts until she was empty except for the acute pleasure, all her focus on one spot, one spot only. The tightness was building in her again and she quieted down, feeling it sneaking up on her, wanting to reach for it, wanting to fall over into that explosion, but Ty pulled away abruptly and eased her legs to the ground.

She blinked at him. Holy shit. He had done it again, and she couldn't tell if it was intentional or not. "I was about to come."

"I know." He reached for her hand and stood up. "Come here. Wrap your legs around my waist."

"I can't. My legs don't work." She wasn't lying. Her entire body felt boneless, and her calves were shaking from the strain they'd been placed under. Her inner thighs pulsed and ached in incompletion.

He didn't bother to argue with her. He just swung her up into his arms with more urgency than gentleness and marched over to the bed. Imogen held on with what little strength she had left while he leaned over and yanked off the duvet one-handed, revealing cocoa-colored sheets, which he deposited her on. She was on her back, sideways on the bed, and he grabbed her knees and yanked her down so that her legs dangled over the side. He stepped in between her knees and pushed inside her.

She loved that moment of first impact, when a man entered her and her entire body moaned and sighed and accepted him, and with Ty, it was even more so. It was primal, possessive, the way he gave that hard thrust, his arms on either side of her, his expression fierce and urgent. Ty was quiet, his lips tightly pressed together, but Imogen couldn't contain her pleasure as he filled her with steady strokes, and she moaned, letting her legs fall farther apart. Wrapping her arms around him, she rested her hands on his back and felt the movement of his muscles as he worked hard pumping in and out of her.

Then he shifted slightly and hit a spot that had her soft caresses turning into hard, nail-scraping grabs as she held her hands in place. Each time he withdrew, his body moved back as well, sending his back into her grip, and she knew she was tearing up his skin, but she didn't care. There should be evidence tomorrow, scratches and bruises to show how hot and hard they had come together. "Oh, yes, right there," she moaned.

"You like that?" he asked, staring down at her with satisfaction.

"Yes. Oh, God, yes, please. Please." He had found an angle that nudged her G spot, and Imogen almost forgot to breathe as he hit her over and over.

She could feel the fullness of him, feel the throb, his growing loss of control, and she raised her hips, anticipating both her orgasm and his. But Ty yanked back all the way out of her, panting, and dropped his mouth to her. Imogen didn't even have time to protest before she was caught by the current and dragged under to the different kind of ecstasy his tongue offered. Raising her arms over her head, she gripped the sheet and squirmed as he tortured her with long licks over her clitoris. It was almost too much, her body sensitive and taut, her legs moving restlessly, feet finding the bed rail to rest on for a better grip, a way to hold herself in place, to ground her under his assault.

When he sucked her clitoris, she arched up off the bed, a gasp flying out of her mouth, but Ty didn't let her stay up. With his hand on her chest, he pushed her back down, moved up, and entered her again.

"Ohmigod," she managed, before she lost the ability to speak.

Then there was nothing, no thought, no words, no anything but the feel of him deep inside her, taking her, their bodies colliding and slapping. Imogen's own excitement grew hotter still when Ty broke his silence and began to let out a grunt of pleasure with each stroke. It was a thrilling, satisfying sound and she dug her nails deeper into his back, needing to hold on, needing to feel him.

Ty pulled out yet again, his movements fast and jerky, and Imogen sucked in her breath at the loss. "No, Ty! Please . . ."

His mouth was on her again and all the logic she had been born with, all her ability to reason and rationalize, completely disappeared. She disintegrated into an insensible, babbling mass of nerve endings, moan after moan emerging as her eyes rolled back in her head and her arms fell to the bed. She couldn't think, couldn't talk, could only enjoy an ecstasy so acute it was nearly painful.

She didn't know if it was a minute or ten before he lifted his head, his lips glistening with her arousal, and entered her again.

This time, she was too insane with want, too close. He stroked once and she felt it rising inside her. When he stroked a second time, harder, her orgasm burst, hot and explosive, from deep inside her, and she yelled out—a warning, a triumph, she wasn't sure—but she wanted him to know that this was it, this was the best orgasm she'd ever had. Ever. Ever, ever.

"That's it," he said, smoothing her hair off her forehead, then clutching a handful hard enough that her head tilted. "Come for me, babe."

"I am." She was. She liked the edgy roughness of his grip, the way he held his rhythm while her body shuddered and convulsed under and around him. The pulse inside was tight and strong, the volume, the intensity, the pleasure overwhelming and wonderful and satiating all at once.

But the best moment of all came while she was still feeling the last vestiges of her own orgasm. She watched Ty as his eyes drifted half-closed, his mouth opened, his erection paused inside her, pulsing, then his orgasm joined hers, his shouts mingling with hers, their bodies tight and connected in shuddering, mind-shattering passion.

It was amazing, to feel him coming inside her, and Imogen smiled up at him with a little laugh as they both reached the end and Ty went still.

"Whoa." He smiled back at her, turning his head to wipe the sweat off his forehead with his shoulder. "Told you you're one smoking hot woman, Emma Jean."

"I have no complaints about you either," she said, enjoying lying flat on her back, his weight heavy and appealing on her, his penis still embedded inside her.

"No?" He kissed her, finishing it off with a nip at her bottom lip. "Not even the fact that I kept you from coming?"

Imogen felt a little aftershock in her vagina from his words and the sensation of his teeth toying with her mouth. "While that was irritating at the time, I see in hindsight that you had a master plan. And I appreciate your willingness to look at the big picture."

"It was definitely meant to benefit you."

"It did, thank you." She raised her hips, wanting to feel that hard hit from him again, even as she knew she was completely satisfied. He just felt so good.

He groaned. "God, you're killing me."

Pulling out of her, Ty moved around on the bed until he was in a proper sleep position. "Come here, babe."

He reached for her, and after Imogen managed to crawl up the bed, he tucked her into his side, his arm around her. He yanked up the covers over them, then let out a mighty yawn.

Imogen had wondered how they would address the sleeping-over issue, if he would want that or not, but his actions were fairly clear that he intended for her to stay, and she was warm and satisfied and sleepy, and her head on his chest felt wonderful. She didn't feel inclined to go anywhere at the moment.

"Ty?"

"Hmmm?" His eyes were closed and his breathing was already evening out.

"Never mind." She had been about to ask something phenomenally stupid, like if he had liked it, or if he thought she was sexy. Questions that stemmed from insecurity and had no business being spoken out loud. If she were logical about it, she would recognize that he had clearly enjoyed himself, and that he must find her at least marginally attractive and sexually appealing to devote the kind of time and energy to it that he had.

She didn't need verbal confirmation from him.

"Alright, good night," he said, his words a little slurred. "But before I pass out, I want you to know that you're the hottest biscuit this side of the gravy boat."

Imogen wasn't sure what the hell that meant, but it was definitely a compliment, and she recognized a warm and fuzzy feeling blooming in her at his unprompted reassurance. She was about to respond when he gave her ass a little smack.

Startled, she looked up at him. But he was already asleep. Obviously the ass pat had taken every last ounce of energy reserve from him.

Snuggling in closer with a silly grin on her face, Imogen stole his body heat and joined him in sleep.

TY woke up the best way possible—exhausted, with stiff muscles and a naked Imogen draped across him. He had always been the kind to snap awake, so as soon as his eyes opened, he was alert and aware that the sun was creeping up outside. The candles he had stupidly left burning had snuffed out while they were sleeping and the room was dim, but full light would be streaming in his windows in another half hour. Imogen was still out cold, her breathing soft and steady, her fingers twitching on his shoulder.

He couldn't resist dropping a kiss on the top of her head as he shifted a little. She had been everything he could have hoped for and then some. Sex with her had been . . . wow. Amazing. Off the chain. Mouthwatering. Hot and exciting and damn satisfying. She had been agreeable and eager, very vocal and very excited, all things he really appreciated. Hell, things he craved. He could admit it, he liked to dominate just a little in the bedroom, and she hadn't fought him on that. In fact, he thought she'd gotten off on it.

Shifting again, Ty tried to get more comfortable. He was sweating his balls off from both his thoughts and Imogen blanketed all across him, one of her legs slung over the top of his. It was a funny thing, his attraction to her. She really wasn't the type he'd ever gone for before. But it was working for him, and he could smugly say it clearly worked for her, too, so there was no reason to worry about the why at the moment. Not when he had better things to do.

Kicking at the covers, he sighed with relief when he succeeded in moving them down their legs and a waft of fresh, cool air hit his overheated body. Imogen whimpered and clutched tighter to him, wiggling so that the warmth of her inner thighs caressed his leg. Ty was instantly hard. Moving his hand lightly down her back, he drew a finger down the seam of her backside and lower still until he found her sex, nicely spread for him because of her leg flopped over his. He stroked inside her, slowly, soothing her with a kiss on her cheek when she made a noise in the back of her throat.

As he moved his finger gently, in no hurry, just enjoying the feel of her soft and moist inside, her body responded by flooding him with sweet wetness. Her hips moved a little and her eyes fluttered open.

"What . . ." she asked, expression sleepy and confused. "Ty? What is . . . ooohh."

"Good morning," he said and kissed her open mouth.

"I thought I was having a sex dream," she said. "But you really are finger-fucking me, aren't you? That is the correct term for it, isn't it?"

His cock throbbed at her matter-of-fact words. "Yep and yep. I thought this was a better way to wake you up than an alarm clock."

"I concur."

Removing his finger, Ty grabbed her by the waist and hauled her all the way on top of him, nestling her mound right on top of his erection. He thought she would take the hint what he wanted her to do, but Imogen just lay on him like a limp noodle, making soft sighs that sounded suspiciously like she might actually fall back asleep.

"Ride my cock, babe," he urged her, moving his hips to encourage her.

"Too sleepy. After coffee I can move, but not before." She yawned into his shoulder.

So she was one of those, groggy and slow to rouse. He could sympathize but he was well aware that he had to leave his house in probably less than two hours and that he needed to eat breakfast and shower. He wasn't going to Martinsville without making love to Imogen one more time, and she was just going to have to deal with that.

He knew the surefire way to wake her sexy little ass up. Even though she was deadweight, she was still a tiny little thing, and it wasn't difficult for him to haul her up the length of him.

"What are you doing?" she mumbled, flattening her palms on the bed to brace herself.

"Sit up," he demanded.

"Why?"

"Because I said so."

She gave a soft laugh and dragged herself to a sitting position on his chest, her eyes half-closed, heavy with sleep, her shoulders slumped, skin pink, and hair messy and tousled.

Damn, she was so gorgeous. Ty reached out and stroked her breasts, her pink nipples.

"Mr. Checkered Flag," she said in amusement. "So bossy. So . . ." She sucked in her breath when he pulled her whole body forward, settling her right onto his mouth. "Ahhh . . . so smart. So right."

God, he liked the sound of that. Her words had him throbbing, and he gripped her hips and ate at her, sliding his tongue up and down and tasting her tangy sweetness. Imogen had grabbed the headboard and her head had snapped back. She was making delightful little mewling sounds in the back of her throat that spurred him on.

He could do this to her all day, just licking and sucking and tasting her arousal, moving his tongue over her most intimate avenue, feeding his own desire with hers. But after a few delightful minutes, Imogen shifted.

"Where are you going?" he asked her.

"I have an idea."

She still looked sleepy as she turned and Ty had no idea what she was going to suggest. He couldn't always predict the direction Imogen's mind moved in. But he figured it out when she reached for his cock.

"Damn fine idea, babe." He lifted her leg over his chest so that he could have full access to her again, and he was flicking his tongue over her again at the exact moment her mouth closed around him.

Ty groaned. There was nothing hotter than that. Imogen's mouth slid over his cock, a warm, moist caress, while he tasted her, her body over his, as they sprawled together in the intimacy of his crumpled bedsheets. They moved together, Imogen's sucking shifting her away from his mouth, then back onto it again. The rhythm got faster, harder, their labored breathing intermingling with the sound of his bed giving a little squeak with each movement.

The more excited she got, the more Imogen relaxed her bottom onto him, and he gripped her hips tightly, wanting to give her the biggest, brightest, most amazing pleasure she'd ever known. Her saliva had slicked him up and he clenched his thighs and her mouth slid smoothly and tightly over his throbbing cock. When she took him deep, Ty's tongue faltered on her while he closed his eyes and groaned.

"Oh, babe," he murmured, knowing she probably couldn't hear him. But damn, that had him about out of his skin.

Knowing he was going to come soon, he renewed his efforts on Imogen, slipping his tongue into her the way he had already figured out drove her wild. Her hips bucked beneath his grip, and he knew he'd hit the jackpot. He worked her, faster and deeper, shifting his focus from the feel of her on his cock to the feel of her soft, sweet insides, and he was rewarded with a trembling in her thighs. Her movements paused on him, then she burst into an orgasm, her moans muffled by the way he still filled her mouth, her body jerking. Ty held on, stroking evenly, enjoying her legs wrapped around him, her weight on him, her hot inner core spread for him to pleasure. Her orgasm was hard and tight, and rolled over him as he kept his tongue buried in her, the tangy moisture an erotic reminder of how much he loved doing this with her. Him doing this to her.

After her shudders had quieted down, Imogen started moving on him again, and Ty sank back a little, still holding her, still feeling her over and around him, but wanting to just close his eyes and enjoy her attention. Her breasts moved over his stomach and her hair tickled his thighs and he forced himself to relax his body, knowing it would make the pleasure more acute for him. Letting himself groan at the feel of her mouth, Ty ran his fingers over her soft smoothness, over the backs of her knees, her thighs, her backside.

When she added her hand to her movements, trailing her mouth with a firm grip on his shaft, Ty forgot about relaxing.

"Yes, that's it," he told her. "Give it to me, honey."

She didn't answer, for which he was hugely fucking grateful. She just kept on doing what she was doing, and Ty held on to her hips and pumped himself into her mouth, taking over the rhythm. Imogen let him, holding her hand and mouth steady while he thrust into her, and Ty gritted his teeth and exploded with a tight groan.

Imogen held steady, taking him, and he rode out the ecstasy, the room hot and bright, his thoughts nonexistent, his body pulsing and throbbing and rejoicing. When his shudders slowed, he brought his thrusts to a stop, and lay on the bed for a second, stunned and depleted. God, she was magnificent. It was another second before she pulled back, then she just turned and shot him a sly smile over the curves of their tangled-up bodies.

Wait a minute. Her lips were shiny, but otherwise clean.

"Did you swallow?" Ty asked, a little shocked.

"Uh-huh," she said. "You don't mind, do you?"

Like he even needed to think about that. "Hell, no. Damn, you are so fucking hot and sexy. I just can't say that enough, Emma Jean. In fact, I'm thinking of giving you a new nickname. I might just start calling you Engine, since that's what you do to me. Turn me on. Rev me up."

"Really?" She shifted so that her legs were no longer on either side of his head. "I turn you on?"

Ty couldn't resist the urge and smacked her retreating ass. She had an adorable, spankable little ass. "Uh, yes, babe, trust me. I am one amazingly lucky guy to have tapped you."

"Tapped me?" She raised her eyebrows, but she looked amused even as she looked confused. "What does that mean?"

"Tap you. Like a keg. Let the fun begin, the spirits flow, open it up . . . I don't know. It's just an expression."

"So I've been tapped?" She rested her chin on his chest and gave him another sleepy smile.

"Yep." Ty kissed her palm. "And I'm going to tap you again on Monday when we're camping, so rest up this weekend while I'm gone."

"Are you leaving today?"

"Yeah, I should be out of here within . . ." He glanced at the clock. "Shit, an hour and a half. Do you want a shower? I'm going to fix us some breakfast."

"I could use a shower." Imogen leaned over and fumbled around for her glasses. She stuck them on her face and widened her eyes. "Ah, that's better. Now I can see."

Ty sat up and leaned against his headboard. "So you really can't see all that well? Damn, girl, you could have lost an eye doing what you were."

She laughed. "I can see something that big. I'm not totally blind."

"True, it is *really* big," he joked. He'd say he was on the high side of average, nothing to either worry about or brag about, and hey, it worked for him. But he enjoyed teasing her.

"I like it. A lot," she said in a voice that was neither joke nor flirtation. It was just Imogen honesty, and that as usual was totally arousing to him.

"Why, thank you, honey," he said, thinking if she didn't shift off of him, she was going to find herself liking it a whole lot more. Since he didn't have a condom within reach and he had to leave, that was not a good idea. Time to change the subject. "You ever thought about Lasik eye surgery?"

"No, not really."

"Too expensive?"

"No, I can afford it. I have a trust fund from my grandparents."

"Really?" Although Ty knew Imogen was educated and had guessed she was from an upper-middle-class family, he'd never suspected she had an actual trust fund. But he reasoned she had to be living off of something while she was in school. "Then why do you drive that shitty car?"

Imogen laughed. "Just because I can afford a new car doesn't mean I should buy one. I didn't know how long I would be in Charlotte, so it seems like a waste of money."

That made no sense whatsoever to him. "A good car is never a waste of money."

"It's just not important to me to have a splashy car with all the bells and whistles. I didn't even get my driver's license until I was twenty-three."

"Why not?"

"I was chicken, and I didn't need one. I rode the bus, the subway, or grabbed a taxi." She propped her hands on his chest and smiled up at him. "And I don't get Lasik surgery because I am not sure I would recognize myself without glasses. I've had them so long it's part of my identity."

Now, that made sense to him. "I can totally understand that. And you wear your glasses well. You are very beautiful."

She sighed. "You say that so earnestly. Like you actually mean it."

He laughed. "I do mean it. Now get up, Engine, and jump in the shower. There are towels under the sink. Come on down to the kitchen when you're ready and I'll have a good Southern breakfast ready for you."

Peeling herself off him, she said, "Is this going to involve gravy?"

"Uh, yeah. You can't be eating a biscuit without gravy."

"I'm not entirely sure my backside needs calorie-laden gravy and buttermilk biscuits."

"Your ass looks amazing, thank you very much. And don't even go there about calories with me. You're rail thin and I am sick to death of women who won't eat. It just sucks the fun out of everything."

"So does gaining weight," she pointed out, though she didn't sound particularly passionate about it.

Ty frowned. "You think I give a shit if a woman has a curve or two? Hell, more for me to play with."

Imogen smiled. "That's good to hear, Ty. That's a healthy attitude. And no, I am not in the business of denying myself foods I enjoy to maintain a completely unrealistic weight goal in order to satisfy society's ludicrous standards of beauty. I am naturally thin and I try to eat healthy for longevity, but I am not going to turn down cake when it's offered."

"Or gravy and biscuits."

She grinned at him. "Right. And I was just curious how you weighed in on the issue, pun intended, since Nikki starves herself."

"It drove me nuts, plain and simple." But he didn't want to talk about Nikki. "Now get in the damn shower."

He smacked her ass again to get her moving.

"Will you stop doing that?" she asked in exasperation as she stood up and padded over to her pile of clothes and bent to pick them up.

"Not if you keep doing that."

She came straight up, ruining the view, and whirled around, her clothes pressed against her naked body, cheeks pink. "You are incorrigible, you know that?"

"Yep. And you like it. Admit it." Grinning, Ty leaned back against his headboard, his arms behind his head, totally naked, with an erection reaching for the ceiling.

Her fingers squeezed her clothes tighter as her eyes crawled the length of his body, but she didn't say anything.

"Admit it, Emma Jean." The need to tease her was replaced with desire at her bold staring, and his voice deepened, roughened. "You like it when I touch you, when I push you down on the bed, when I fuck you. When I spank you. Tell me you like it."

Visibly swallowing first, she whispered, "I like it." Then she turned and rushed into his bathroom, slamming the door shut behind her.

Ty banged his head back against the wall, mentally berating himself. He should have kept his damn mouth shut. Now Imogen was skittish and his dick was throbbing with a want that couldn't be satisfied at the moment.

Climbing out of bed gingerly, wondering how he was going to shove his erection into a pair of boxers without it snapping off, he figured he got what he deserved.

And maybe if he shoveled enough grits in his mouth, he wouldn't beg Imogen to come to Martinsville with him so he could make love to her sexy little ass every free second he had.

TY wasn't kidding when he said he was going to make a big Southern breakfast. Imogen sat across from him at his kitchen table and watched him plow his way through eggs, ham, hash browns, three biscuits with gravy, grits, and a hunk of French bread with butter. If she ate that much food, she could guarantee she would be writhing in agony before vomiting.

But she was absolutely starving, not to mention she had a point to prove that she was no Nikki, so she ate a smaller portion than Ty of everything, except for the grits. Those she just couldn't handle, and while she didn't want to offend him, she wouldn't make herself swallow them either.

He noticed, unfortunately, and commented on it. "You're not eating your grits."

"I don't like them. It's a texture issue. I've tried but I can't have something wet and gelatinous and creamy in my mouth like that. I just can't get it down my throat."

Ty paused with his biscuit halfway to his mouth and let out a huge laugh.

"What?" she asked, baffled. "What's so funny?"

"That sounds like a fair description of what wound up in your mouth not even an hour ago, and you didn't seem to have a problem with that."

"Oh!" Imogen felt her cheeks heat up. He had the uncanny ability to bring everything back around to sex. Not that she was complaining. "It's not the same thing at all," she said, though she honestly couldn't say why not. "I guess passion alters everything."

"No doubt about that."

Now she was intrigued at the thought, and she smiled a little as she mulled it over, pushing her fork around her plate. "I mean, think about it. What differentiates sexual fluids from other viscous fluids? Snot has a very similar consistency to, say, vaginal fluid, yet no one wants to slide their tongue through snot. It seems that the origin of a slippery liquid alters the reaction it receives, with total extremes, one being gross and one sexy. Hmm. Very interesting, don't you think?"

Imogen glanced up to see Ty holding his fist over his mouth, his face turning red. "Are you okay?"

He shook his head no, but before Imogen could jump up and Heimlich the biscuit out of his windpipe, he swallowed hard and let out a wet, choking laugh.

"Oh, my God. Are you trying to kill me?" His eyes watered as he choked and laughed, laughed and choked, pounding on his chest.

"What?" she asked, mystified.

"Do not say things like sliding your tongue through snot while I am drinking coffee, babe." His laughing and coughing settled down and he shook his head at her in amusement. "You are absolutely hilarious. I love the way you look at things."

Wow. Ty thought she was funny? No one had ever indicated they found her in any way humorous before.

He thought she was sexy and funny.

Imogen smiled back at him and thought she could really, really get used to this.

CHAPTER
TEN

TY shoved miscellaneous crap into his suitcase and glanced around his bedroom. He was late and undoubtedly going to arrive in Martinsville forgetting something seriously important. But he had underwear and he had his toiletries bag, which stayed packed all the time, so he wasn't sure what else mattered. He shoved gym shoes into the bag and dialed Toni on his cell phone.

"Where are you?" Toni asked suspiciously after greeting him.

"At home."

"You're going to miss your plane," she said matter-of-factly.

"No, I'm not." He didn't think. Ty zipped his bag and glanced around the room. Nothing important jumped out at him so he grabbed the duffel and headed toward the door. "Listen, I need you to get a copy of *Much Ado About Nothing* on audio for my laptop. E-mail it to me and I'll download it at the airport."

"Yesterday it was a guidebook on how to marry a driver, to-day it's Shakespeare. Interesting."

Ty chose to ignore that since he was in a hurry. "And see if you can get me some kind of study guide or Cliffs Notes to go with it."

"That might be tricky on audio, Ty."

He wanted to sigh, but he didn't. Sometimes it was just damn irritating to not be able to read. "I know, but please try."

"Okay, I will. So you need this before you board?"

"Yep."

"I'd better hurry then. Anything else?"

"Yes." Ty glanced at the clock in his kitchen, winced, and sprinted toward the garage. He shouldn't have lingered over breakfast with Imogen. "I need to cancel everything on the sched-ule for Monday and Tuesday."

"*What?*" Toni shrieked at him.

"You heard me. And book me a campsite at Lake Norman for Monday night."

"I can't do that. You can't just cancel everything."

"Is there anything vital? Any sponsor events? Charity ap-pearances?"

There was a big long pause, then Toni admitted, "No."

"Then a man is entitled to take twenty-four hours off once in a great while. I usually work seven days a week during the sea-son. I can miss one lousy Monday."

Toni sighed as Ty hopped into his car, tossing his duffel bag on the passenger seat. "Fine. What kind of campsite? Are you taking your coach?"

Imogen would probably love the idea of spending the night in the tricked-out motor coach that he lived in every weekend at the various tracks he raced, since given the amount of time he spent on the road, his coach was almost as comfortable as his house. But that wasn't what he had in mind for Imogen—he wanted a simple, stripped-down experience with her. "No, tent camping."

"You haven't done that in a while. Are you going alone?"

"No. And get a site as remote as possible." He didn't want to share Imogen's company with a crowd of neighbors.

"Do you think that's a good idea with Nikki? She's not really the outdoorsy type from what I can tell."

Peeling out of his driveway, he told her, "I told you Nikki and I broke up. I'm taking someone else camping."

"Wow, that's a two-day turnaround from one girlfriend to the next. Impressive."

Ty rolled his eyes even though she couldn't see him. "Thank you. Though I can't really call her my girlfriend. Yet." He would like to, though, and that surprised him. He hadn't thought he was in the market for a more serious relationship, but Imogen had him thinking all kinds of crazy thoughts.

"Alright, let me off this phone so I can run around and do all this extra work you just dumped in my lap with no warning."

It was a good thing she did her job without complaining. Ty grinned. They did work well together, despite her grousing and his protesting. "Thank you, gorgeous. I'll make it up to you."

"Sure you will. I wait with bated breath for that. Please." But then she ruined the bite of her remarks by adding, "And if I can't find the notes for *Much Ado* on audio, just call me and I'll walk you through the story. I've always been fond of old Will."

Ty was touched by that and he smiled. "Thanks, I appreciate it. You are a dream, Toni."

"Yeah, yeah. Whatever."

"OH, boy," was Tamara's opinion when Imogen admitted to her two friends she had slept with Ty.

"You shitting me?" Suzanne asked. "Was he any good?"

They were in a Mexican restaurant that had beco me their favorite haunt for cheesy food and the occasional margaritas. Tamara looked worried, Suzanne gleefully pleased.

Imogen sucked down her drink nervously and nodded. She had felt compelled to share her night with Ty with her friends, but now she felt strangely uncomfortable that she had.

Suzanne grinned. "Like he took you to regions on the passion chart previously uncharted good, or like taking a bubble bath kind of good? You know, relaxing and satisfying, but not something you're going to remember a week later."

Clearing her throat, she willed herself not to blush. "The first one."

Now Suzanne laughed. "Yee haw. That's what I'm talking about. So, what is he like? Is he hung?"

"Suz!" Tamara protested, dropping her fork onto her plate. "I don't think that's any of our business."

"Why not?" Suzanne looked unfazed.

Imogen didn't really want to discuss Ty's penis size with her friends, but she had to admit, Suzanne's enthusiasm for the event was helpful. She was feeling a little strange about their night together herself. She was so glad she had experienced what she had with him, and she had enjoyed herself immensely, both physically and emotionally. Which was the crux of her concern.

She liked Ty.

She always had.

Even when she had tried to convince herself she was just physically attracted to him, she had known all along that she had a bit of a crush on him.

Now that she had gotten, well, down and dirty with him, that crush had amplified, and that scared her.

Ignoring her enchiladas, Imogen sighed. "It was so, so good. I think that's a bad thing."

"Why, sweetie?" Tamara asked, looking concerned. "I think it would be bad if the sex sucked, but good sex shouldn't be a bad thing, right?"

"Not in my book," Suzanne said.

Imogen didn't answer right away, and Tamara said, "You like him too much, don't you? This isn't casual for you, is it?"

Yikes. "Of course it is," she protested. "I mean, where would it go? He's a race car driver who likes being outdoors; he's impulsive, reckless. I'm methodical, logical, addicted to air-conditioning. It would never work, and I know that. I just wanted to do it anyway, and I think that was a miscalculation on my part. Because now I know what sex with him is like. And it's amazing."

"Why? What's he doing exactly?" Suzanne turned to Tamara. "I bet he's hung."

Tamara smacked Suzanne on the arm. "Whether a man is hung or not isn't the only thing necessary to have amazing sex with him."

"Are you saying Elec isn't hung?" Suzanne asked.

The expression on horror on Tamara's face actually made Imogen smile.

"Of course he is," Tamara said. Her hands came up to indicate size before she quickly dropped them. "It . . . *he* keeps me very happy."

Now Suzanne and Imogen were both laughing.

"Anyway," Tamara said, waving her hand around. "This isn't about me and Elec. This is about you and Ty. I don't think you can assume that future sex is ruined for you. Just look at this way—if Ty could give that to you, so can some other man. He opened a sexual door for you, and that's a positive outcome."

"You going to do it again with him?" Suzanne asked, studying her carefully.

"She just said she isn't," Tamara said.

"No. I didn't. And yes, I actually am." Imogen took another massive sip of her drink.

"I knew it," Suzanne said triumphantly.

"You are?" Tamara asked in disbelief. "Are you sure that's wise?"

"Since when does being wise come into play when you're coming?" Suzanne asked. "The girl got her freak on and she wants to do it again. No mystery there."

"Yeah, but if she's worried about getting emotionally involved with him, seeing him again might not be the best thing to do."

Suzanne looked like she could care less about that. "So when are you seeing him again? Are you just going to his place to do the nasty or what?"

"He's taking me camping on Monday."

"Camping? That sounds like fun. I like camping."

"I don't," Imogen said. "At least, I don't think I do. I've never been in a tent in my life, unless it was the catering tent at a garden party."

"So why are you going, then?" Tamara asked.

"We made a deal. I'll go camping if he reads *Much Ado About Nothing*."

"And he agreed to that?" Suzanne asked skeptically. "I'd watch him, if I were you. He'll haul your ass out into the woods and never pick up that play and read it. You get play payment up-front."

"He wouldn't do that," Imogen protested. "Would he?"

"I think it sounds kind of, I don't know, romantic," Tamara said. "Like he's trying really hard to impress you and to find common ground with you."

Suzanne's opinion of that was clear from the height of her eyebrows. They had disappeared under her side-swept blond bangs.

But Imogen was inclined to agree with Tamara. At least that's what the soft and foolish pounding mass in her chest wanted to believe. It was stupid, she knew that. She was, to be highly overdramatic, which she never was but for once just needed to be, at risk for having Ty drive his race car over her heart and grind her into the asphalt.

The knowledge of that didn't seem to be stopping her.

"Aside from all of that, which is confusing enough, I have thoroughly ruined my thesis," Imogen said. "I was supposed to be following the *Six Steps*, or at least attempting the initial steps to see if I could secure interest from a driver."

"I think you secured interest all right."

That was true. "Yeah, but that wasn't from following the rules. I think I've broken about every single one with Ty."

"And the goal with Ty isn't to marry him," Tamara said.

True, but did she have to point it out so baldly?

"Of course not."

"What are these stupid six steps anyway?" Suzanne asked. "I've been sweating my ass off at the gym with you and I haven't even heard the rest of them. If they're cracked, I'm not doing them."

"Okay, well, Step One is getting date ready. Step Two is meeting him. Step Three is your first date. Four is getting in good with his friends and maintaining your own life. Five is adding intimacy and becoming exclusive. Six is letting him know he can't live without you."

Tamara and Suzanne both stared at her. "That's it?" Suzanne asked. "That's supposed to snag you a husband?"

"That sounds sort of like how every relationship goes to me," Tamara added. "Those aren't steps you can control either, I might add."

While Imogen agreed that the whole concept of a dating manual securing any woman eternal bliss in marriage was far-fetched, she did think that at least the steps were practical. "Of course you can. I think that is actually the success of the book. These are all normal dating and mating behavior patterns, but this book gives women control, whether it's an illusion or not. Before you even meet him, you diet and exercise, check your wardrobe, etc. You learn about stock car racing, which is both his passion and his career. You learn about him. So when you do finally have the chance to meet him, it's allowing you to put your best foot forward to secure his interest."

"You didn't do that with Ty?"

"Not so much," Imogen admitted.

"Yeah, but he's digging you."

"I don't think that's my point," Imogen said, feeling a little exasperated with her whole thesis in general, men in particular. "My point is perhaps that the success rate is higher if you go into a relationship more methodically than impulsively. So I slept with Ty. That is not going to result in marrying him. If I had done it per these directives, maybe I would be at some point." Saying that out loud made her a little hot in weird places, and she instantly regretted those words coming out of her mouth.

But her friends didn't seem to think it was odd. They both just looked puzzled and unsure.

"I don't know . . ." Tamara said. "I met Elec by accident, when I was tipsy drunk on a date with another man, frantic because I'd lost my purse. Not exactly my best foot forward, and yet we had sex that first night, again not following these rules, and we're doing just fine, thank you very much."

"And I would argue that Ryder and I followed those rules to the letter and we're divorced, so go figure."

"Which all really means that my thesis just sucks," Imogen said, feeling torn between wanting to scream and wanting to burst into tears. "It's a big, complicated mess and I don't know how to fix it." She had never screwed up a paper or project so badly in her entire academic career, and to do it now, with the mother of all projects, her thesis, was inconceivable.

"Well," Tamara said. "I think part of the problem is there is no way to accumulate enough data to prove or disprove your theory if you're the only one attempting to follow the rules. I think you need to approach it from a different angle. You need to become the Myth Buster of Sociology and question, is this true or not true?"

Given that Tamara already had her master's degree in sociology, Imogen was eager to listen to any advice she could give. "I guess that was my intent originally, but I'm no longer certain how to do that."

Tamara sipped her margarita. "You interview as many driver's wives as you can. If you interview fifty wives, you can ask pointed questions that determine if their path to marriage even remotely resembled the rules in that book. If you develop questions regarding their previous knowledge of stock car racing, whether their meeting was accidental or intentional, their first date, how long they dated before getting engaged, etc., you can classify them as having followed the rules or not. Check your percentages of rule followers versus non–rule followers and call it good."

There was some merit to Tamara's suggestion. It was certainly more logical than running around trying to flirt with men she wasn't interested in. "Except how can I argue that the book works or doesn't work when none of the subjects were aware of its rules to follow them or not follow them?"

"Toss out the concept of whether or not the book itself works. The myth you are busting, or potentially proving, is that, in the subculture of stock car racing, there is a discernible pattern to dating and subsequent marriage. That is the basis to the theory of the book. If there is no pattern, how can the book work for the majority of readers? I would assume your conclusion would be that given the uniqueness of individuals and their courtships, there is no way to follow rules and guarantee marriage."

This was sounding more and more appealing to Imogen. "This just might work."

"Good, because I'm glazing over from this conversation," Suzanne said.

"Sorry," Imogen said, frowning at her enchiladas. "This is just so much more stressful than I expected."

"I know and I'm sorry. I wish I could help," Suzanne said, looking a little contrite for her remark. "And I'm sure tossing mattress play with Ty onto all of this isn't helping your peace of mind." Then Suzanne grinned. "But I bet it's helping other things, if not your mind."

True enough. "So what on earth do I pack to go camping?"

"Jeans. T-shirts. Boots. It's going to be hot again this week, in the eighties, so pack a bathing suit," Tamara said.

"And your tiniest, sexiest underwear," Suzanne added.

Imogen tried to picture feeling sexy on the damp ground in a tent and could only feel a serious amount of trepidation. "Are there bugs camping?"

Tamara and Suzanne exchanged a look. "Probably," Tamara said.

"Animals?" Were there bears in North Carolina? Imogen didn't even know.

"Maybe," Suzanne said. "But they shy away from humans. Except for raccoons and skunks. They'll come right on up if you have food or garbage lying around."

Wonderful. "Can't wait," she said weakly. "Everyone should be open to new life experiences, right?"

"Don't worry about the skunks," Suzanne reassured her. "Just concentrate on the fact that if anything is going to be open, it will be your legs."

More likely she'd be too afraid to take her clothes off, but she did appreciate Suzanne's optimism.

"I can practically hear your brain creating a list of all the things you aren't going to like about this trip," Tamara said. "Just relax and enjoy yourself."

"Do I know how to do that?" Imogen asked honestly.

Her friends laughed, and Suzanne actually descended into a snort.

"You enjoyed last night, didn't you?" Tamara asked.

She nodded. "Oh, yeah."

"So it's the same thing, just in a tent."

Right. Sex in a tent. No different than a bed, really. Just harder. And earthier. And buggier.

The only conclusion she could reach if she was willing to go to such lengths to spend time with Ty was that she was seriously infatuated with him.

And that was almost scarier than the thought of running into a bear while covered in honey.

RYDER Jefferson was heading to a preliminary meeting with his crew chief in Martinsville when his cell phone rang. Striding across the motor coach lot, he pulled it out of his pocket and glanced at it.

"Shit," was his opinion. It was his ex-wife, Suzanne. If she was calling him, it usually meant she wanted something from him.

They'd been getting along just fine lately, which was probably because they hadn't been seeing much of each other since a dinner party incident back in May when she'd tossed a pie in his face. He still hadn't figured out what that was all about.

Deciding to ignore her call, he sighed when he realized she had hung up and was calling again. Knowing Suzanne and how tenacious she was, she'd keep calling until he answered.

"Hello, Suz, how are ya?" he said, slowing down his gait as he headed for the track.

"Are you busy?" she asked. "Do you have a minute to chat?"

Well, now, that was a good start. She was being all polite and agreeable. "Yes, this is a fine time. Just heading to a meeting. What's up, darlin'?"

"Why didn't you answer, then?" she asked caustically.

Ryder rolled his eyes. So much for a good start. "I did answer."

"But you didn't the first time . . . Oh, never mind. I didn't call to fight."

"That's reassuring." Because when he fought with Suzanne, he always felt like he was driving the short track blindfolded and she was the wall.

"Listen, did you know Ty is banging Imogen?"

Ryder stopped walking and stared blankly at the fence surrounding the track. "Huh? Who's Imogen?" And why did Suzanne feel the need to tell him she was sleeping with Ty?

"Tammy's teaching assistant. You met her at Tammy's house a few times and at the wedding. She's become a really dear friend to me and I'm all sorts of worried, Ryder. I think she and Ty are like oil and water, and while she is saying the sex is freaky-deaky, I just don't know if I should encourage this."

And this involved him how? "Umm . . . Suz?"

"Yeah?"

"Didn't we have a talk about interfering in other people's love lives a while back when Tammy and Elec were first getting it on?"

"I was right to interfere with those two. They might have kept insisting they didn't want to date if I hadn't thrown that dinner party."

"*We* threw that dinner party. Then you threw a pie in my face." Apple. He could practically still feel that sticky mess ooze down his nose and chin and taste the sweet tartness on his lips.

"You deserved it," she said breezily. "And this isn't about you. This is about Imogen and Ty and their happiness. We can't be letting Ty take her for a ride. She's just not the kind of girl who is into casual sex."

Ryder rubbed his forehead, wondering if he really was

supposed to give a shit who Ty was sleeping with. If the guy had a thing for the skinny chick with the glasses, more power to him. Ryder wouldn't have thought she was Ty's type, given that she was pretty in a more conservative, understated way than Ty's usual full-blown beauties, but it wasn't really any of his business. "I believe you said Tammy wasn't that kind of girl either, and she was all about bouncing Elec. I just think we need to let people work these things out themselves, darlin'."

"If Ty breaks Imogen's heart, I'm going to be seriously pissed off."

"I don't imagine Ty is really taking your feelings into account, nor should he. It's his life."

"So here's what we need to do," Suzanne said as if he hadn't spoken at all. "I need to see the two of them together and decide for myself if Ty actually likes her or if he's just playing her, so you and I need to have another dinner party."

The hell they did. "No. Absolutely not. It's none of our business and I'm not taking another pie in the face to support your meddling in your friends' love lives."

"Oh, I wasn't going to make a pie. I was going to bake a pineapple upside-down cake."

Damn her. She knew that was his all-time favorite dessert. He paused, closing his eyes to gather his willpower. "No . . . it's not a good idea."

"I'll bring one to the dinner party, then I'll follow up with the dessert of your choice on the first of the month for the next three months."

"Sold." The woman knew exactly how to manipulate him. He had a killer sweet tooth, and Suzanne had always been able to bring him to his knees with her amazing baked goods. It was something he should probably be ashamed of, but it was only one dinner party, and chances were Suzanne would do it with or without him, so he might as well reap the benefits of cooperation.

"I'd better make sure I leave condoms on the counter in my bathroom. Last time we did this, Tammy and Elec ransacked my medicine cabinet before doing the deed in my bathroom. Maybe we can just eliminate the stress of that for them and the cleanup for me. There was aspirin flung all over the place."

"Imogen and Ty are not going to be doing it in the bathroom," Suzanne said, scoffing.

"You said that last time." Frankly, it seemed the only one not having sex lately was him, bathroom or anywhere else. He didn't even want to contemplate the last time he had been with a woman, because it was bound to make him cranky.

"Alright, so maybe they'll have sex in the bathroom. Imogen is blushing every time his name comes up. But I guess that doesn't matter if he's treating her well and is serious about her."

"Easy for you to say since it's not your bathroom. So when are we doing this little night of forced fun?"

"A week from Monday. This Monday, Ty is taking Imogen camping."

Ryder tried to picture serious and studious Imogen hiking through the woods in her sweater set and shiny black handbag. "She doesn't really seem like the camping type."

"She's not. Which is why I'm worrying. She's willing to get dirty for him and that scares me."

Not wanting to explore Suzanne's logic with her, given that he still didn't really think it was any of her business, Ryder just said, "What do you need me to do?"

"Just invite Ty. I'll invite everyone else."

"Okay. And I guess there will be one good thing about this."

"What's that?"

Ryder grinned. "Nikki won't be there."

Suzanne laughed. "No kidding. Lord, that girl tries my patience."

"You and everyone else." Ryder honestly hadn't been able to figure out how Ty could stand five minutes with the girl.

"Alright, I'm going to let you go. Thanks, Ryder."

That was nice to hear. "You're welcome, Suz. You have a good heart to care about your friends, ya know that?" Even if it was misguided, he knew Suzanne's plans came from a place of concern.

"Thanks. I'll talk to you later. I lo—"

Ryder froze as Suzanne cut her sentence short. It had sounded like she had been about to say "I love you" before she hung up, just like she used to.

"Bye," she said quickly, and then Ryder heard nothing but a dial tone.

It must have just been habit, conditioning, from when they were married. Suz didn't have those kinds of feelings for him anymore. Ryder frowned at his cell phone before jamming it back into his pocket. He and Suzanne had been divorced for damn near two years. This was his reality.

So why did he suddenly feel lonely as hell?

"Ryder, what's up?"

Grateful for the distraction from his unexpected thoughts, Ryder looked up to see the very man he and Suzanne had been discussing striding toward him.

"Hey, Ty, not much. How about yourself?"

Ty looked like he was in a great mood. He was whistling a cheerful tune. He paused and gave a grin. "Same old, same old."

Because he was mildly curious, Ryder shifted on his feet and said, "Heard you're not seeing Nikki anymore. You don't look cut up over it."

"Nope. I should have ended that a good long while ago." Ty shrugged. "But it doesn't matter. I've started seeing someone else this week, and it's looking good."

"She put that stupid grin on your face?"

Ty laughed. "I imagine so. You remember Imogen Wilson, Tammy's student? It's her."

"No kidding?" Ryder pretended like he didn't know. "She's a nice girl. Not your usual type, but she definitely seems like she has her act together."

"She's not my usual type, but maybe that just goes to show you I've been barking up the wrong tree. Imogen is the whole package, you know what I'm saying? She is beautiful, sexy as hell, and smart. I mean, we have great sex *and* great conversations. Who knew that was possible?"

Ty looked so bemused at the concept, Ryder grinned. "I think a lot of people knew that was possible. You're just a slow learner. But I'm glad things are going good for you."

Suzanne's fears about Ty playing Imogen seemed totally unfounded to Ryder. Ty looked like a man with a massive crush.

"Things are damn good."

"Well, bring her around my place next Monday. Suzanne is throwing a dinner party."

Ty's eyebrow went up. "How did you get roped into doing that again?"

Ryder realized he'd never been told what excuse to give for the party, so he just shrugged. "I don't know. You know I have a soft spot for Suz and she likes these things. Please say you'll be there or she's going to give me hell."

Ty clapped him on the shoulder and grinned. "Sure, we'll be there. But you might want to think about why it is you're whipped by a woman who's not even doing the dirty with you."

He had no intention of thinking about that and hated being reminded of it. "Screw you, McCordle."

Ty laughed and said, "I think you're the one getting screwed. Screwed over."

Ryder felt a wave of anger roll over him.

It was becoming more and more clear to him that he and Suzanne had some unfinished business.

But he wasn't going to deal with that now. He had a meeting to attend. So he told Ty in total irritation, "Suck my dick."

Which only made Ty laugh all that much harder.

CHAPTER

ELEVEN

IMOGEN smiled across the table at Tabby Stephenson, an attractive woman in her midthirties who had been married to driver Jack Stephenson for the past seventeen years.

"Thank you so much for agreeing to be interviewed," Imogen said, glad she had chosen to meet Tabby in the quaint tearoom. It seemed like the appropriate place to discuss dating and marriage.

"Oh, are you kidding? What woman doesn't like to tell the story of how she met her husband?"

"One who isn't happily married."

Tabby laughed. "True enough. But I have been about as happy with Jack as a woman can expect to be, so I'm happy to tell you whatever you're willing to listen to." Tabby tucked her honey-colored hair behind an ear. "Jack will love this, by the way."

"Good. I certainly appreciate you both being so agreeable. So to start off, just tell me how you met Jack. Was it by chance or did you have your eye on him? Was he already racing profession-ally?"

"Not at all. I was only fourteen when I met Jack. He was sixteen and a total hell-raiser. We didn't go to the same school because I was in the eighth grade and he was a sophomore in high school, but I met him at the ice cream shop after church one Sunday. My older sister and I were allowed to walk up there by ourselves for a cone, and that's where I saw him, drinking a shake and showing off the engine of his stock car to his buddies. Honey, I took one look at that backside in those worn Levi's and the whole boy-girl thing clicked for me. I'd never looked twice at a boy before that, but between those jeans, his devilish grin, and that deep, sexy laugh, I was just gone."

Imogen watched Tabby sighing at the memory and she smiled.

" 'Course, he didn't notice me at all. I was still in middle school and I had zero fashion sense. I was wearing a denim skirt that damn near hit the ground since I'd just come from church. I was so fascinated by him, so upset that he wouldn't look at me, that I didn't even finish my ice cream cone."

Imogen remembered that feeling herself, that longing, that moody, desperate need for a boy to notice you when you were fourteen. Not a pleasant thing. Of course, she hadn't really en-joyed the twenty-eight-year-old version of it either as she had lusted after Ty for months.

"I wanted to hang around until Jack left so I made up an ex-cuse about having to use the bathroom. Told my sister I was hav-ing intestinal issues and might be a while." Tabby grinned. "Cindy was always impatient so she left me and walked home by herself. She got chewed out for leaving me there, and for walking alone. But anyway, once I was rid of her, I ordered a soda and tried to figure out how to talk to him, but in the end, after thirty minutes,

I couldn't work up the courage, so I headed across the parking lot to walk home. This creepy guy in his thirties called out and offered me a ride, and I was freaking out. I lived in a small town in Alabama and my mother had warned me all about crazies who would molest and rape a girl and ruin her life if he didn't beat her to death or set her on fire or something sick like that." Tabby shook her head and gave Imogen a rueful look. "Putting the fear of God into us worked, but I can't help but think there was a better way to do it than letting us believe we'd be barbequed if we talked to strangers."

"With my mother, it was Mace," Imogen said. "Living in Manhattan, I usually felt safe because there were always people around, but my mother made my carry Mace at all times, and I'm sure it was the smart thing to do. Of course, if I had ever been attacked, I probably would have dropped the stupid can before I could use it."

"No kidding." Tabby shrugged. "So, I freaked out, of course, and was going to run back into the ice cream shop, but suddenly there was Jack, standing next to me. He tells the guy to move along, that I'm with him, and he shouldn't be talking to teenage girls anyways."

"The guy looked annoyed, but he did leave right away, and then Jack looked at me and asked if I was alright. I nodded, because I had no spit left in my mouth and couldn't talk, and then he offered me a ride home. I nodded yes." Tabby grinned. "And then he yelled at me for being stupid enough to accept his offer of a ride and how did I know he was any better than that other guy? So then I was mortified, and he marched me into the store and made me use the pay phone to call my mother to come and pick me up. He even got on the phone and told her in a very respectful voice that a rather unsavory man had been talking to me and he felt that, for my safety, she should come on up and fetch me. And the whole time I'm thinking not only is my mother going to be furious with me, this cute, cute boy thinks I'm a foolish little girl."

"That does sound rather mortifying," Imogen said sympathetically, adding some sugar to her tea. "So what happened?"

"I politely thanked him, then sat down at a picnic table outside, assuming he was done with me and pretty much just wanting to die. But he sat down on top of the table, feet on the bench, and started talking, telling me how he's going to be a famous stock car driver and telling me all about his car. I didn't know squat about racing, which seemed to please him as much as if I had been a fan, because this gave him the chance to tell me everything from the ground up. He told me his name was Jack and he told me that he'd seen me in church, that I always sat in the eighth row next to old Mr. Hodgkins. Now I was shocked that he could know that, when I'd never seen him before. I mean, I would have noticed him, right?" Tabby held her teacup in front of her mouth and smiled. "But he told me he knew where I sat because he was always looking down on me. He sang in the choir and he was up in the loft every Sunday. And my heart just about exploded in my chest with excitement. I mean, a choirboy? Even my mama couldn't object to that, right?"

Imogen pondered that. "Mothers can always find something to object to, but that was a definite notch in his favor, I'm sure."

"Exactly. So then, proving he hadn't been listening all that hard in church about lust and lying, he led me around the side of the shop on the pretext of picking me some scraggly wildflowers. He asked me for my phone number and he asked me to the movies. Then he kissed me." Tabby put her hands on her cheeks. "I was so shocked, both at him, and at me for letting him. But have mercy, it felt fine. I'd shared a kiss or two with a boy before, but this was something else entirely, and I still had the taste of him on my lips when my mama pulled into the parking lot. And we've been together ever since."

"You stayed together all through high school?"

"Yep. We never broke up, not even once, not even for a day. Jack started racing on the local track and worked his way up to earning a little bit of money at it while I was finishing school. We started out dirt poor with nothing but our faith in the future and our love. We've been together twenty-one years and had all manner of ups and downs, and yet marriage and loving Jack have never been hard. Life has been hard at times, but marriage never has been. Now we have four beautiful, occasionally bratty kids, a gorgeous house, and Jack's career, and I feel very blessed."

Imogen had a lump in her throat staring across the table at the pure contentment on Tabby's face. She loved her husband, and he loved her, and they had built a life together.

She had never expected to pine for hearth and home and a man to call her own, but at that moment, watching the joy of one woman's love for her husband, Imogen truly felt the ache of wanting that for herself.

Tabby's cell phone chimed in her purse and she gave Imogen a shrug of apology. "I'm sorry, I'm not usually the rudest woman in the world, but do you mind if I see who this is? I want to make sure it's not the kids or Jack. We have a deal that he always calls me when he arrives at the next racetrack so I know he made it safely."

"Sure, of course. I don't mind." Imogen was pondering anyway, thinking that Tabby's story of meeting and falling in love with Jack didn't follow the *Six Steps* at all.

Tabby checked the screen on her phone, then said, "It's Jack. Let me take this. I swear I'll only be two minutes."

"No problem. Take your time." Imogen pulled out her own phone, aware of exactly who she was hoping to have a voice mail or text message from. Not that she was really expecting Ty to contact her until he had the camping details, but she couldn't help but think it might be nice to hear from him since she had just spent the night with him.

Pulling out her own phone, she got excited for half a second when she realized she did have a text, until she opened the message and realized it was from Evan Monroe. He was asking if he could call to make plans to go out to dinner.

Oy. This was what she got for flirting with a man she wasn't really attracted to. Now she had to find some way to turn him down without being rude or hurting his feelings.

Regardless of whether she and Ty ever shared more than a few steamy nights together, this was definitely a lesson worth learning. Tabby had spent twenty-plus years happy with her husband because from day one there had be an indisputable attraction between them, and it was starting to occur to Imogen that, dating guide or not, that was not a feeling you could force, either in yourself or in the other person.

Tabby said into her phone, "I love you, too, you handsome man." Then she tucked her phone back into her purse and said, "Where were we?"

Good question. If Imogen only knew where she was and what she was doing, she would feel much better, but for the first time in her life, logic seemed to be failing her.

TY was keyed up with excitement and a fair amount of nerves when he pulled into Imogen's apartment complex to pick her up Monday morning. He'd had a lousy race the day before, finishing eighth, which earlier in the year would have pleased him, but with only four races left in the season, left him dissatisfied. He was still in contention for the overall championship, and every point counted. To that purpose, he really shouldn't be taking today and tomorrow off. He should be sitting down with the team and assessing what had happened on Sunday and going over the car for Atlanta.

But he had already made plans with Imogen and he didn't want to cancel them. One, because it would look rude. Two, because he wanted to spend time with her. Lots of quality time naked. That was good for his physical and mental health and surely that was good for racing performance. He would just have to haul his butt back on Tuesday and head straight to the garage. In the meantime, he needed to make sure Imogen was having a great time camping and he needed to display a working knowledge of *Much Ado About Nothing*.

He'd struggled with the play all weekend, listening to it on his iPod whenever he had a spare few minutes. He'd gone jogging and listened to it, eaten breakfast at the Waffle House solo and listened to it, and sat in his lawn chair outside his coach, trying desperately to make sense of what the voice actors were saying. He tried really damn hard but, in the end, had only had a basic outline of the story. Calling that good enough, he'd called Toni and had her confirm he was at least in the right ballpark. Then he'd asked her for the most romantic quote of the play. Toni had indicated that *Much Ado About Nothing* wasn't exactly Shakespeare's most swoon-worthy play, but she managed to find a passage that Ty thought sounded pretty darn hot. He had made her repeat it to him four times so he could commit it to memory. That was one thing Ty could say about his brain—he had a good memory, probably because he couldn't really write anything down.

Going over the quote in his head, he was confident he had it right, so Ty turned off the car and got out, sniffing the air. It was warm already, and they were looking at temperatures in the eighties, the last gasp of summer before fall really kicked in. Perfect weather for camping.

Imogen looked sleepy and grumpy and damn adorable when she answered the door. She had her hair in a sleek ponytail, her face free of any makeup, her glasses sliding down her nose, a frazzled and unfocused expression on her face. Dressed in what Ty would deem dressy jeans, an expensive-looking black-and-white-striped short-sleeve sweater, and little black shoes, he realized she had a different understanding of camping than he did.

He also realized she hadn't had her coffee yet when she said, "Why does anyone get up this early on purpose?" by way of greeting.

Ty reached out and pushed her glasses up her nose. He gave her a soft kiss. "Me. And if you show me your bag, I'll toss it in the car and we'll run you through the drive-thru at McDonald's and get you a coffee."

For a second, she just stared at him, clearly flummoxed. "Okay. Good. Coffee is good." Then she looked around her apartment, which was far more cluttered than Ty would have ever guessed. "My bag is still in my bedroom. Sorry for the mess." She moved a pile of books from the couch to the coffee table on her way by.

"This is a great apartment. I can really see your personality." It was true. While there was an amazing amount of clutter, books and papers scattered on every available surface and even stacked on the floor, the furniture was eclectic and comfortable, a hodgepodge of antique lamps and chandeliers, modern glass tables, and a soft white slip-covered couch. Everything looked sort of worn and soft and touchable, the early-morning light from the big picture window bouncing off the glass tables and heavy crystal chandeliers. She had a theme to her artwork; every oil painting hung on the walls was a portrait of a woman, from one wearing a huge ball gown to one in a canary yellow suit. She also had a vintage eyeglass collection, displayed on a chest of drawers painted a soft, chipped yellow.

Ty was so busy checking out her place, he didn't notice the tiny backpack she was reaching for in the doorway of her room.

"That's it. I can carry it." She lifted it up one-handed and slung it over her shoulder, which indicated to him it wasn't all that heavy.

Eyeing it dubiously, he said, "Okay, then. Guess we're all set." In his entire life he had never met a woman who could pack everything she needed for an overnight camping trip in a backpack. But then again, he was familiar with Southern women, who wanted to be prepared for anything at all times. Imogen was from New York. They lived in tiny apartments, they walked all over the place. Chances were she had learned to streamline, to take only what she needed.

Ty's mother had been known to pull pedicure kits out of her camping gear in case anyone had tired feet or a blister after a day of hiking. And the food supplies had nearly flattened the tires on the family station wagon when he'd been a kid and they'd headed out on road trips. His father had never discouraged her and, in fact, had been grateful a time or two when his mother had whipped something totally improbable out of her purse, like a sugar packet or a whole bottle of antacids.

Imogen's backpack was mildly unnerving, but he didn't want to call her out on it and make her feel like she had done something wrong.

But he did feel compelled to ask, "Do you have boots in there?" She'd slip and break her neck if she tried to hike in those little shoes.

"Yep." She patted the bag with her free hand.

"Okay, good. Let's pump you full of caffeine and hit the road."

It was only thirty miles to Lake Norman, but it took almost every one of them and a large black coffee before Imogen appeared to wake up. For most of the drive, she rested her head on the window with her eyes closed and Ty listened to the radio and stole glances at her, feeling a little foolish. She was so damn pretty and he was experiencing the weirdest sensation every time he looked at her, a sort of bizarre tenderness that he didn't really understand. He'd never dated a woman like her, and he felt almost unsure of himself, like he'd fallen back about a decade and was an eager twenty-year-old desperate to impress a girl.

It wasn't a comfortable place to sit, and the silence wasn't helping.

He was grateful when she sat up and yawned and said, "Sorry. I'm not much of a morning person."

"I kind of caught on to that. Maybe I shouldn't have hauled you out of bed so early."

"It's okay." She drained the remains of her coffee. "I'm good now. Are we almost there?"

"Pulling in right now."

"It's very beautiful," she said, looking out the window at the huge canopy of trees on either side of the winding road. "Very green."

That almost made Ty laugh, but he held it in. "There's a deer family to the right." He pointed to them.

Imogen started. "Wow. They're big. And close to the road." She shot him a wary look. "What other kinds of animals are there here?"

"Squirrel, deer, opossums, rabbit, foxes, maybe coyotes. Nothing out of the ordinary. Nothing dangerous." He wasn't going to mention that occasionally a venomous cottonhead snake was spotted.

"Coyotes? That sounds dangerous."

"Nah. They run as soon as they see you." Ty made a mental note never to leave Imogen alone for the next twenty-four hours. In all his years tromping through the Lake Norman State Park, he'd never seen a coyote, and with his luck, Imogen would have a whole pack tear past her and he'd never get her back in the woods.

That thought gave him pause. Did he want to get her back in the woods? He'd reserve opinion on that until they were on their way out of the park instead of the way in, but he suspected the answer might be yes.

"Alright, we're looking for a sign for a turnoff called Camp Lane. How original is that? If you spot it, give a yell." Ty had been to the site before, but it had been a couple of years, and he knew he couldn't find the turnoff on his own. He also suspected he wouldn't be able to decipher the sign, so he'd put Imogen on the task.

"Okay. So what does one do exactly while camping?" she asked, her hands folded neatly in her lap.

Ty grinned at her. "We're going to go hiking. Swimming. Fishing. And we're going to make love in a sleeping bag. Or maybe on the sleeping bag. Depends how impatient we are to get to it. Does all that sound alright with you?"

"I think I can handle that," she said briskly, pushing her glasses up her nose.

"Good." He was bemused by her. "And you're being very polite not to ask, but I want to reassure you that I did read *Much Ado About Nothing*." In a roundabout sort of way. "So I upheld my end of the bargain. I'm not sure I could write a term paper on it, but I think I can have a reasonable discussion with you about it."

She smiled for the first time since he had picked her up. "Thank you. Did you like it?"

"Yeah, I did." He had to admit, it was an entertaining story. "I was right about Beatrice, you know. Total man hater. And she's ticked at herself for what she perceives as her own personal weakness for falling in love with Benedick."

"That's true. She certainly fights the feeling."

"What's so wrong with falling in love anyway? I always imagined it was kind of a good feeling. There wouldn't be damn near as many songs, books, and movies about it if it wasn't."

"I think Beatrice sees love and passion as a way in which a woman turns over control of herself and her love to a man, not a desirable thing in a time period in which women were essentially the property of their husbands."

"That's understandable. But fear almost causes her to spend her life bitter and alone rather than take a chance on happiness with a man. Sometimes you have to take a risk, not knowing exactly how it's going to turn out."

"Oh, there's the road we need," Imogen said, pointing to her right. "Camp Lane. And I don't think I'm much of a risk taker."

"Cool." Ty pulled into a gravel parking lot and stopped the car. "No? You're not a risk taker? I think I probably am."

"Since you risk your life every Sunday, I would say so, yes."

Ty shrugged. "I don't see racing that way. Sure, you can wreck, but given all the thousands of times we all drive on a track, serious accidents don't happen all that often. You're probably more at risk of an injury in an accident in that piece of crap you call a car than I am in my safety-first stock car."

"Maybe you're right." Imogen ran her finger along her bottom lip. "Do you think there are personality types that are truly incompatible? Like can a cautious person and a risk taker actually tolerate each other long term? Or a highly sexual person live with someone who has a low libido?"

"The first one, yes. The second one, no. If one person is wanting some action all the time and the other is constantly begging off? That's going to be a huge source of tension." He could say with absolute certainty that he would be really frustrated if he was with a woman who thought having sex once a month was plenty. He'd get more if he was single. Of course, the upside to a relationship was that when you did finally get around to sex, there would be intimacy along with the physical connection, but he still didn't think he would be anything short of chronically horny and irritable if he had access to a woman but got the black flag every night.

"I think I would have to agree. One person will always feel like they're having to ask for sex instead of sharing it freely with each other. And the person who is not highly sexual will fall into a pattern of simply giving in to the other in order to stave off the argument, which isn't conducive to intimacy or uninhibited and enthusiastic sex."

Ty gave Imogen a long look. "Are you trying to tell me you gave in last week to prevent an argument?"

She snorted. "Hah. If anything, it would have to be considered the other way around. I offered it even before then, and you turned it down."

"I explained that. We're not going there again, are we?" Because that didn't sound like anything he wanted to bumble his way through a second time.

"No, we're not. I said I understand and I do." She smiled at him, a wicked gleam in her eye. "I mean, it's okay if you're the one with the low sex drive. We'll just have to adjust and learn to accommodate that."

Well, wasn't Imogen the funny one? Ty refused to give her smug little self the satisfaction of smiling, even as he thought her wit was damn amusing. "Oh, is that right? I'm the one with the low sex drive?"

He leaned over and kissed her hard, his tongue thrusting inside her mouth as he tasted the traces of her coffee. He ransacked her, squeezing her breast with one hand as he buried the other into the hair of her ponytail. He kissed her until her glasses had fogged up from their heavy breathing, her nipples were tight buds beneath his fingers, and he would bet his career she was sopping wet in her panties.

Imogen yanked herself back from him and sucked in a deep breath. "I . . ." she panted, "was being facetious."

"I know." Ty grinned. "But it gave me a good excuse to feel you up."

"I thought we had established you never needed an excuse."

Brushing his finger over her nipple, loving the way her mouth slipped open on a breathy sigh and her eyelashes fluttered rapidly, Ty kissed a trail down her jaw. "I don't think that we did establish that. But it's nice to know I have the green light at any time."

"Well." She tipped her head a little to give him better access. "Maybe not at just *any* time."

"No?" Ty loved the way her skin felt, smooth as satin, free of makeup, just fresh and clean beneath his lips. "What times are off-limits?"

"In the presence of other people should be off-limits. I think that covers most awkward situations that might arise."

"But in the woods is okay?" Ty was getting hot in the car, an erection pressing hard against his jeans. There was something about the way Imogen looked at him, so intelligent, yet so trusting that he could give her pleasure, that just did him in every time and made him want to strip her and lick her from head to toe.

"I would imagine the woods are okay."

Ty pulled back. "Then let's set up camp, babe, before I regress to seventeen and try to nail you in the backseat."

Imogen glanced in the backseat and just wet her bottom lip.

Fighting the urge to groan, Ty said, "No. We're not having sex in this car. There are a million better places right on up this path, so change your shoes and let's head for the site."

"Why do I need to change my shoes?" she asked, pulling her backpack up from between her legs.

It was possible he might have failed to mention to Imogen that their site was so remote it wasn't drive-up. They had to hike several miles from the car to get there. "We just need to go off-road a bit here to get to the site." He tried to downplay it as he opened his door. "So maybe boots would be a better choice."

Ty got out of the car before he could see her expression. If she was irritated, frankly he didn't want to see it. He had packed light, since it was only an overnight, but between water and food and all the necessities like a sleeping bag, bug spray, and a flashlight, he was loaded heavily on his back when Imogen stepped out of the car wearing different shoes. Which, while technically could be called boots, weren't any hardier than the little flats she'd had on. These were shiny black ankle boots and looked to cost somewhere in the hundred-dollar range. At least they were flat and appeared to have a tread.

"These were the only boots I had," she said apologetically. "Other than my fur-lined snow boots, and I thought that was perhaps overkill."

Ty grinned. He liked the way Imogen figured out the score immediately. She was definitely trying, despite not really knowing a damn thing about camping, and he really appreciated it. "Probably snow boots would be overkill. But I'm sorry, babe, I should have picked you up some hiking boots or given you better suggestions on packing. I hope your feet don't start to hurt."

"They shouldn't." She smoothed back her ponytail. "I wore these tromping all over the Village when I was in school."

"Alright, well, if they do, you let me know." Ty winked. "I'll carry you."

She laughed. "I think that will be completely unnecessary, but thank you. Do you need me to help with anything? You have a lot of . . . stuff on your back."

"Could you grab that little cooler? Then just your backpack and we're good to go." Ty started down the path to the site. "So you went to college in New York, too?"

"Yes. NYU. I probably should have gone away from home for school to assert my independence, but it seemed a little ridiculous when there were so many quality schools to choose from in New York. I did live in the dorm, so that helped, but this little adventure in Charlotte is my first time living out of New York."

"Do you like it here?" he asked, aware that the answer actually really mattered to him. He'd hate to think that she was going to skip out of town in a couple of months.

"I do," she said thoughtfully. "More than I thought I would.

I like the people and the slower pace. I like the trees." She stumbled on the rough trail and grinned. "Well, I like looking at the green trees from afar and I like the idea of a tree in the yard of a pretty little house. I'm not sure how I feel about the forest here swallowing me whole. The verdict is still out on that one."

"If you're going to stay, you should get a better car." Imogen's car downright offended him, and she wasn't safe driving around in that rattletrap.

She smiled. "Maybe. I hadn't intended to stay here more than eighteen months."

That meant she would possibly be leaving after Christmas, then, and he didn't like the thought of that at all. Hell, they'd just gotten started on this whatever it was they were doing. He wanted to follow it and see where it could go.

"Charlotte's a nice town," he said, instead of saying anything he really wanted to, because it was too damn soon in their relationship and he would look like a total jackass if he let her know that he was already thinking beyond another night together. That he was thinking maybe they could try on dating, for real.

"Yes, it is," she said simply.

He let it drop, knowing he would say the wrong thing if he continued the conversation.

After ten minutes of silence, Imogen was starting to huff and puff a little as they walked down the path, their boots crunching on the sticks and other debris. Ty felt a little guilty for the long hike, but then without warning, she stopped walking and just looked around her. She turned in a complete circle, gazing up at the sky, before closing her eyes and breathing deeply.

When she reopened her eyes, she was smiling in wonderment. "God, Ty, it really is beautiful, isn't it? Everything is so verdant and alive, the sky so crisp and blue, the smells so unusual and fresh. Even the air feels different. Damp. Earthy. Thank you for suggesting this."

She was beautiful. She was verdant and alive, unusual and fresh. Damn, if he wasn't struck a bit dumb by the sight of her standing there glowing with curiosity and appreciation for the world around her. "It's a pleasure to share it with you," he said. "And if I wasn't hauling twenty pounds on my back, I'd show you how much more pleasurable it could be."

Imogen laughed, and the sound sent birds scattering from the red maple behind her. The sunlight that streamed in between the canopy of leaves danced across her face, and her eyes sparkled.

Ty had no words to describe how she looked, how he was feeling.

And suddenly the meaning of the quote he had memorized from *Much Ado About Nothing* became clear.

So he said to her, "'Silence is the perfectest herald of joy.'"

Imogen's laughter died out and her hand curled into a fist on her chest. "What did you say?"

"'Silence is the perfectest herald of joy: I were but little happy if I could say how much. Lady, as you are mine, I am yours: I give away myself for you and dote upon the exchange.'"

"Oh, my God," she whispered. "Act Two, Scene One. Claudio describing his joy in being with Hero."

"It definitely suits how Ty feels about being with Emma Jean right now," Ty said, shrugging off his heavy camping backpack and dumping it on the ground. The hell with it. They'd get to the site eventually.

Her eyes widened and she made a sound in the back of her throat. "That . . . that. Oh, my. You . . ."

It seemed he wasn't the only one having trouble finding words.

Ty closed the distance between them, took the cooler out of her hand, and set it on the ground. Then he pulled her into his arms with more passion than finesse and took her mouth beneath his.

"I've been thinking about your lips all weekend," he told her, kissing her over and over, hauling her as tightly up against him as he could manage.

Her response was to grip his shoulders and kiss him back, dipping her tongue inside his mouth to flirt with his. They were plain old making out, fast and furious, and Ty wanted to feel more of her, all of her, wanted to bury himself inside her right there on the trail.

He loved that sound, the moment when her breathing shifted, when it went ragged and hot and desperate, the sound that told him he could take and she would give. Glancing around, Ty eyed the nearest tree with a large, wide trunk.

"Turn around," he told her urgently, popping the button on her jeans and unzipping them. "Walk to that tree."

"What? Why?" she asked, but she did it, wiping her moist lips and swiveling her hips in a seductive invitation.

Ty followed her, hell, stalking her, and when she reached the tree and started to turn back toward him, her mouth open to question, Ty just took her and pushed her back against the tree trunk, his hand slipping down into her unzipped jeans at the same time he claimed her lips again. He closed his eyes on a rush of lust, the feeling hot and wet in his mouth, just the way she felt beneath his finger when he slid inside her. Her moan sighed softly past his ear, and Ty started tugging her jeans down.

"What are you doing? You can't be serious," she said, even as her hands lifted over her head and braced against the bark. She was still wearing her backpack, and it caused her chest to arch out toward him, a temptation too great to pass up.

Ty sucked her nipple through her shirt as he finished shoving her jeans and panties down to her knees.

"Wow, you are serious, aren't you?" she asked, sounding completely scandalized, yet oh, so turned on.

Raising his head, he said, "Yes, I'm serious." He used one hand to unzip his own pants and release his erection, and the other to stroke her slick inner thighs.

"Oh, Ty, yes."

Yes was right. She felt so good wrapping around his fingers, he wanted his cock in there. "Spread your legs for me."

He loved that Imogen didn't protest or demur or act like she didn't want it just as much as he did. She just turned her knees out and dug her nails into his shoulders and waited for him to fill her.

Which he did.

They groaned in mutual pleasure. Ty paused for a split second, to torture himself, then he stroked in and out of her, hard, fast, pounding at her, in her. He felt out of control, desperate, consumed by the need to take her, to make her scream his name in the woods.

Their rhythm was so furious that Imogen's sounds of pleasure were short, quiet little pants, punctuated by the occasional breakthrough full-on moan when she caught enough breath. It was beautiful against the silence of the trees.

Until they heard a rustling and snapping.

"What was that?" Imogen asked, her eyes flying open. "Oh, my God, is that a bear?"

Shit. Shit. And shit. Ty pulled out of Imogen, zipping her pants up quickly and stepping back away from her. "Worse. It's people coming down the trail." Ty tucked his erection in his jeans and winced. "Damn, that sucks."

"People? People are coming?"

"Yes." He could hear their voices now. Ty reached out and yanked her off the tree trunk, where she'd looked frozen mid-fuck, and gave her a quick kiss. "Time to move along, babe."

Imogen checked her zipper and gave a nervous laugh. "Well, that's embarrassing. And really disappointing."

"Tell me about it." Ty slung his pack over his back and tried not to think about the unsatisfied ache down south. Walking gingerly, he looked around. They were missing something, but between the sex and the sudden stop presatisfaction, his brain was blank.

Wiping her lips, she craned to see down the trail. "Oh, geez, here they come. Where's the cooler?"

"The cooler. Right." That was what they were forgetting. Ty had dropped it on the edge of the trail, just before he had marched Imogen up against the tree trunk.

Imogen bent over to pick it up and her backpack slipped over her shoulder, sending her stumbling forward.

"You okay, babe?" He started toward her, but she giggled.

She righted herself and turned around, smiling. "I can't believe we almost got busted."

Ty grinned back. "Almost is the important thing. But they're here, so mum's the word."

A man and a woman in their midthirties came enthusiastically trekking up the trail, which reassured Ty that at least if they had gotten busted, it wasn't by a pack of Boy Scouts or anything. He would have felt terrible if a kid had seen them doing the deed. Of course, he hadn't given that possibility much thought before he'd started tearing down Imogen's pants.

"Hey, how's it going?" Ty said, nodding politely as he stepped aside to let them pass.

They smiled and greeted him. Then the man did a double take.

Uh-oh. Ty braced himself.

"Say, aren't you Ty McCordle? The number sixty car?"

Ty plastered on a smile. "Why, yes, sir, I am. How are you doing today?"

"Just fine, just fine, thanks." He shook his head and adjusted his ball cap. "Wow, what a coincidence, you being here and me stumbling on you. You're a fantastic driver. Been rooting for you all season."

"Well, thank you, I appreciate it. Hoping to finish out the year strong, but there are some really good cars and drivers out there."

"True, true." The man turned to his companion. "Look at this, Lisa, it's Ty McCordle. Can you believe it?"

Lisa shook her head no rapidly. She looked a little awe-struck.

"What are you doing here? Just hiking and taking in a little R and R?" the man asked.

"Yep." Ty put his hand on the small of Imogen's back and rubbed it to reassure her, knowing she had to be thinking if this couple had walked only a touch faster, they might be having a different conversation. Hopefully if he had been caught bare butt, no one would have recognized him, though. He didn't imagine much of his fan base was familiar with his backside. "How about you?"

"Yep. Me and the wife are on a long weekend. It's our fifth anniversary this past weekend."

"Congratulations."

The man beamed at them. "Thanks. This your girlfriend?"

Ty fought the urge to sigh. He loved and appreciated his fans; he truly did. They made the sport both profitable and a hell of a lot of fun. They kept the energy level high and spurred him on to do the best he could week after week. But there were times when a man wanted some peace and privacy, and this was one of them.

"This is Imogen." That was a respectable way to avoid the question, because he had no clue how to really answer. He didn't think they were dating officially yet, but he wanted to be. It just wasn't something he wanted to discuss with total strangers on the trail. "We're just doing a quick one-night stay here. I have to get back and plan for Atlanta."

That effectively diverted the man. "Right, sure, of course. Coming down to the wire, aren't you?"

"Jim, maybe we ought to let them head on their way," his wife said, nudging him.

"Right, of course." The man flushed red. "Well, nice meeting you both. Wow. Ty McCordle."

"You, too. It's been a pleasure." Ty stuck his hand out and shook the man's firmly.

"Happy Anniversary," Imogen said to both of them.

They beamed. The wife relaxed a little. "Thanks." She shot a sly look at Ty, then back to Imogen. "Enjoy your day and *night*."

The woman might as well have winked at Imogen. Ty felt almost sheepish as he followed Imogen, who smiled and waved, then started up the trail. The couple waved back and continued in the opposite direction.

"Does that happen to you often?" Imogen asked. "People recognizing you?"

"Sometimes." He had discovered there was no rhyme or reason to when it happened. It had happened in all sorts of different places, with all different age ranges. Stock car racing drew a wide audience.

"Well," she said. "Given that you are in the public eye and

recognized, perhaps we should exercise a little discretion in the future."

He loved the way she said that—in the future. Implying there would be a future, in her very prim yet, to him, provocative voice.

Ty reached out and swatted her ass. "*Perhaps.*"

Imogen squawked and reached around to try to smack at his hand. "Ingrate. I'm trying to look out for your public image, but if you want to tarnish it, I suppose I can't stop you."

Which made him laugh. "No, you can't stop me. And the only thing I'm going to tarnish is your chastity."

She shot him a sultry dark-eyed look over her shoulder. "I think you already have."

"Oh, yeah? Tell me how." Ty wanted to hear it from her lips, wanted to hear a description of all the things he had done to her.

But she just smiled and said, "I'm not talking about this until we are at our campsite and safely in a tent, where no one can see or hear us."

He would just have to walk faster, then. "Fair enough," he told her. "Because I'm planning to pick up where I left off."

Imogen said, "I'm counting on it."

Damn it. She was smoking hot as usual, and he couldn't wait to get her into his sleeping bag.

CHAPTER

TWELVE

IMOGEN sat gingerly on a rock and watched Ty moving around the campsite, inspecting the platform tent, hauling wood to the fire circle, and unpacking supplies. Her feet were killing her and she wanted desperately to pry off her boots and rub them, but she knew it would only make Ty feel responsible for her poor choice of footwear and she didn't want him to feel guilty. It was her fault, not his, that she was inadequately prepared for an outdoor adventure.

Aside from the feet, though, and nearly getting caught with her pants down, literally, by total strangers, so far, so good. The park was beautiful, and she had been in awe standing in the quiet staring at the serenity of the wilderness and at the vastness of the sky. And then, in that moment of unexpectedly pleasant discovery of the majesty of the woods, Ty had tossed out Shakespeare at her.

That had stunned her, wowed her, aroused her. In that moment, with Claudio's words for Hero flowing off Ty's lips, Imogen had known that her heart was in jeopardy. Ty was thoughtful, interested in her career, her likes, her opinions. He wasn't even remotely uptight or pretentious or conceited. When that man had spoken to him on the trail, he had been humble and almost sheepish about being approached. Ty delivering that line from Shakespeare had been wildly romantic, yet at the same time, there was nothing too gushy or melodramatic or whiny about him, as sometimes overly romantic men could become. Ty was all man, as was evidenced by how he'd followed up that quote. He had shoved her against a tree trunk, and shown her exactly how much he wanted her.

Squeezing her knees together, Imogen swallowed hard and admired Ty's butt when he bent over to grab the sleeping bag out of his giant backpack. If she were inclined to write poetry, she could pen a sonnet regarding the beauty of his backside in denim. Not many things in her life had drawn such a tactile response from her. She always wanted to touch his bum when it was in front of her. Always. Hell, whenever it was in touching distance, she wanted a crack at it, no pun intended.

Maybe she hadn't consumed enough coffee yet, given the wild and ridiculous nature of her thoughts. It had to be almost 10 A.M., and one cup was way below her daily average for this time. She usually got up about eight and, two hours later, was on her third or fourth cup. Lack of caffeine and the arduous nature of the hike were clearly making her punchy, because she was waxing poetic about the man's backside and not feeling the least bit concerned about the physical discomforts of camping that lay ahead. She had already seen Ty toss a spider out of the tent and she hadn't even winced.

All she could think of was what difference did animals, insects, cold, and the lack of a comfortable bed matter when she was spending time, naked fun time, with Ty?

It seemed that feeling the way she did just might indicate that she was more emotionally involved with Ty than she cared to admit. It might even be that she was potentially falling in love with him, which was more than alarming. Yet she had never been in love before, she was certain of that, so how could she possibly know if she was even remotely close to feeling that exalted emotion for Ty?

What she did know was that she was sitting on a rock, a hard, dirty rock, in the middle of nowhere, with mosquitoes flitting around her face, with aching feet, and yet watching Ty, she just wanted to sigh in moony, googly-eyed girl fashion.

"How could you remember that quote from *Much Ado About Nothing*?" she asked him.

Ty glanced her way and tapped his head before returning to the task of making some kind of sculpture with the wood in the fire pit. "I have a good memory."

"Obviously. But what made you think of it?" She shouldn't ask, shouldn't ruin a good moment by probing into the why of it. She should just enjoy the fact that he had said it and stop always searching for answers and explanations. So she quickly added, "Never mind. You must think I'm akin to a preschooler, always asking why."

Standing back up, Ty looked over at her, his expression unreadable. "Why shouldn't you ask why? If you're curious, there's nothing wrong with asking. And I'll tell you why I thought of it . . . Watching you on the trail in the quiet of the woods, I was just grateful to be with you." He shrugged. "That's all. And Shakespeare's words are better than mine."

There it was again, that fluttering-butterfly feeling in her chest and the urgent need to heave out a massive sigh of aching contentment. Imogen had never really experienced this level of infatuation since early high school, and it was weird and wonderful and illogical. But having spent the past few days interviewing six more wives of drivers, Imogen had definitely seen a pattern—nothing about love was logical. Plain and simple.

Not that she was in love with Ty.

That was ludicrous. But she was in serious like.

"I think that any words spoken with sincerity are of value." Imogen leaned back on the rock and let the sun wash over her face as her eyes drifted close. "Thank you for bringing me here."

"The pleasure is truly mine." Ty was moving around, his boots crunching in the sticks and leaves. "And maybe you should hold off on the thanks until tomorrow morning. After a full day you just might change your mind."

"What are we going to do?" She was hoping it involved the sleeping bag inside the tent and Ty doing delicious things to her with his mouth.

"Right now we're going fishing."

"Oh." That didn't quite have the charm of sex, but she could roll with it. Imogen opened her eyes and glanced around. Just trees and more trees. "I don't see any water."

"We have to hike there."

Right. Of course.

"And wear your bathing suit under your clothes so we can go swimming afterwards."

Swimming sounded more appealing than fishing, hands down. "Okay. Where should I change?"

Ty grinned. "There's no cabana here, babe. You can change right where you are, or you can go into the tent."

Imogen felt her cheeks heat up at the thought of just stripping where she was and wriggling into her bathing suit with who knew what's eyes on her. "I'm not changing out here, there are probably animals lurking all around us."

Standing with his hands on his hips, he raised his eyebrows. "Why the hell would that matter?"

Just the thought had her crossing her arms over her breasts. "I would be naked! What if there's a bear or a deer or something watching?"

Ty started laughing. "Do you think the bear's going to video-tape you and put it up on the Internet? They're animals, they don't know the difference between you naked and you wearing a prom dress."

It did sound irrational when he put it that way, but she had never changed outside in her entire life and the concept was for-eign and disconcerting. "I'm changing in the tent," she told him, standing up. "And I may just come out wearing a prom dress, smart-ass."

He laughed harder. "I would love to see that."

"No, you wouldn't," she assured him, reaching for her back-pack. "I was gawky and nerdy in high school and my dress was this horrible cotton candy blue that my mother picked out. It washed my skin tone out and I looked like I'd just had the flu for a month. My date went with me under the pressure of his best friend, who was going with my best friend, and he ignored me all night until he got drunk then tried to grope me. I gave him a shove and he threw up in the cab."

"Wow. Sounds like a blast."

"Not so much." Imogen walked toward the tent. "How was your prom?"

"Actually, it was a good time. I took this girl Mindy. Real

sweet and cute. And according to locker room gossip, a sure thing."

Imogen paused on her way into the tent, and glanced back at him from her hunched-over position. "Was she?"

Ty winked. "Oh, yeah. Why do you think I had such a good time?"

She rolled her eyes at him. "Guys devote so much time and energy to the pursuit of sex it's a wonder they accomplish anything."

"And explain how exactly girls are different?" Ty sat down on the rock and yanked his boots off. "How many times have you thought about sex today?"

"Hardly at all," Imogen said. Ty had taken off his socks and he was removing his jeans, leaving him in a T-shirt and boxer shorts. Clearly the thought of a bear seeing him in the buff wasn't a concern for him. "Okay, that's not accurate," she admitted, because she never could lie. "I've pretty much been preoccupied with sex since the moment I woke up."

He smiled. "I like that you're honest about it."

Then he removed his T-shirt and his boxer shorts and was standing there in the clearing 100 percent naked. Imogen's mouth watered and she had a sudden flashback to the feel of him inside her on the trail, her backpack against the tree trunk, her jeans partially down, his urgent thrusting inside her. She swallowed hard as her eyes raced across his hard, muscular body.

Ty pulled on his swim trunks and said, "What are you waiting for, Emma Jean? We're burning daylight here."

The look on his face told her he clearly knew what she had been doing and he was enjoying it.

"Don't come into the tent," she warned him. "If you do, we'll never end up fishing."

A squirrel had hopped onto the rock next to Ty and he turned to the furry creature and said, "Does she really think I care that much about fishing?"

"You'd better care. Or why else am I enduring it?"

"She's got me there," Ty told the squirrel.

The animal dropped his nut and ran away, and Imogen retreated into the musty, damp tent to change and try to work up some enthusiasm for dropping a wire into the water and waiting for a fish to hook himself onto it. Just the thought made her lip curl.

Maybe she should have just lured Ty into the tent after all.

IMOGEN was sitting next to Ty on the seat of the rowboat, diligently following his instructions as he showed her how to cast her line and how to reel it in. Ty liked that even though she clearly wasn't comfortable with being in the boat or casting the line, she was willing to try it.

She was chewing her lip rather industriously as she practiced with her rod. "Damn it," she said when her line got no farther than the floor of the boat, hooking the rubber of her boot.

"You're getting it," he told her, releasing the hook so she wouldn't attempt it herself and manage to impale her finger with the sharp end. "Try again."

She did, and this time her line sailed and dropped nicely into the water.

"Good one."

"I did it." She smiled. "Well, you learn something new every day, don't you?"

"That's the hope," he told her. "And even if you don't, you know what they say—every day aboveground is a good one."

Imogen gave a startled laugh. "That's rather macabre, yet drives home a crucial point."

What she said. Ty grinned at her, fascinated as he always was by Imogen's speech patterns. There was something damn adorable about when she slipped into her thinking mode.

"Reel your line back in. You need a worm on it now for this to work."

"Oh, I guess I don't have a worm, do I? Maybe I should have put one on before I threw this perfect arch. I might have caught seven fish by now."

"Not likely." And he was further amused because he was starting to recognize that when Imogen was enjoying herself, she got flippant. "But it's possible, and I take complete responsibility for that missed opportunity."

Imogen reeled her line in and Ty took the lid off the Styrofoam cup holding the bait and held it out to her. "Pick your worm."

Most of the women he had dated in the past would have squealed and protested and insisted he do it for them. Aware that he just might be testing Imogen, he waited for her response.

"Just grab any one I want?"

"Yep. I'll show you how to put it on the hook."

"Okay." Imogen frowned in concentration. "This one looks appropriately plump and enticing to . . . What kind of fish are in this lake?"

Ty felt the corners of his mouth turning up. So far, she was passing the test. "Uh . . . crappie, bluegill, and yellow perch, and a couple varieties of bass."

"Crappie? I don't want to catch one of those." Imogen put her fingers into the cup and gingerly removed a worm. "This is a bass-catching worm, I'm certain of it."

"Absolutely. It's written all over him." Ty plucked a worm

out for himself and showed Imogen how to put it on the hook. "See? That's it. Just watch your fingers."

"I would have thought baiting fish would have gotten more sophisticated these days."

"We're just pleasure fishing. We don't need anything special."

"It's very nice that you can rent the boat, get the fishing license and all the accoutrements right here at the lake." She crammed her worm onto her hook. "There. I'm good to go."

"Just cast your line again, then."

Imogen was staring at the worm. "So . . . does the worm die when I jam that hook through him? Because he looks like he's still moving."

"No. Worms can actually survive parts of their body being chopped off."

"That's impressive." She lifted her rod. "But does the worm drown, then? Or is it still alive when the fish eats it?"

"I have no idea how long it takes a worm to drown."

"Maybe I should just kill mine now, then, so as not to prolong his agony."

Trust Imogen to consider the consequences of fishing to the worm. She didn't look particularly upset or disturbed, she was just clearly thinking it through.

"If that seems appropriate to you, go for it. I'm tossing mine in, because I suspect the fish likes a wiggling, live worm better than a dead one."

"Really? They have discerning tastes?"

"I would just think a moving worm would attract their attention more than a dead one. They might just think it's debris floating in the water if it isn't wiggling around."

"Oh. That's a valid point." Imogen lifted her rod and spoke to her worm. "I'm sorry, but try to remember you are a part of the circle of life." She cast her line. "Speaking of which, I'm hungry. I should have brought some snack foods."

"I did." Ty reached into his smaller, portable backpack. "Water, pretzels, and granola bars. And if you're nice to me, I'll share."

She pushed her glasses up on her nose and trained those big wide eyes on him. "You promised to take care of me on this camping adventure."

Ouch. She went for the jugular. "Fine. Here's some water." He tucked it between her legs. "And do you want pretzels or a granola bar?"

"Both."

Of course she wanted both. Ty pulled out some antibacterial gel and squirted it into his hand. "Hold out your palms."

"I can't. I'm holding the rod."

"Well, then one of them."

She did, gingerly, and he put gel in her hand. Sticking the rod between her legs with the water, Imogen tried to carefully rub her hands together. "If I drop the rod, grab it," she ordered him.

"Of course." Ty watched her, trying not to grin. She did everything so cautiously, so precisely. When she held her palm out, he dropped three pretzel twists in it and she popped them in her mouth.

"Whew, it's hot out here on the water," she said when she was finished chewing, wiping her forehead with the back of her hand.

"Drink your water."

"I don't want to."

"Why not?" Ty drank some of his just to make a point.

"What if I have to go to the bathroom? We're on a rowboat in the middle of the lake."

"You go in the water."

She shot him a look of horror. "I am not a man."

"So I noticed."

"Therefore, I cannot take aim and just send it into the lake."

"Yeah, but we're going to go swimming soon, so go then."

"In my bathing suit?" Her nose wrinkled in disgust. "No, thank you."

"So take your bathing suit off and go skinny dipping. I'd like that."

"We're in public. We'll get caught. We'll get arrested."

She had an answer for everything. "So you're just going to dehydrate?"

"It is a conundrum," she admitted. "I am really thirsty. And hot."

There was no questioning that. "Here, I'll hold your rod. Take a sip of your water before you overheat. One sip won't make you have to go to the bathroom. Taking your jeans off will cool you down, too, and we're going to want to go swimming soon anyway. Just be careful moving on the bench. You don't want to capsize us."

"No pressure or anything," she said, handing him her rod. After sipping her water and handing it to him, she unsnapped her jeans and began delicately tugging them off.

Ty blatantly watched. Her ponytail flopped around and her glasses slipped down her nose as she tried to wiggle out of her pants with as little movement as possible. After a couple of precarious minutes, she had them in a puddle on the bottom of the boat and had her flip-flops back on her feet. Imogen was wearing black bikini bottoms with a little tie on each side, and Ty appreciated the nice view of her long, pale legs.

"Better?" he asked.

"Much." She took her pole back from him. "Thank you."

They sat in companionable silence for a few minutes, the sun hot on his arms, a sleepy and pleasant lethargy stealing over him. Now, this was the way to spend his day off—out on the lake with a woman whose company he really enjoyed.

Imogen sat up straight suddenly. "Oh, something's happening!" She had a look of fear on her face and held her pole like it had suddenly come alive.

"Hold steady," Ty said, leaning over and peering out into the water. He could see the ripples of movement where her line was cast. "Okay, just start reeling it in, slow and steady."

"Just turn the little handle thingie?"

"Yep."

"Okay." Imogen took a deep breath and started reeling in her line.

Ty reached over to feel the line. It was taut and there was definitely something on it.

"What are you doing?" she asked, pausing.

"Just checking it. Keep going."

She did, biting her lip and spreading her feet to brace herself. Ty just sat and watched her, enjoying the concentration on her face, appreciating the beauty of her face in profile. He turned to the water right at the moment a striped bass emerged, dangling and flopping on her line.

"Alright!" he told her, pulling the line forward so that the fish fell on the floor of the boat. "You got a bass, babe."

"I did?" Imogen stared at the fish jumping around, then smiled. "Well, of course I did."

Ty laughed. "Exactly." He released the fish from the hook and dropped it into the small cooler he had brought with them. "Very impressive."

Imogen beamed at him. "I caught a fish. Wow. I can't wait to tell my mother. She'll never believe me."

"What's your mother like?"

"She's like me, actually. Logical, boring. She owns an art gallery."

Somehow that didn't surprise him. He knew the world of art galleries and traffic and fine dining was Imogen's home, but sometimes he had a hard time swallowing it. While she had big-city polish, she also had small-town curiosity.

"Babe, there is nothing boring about you at all." He meant that straight up. She entertained him every second she was with him.

"Thanks." She gave him a sheepish smile. "So do we keep fishing? Is there a goal in mind for the number of fish we want?"

His goal had simply been to relax and introduce Imogen to something he enjoyed, nothing more. "Nope. In fact, I'm thinking we should jump in and go swimming. I didn't bring these inner tubes with us to let them go to waste." Ty shucked off his T-shirt. "You ever been tubing?"

"I don't even know what it is, so I don't imagine I've done it."

"I don't know," Ty said with a grin. "Sometimes you do things without knowing they have a name, and then you find out that the thing that gives you so much fun and pleasure is actually called something."

She shot him a suspicious look. "You're talking about sex again, aren't you?"

Ty touched his chest. "Did I mention sex? I think you have a dirty mind, girl."

"Probably," she said. "Because right now I'm wishing we were back in the tent instead of in this wobbly boat."

That made him grin and go hard, all at once. "Don't worry, we can make something work." He tossed the two tubes he'd brought with them into the lake and glanced around. They hadn't seen anyone in the whole hour they'd been out on the water, which was a good thing. "Now we just jump in."

Ty stood up and dove into the water, hearing Imogen shriek behind him when the boat rocked. He hit the water in an arc and came back up to see Imogen gripping the sides of the rowboat. "Come on in, the water's nice."

"It's October, you know. Isn't the water cold?"

"Nah. It's over eighty degrees outside, the sun is shining. If this was spring, it might be chilly, but the water holds its temperature in the fall." It was a little brisk, but he wasn't going to admit that. Ty paddled over to an inner tube and climbed into it. He sank in and relaxed. "You don't know what you're missing."

"That's tubing? You just lie in a black rubber doughnut?"

"Well, I guess technically tubing is moving down a river in your inner tube, but we've got a lake, not a river."

Ty dipped his fingers in the water and flicked some in Imogen's direction. It hit her on the arm and she stared at it like it was acid.

"Hey. Watch it."

He did it again.

She was fighting the urge to laugh, he could tell. But she didn't say anything, just carefully took off her glasses and tucked them in the pocket of her jeans. She stripped off her T-shirt, revealing a whole lot of Imogen in a tiny black bikini. He wasn't sure why, but he wouldn't have taken her for the string bikini type, but it was barely there, and he was thoroughly grateful. She stood up cautiously, back hunched over, clearly not even aware of the power she could wield over him posing in that bikini.

Instead, she pinched her nose shut with her fingers, which he found absolutely adorable. Then she jumped, feetfirst, in the most ungraceful, sinking-stone leap Ty had ever seen, covering him with water from head to toe from the massive splash.

He was shaking his head like a dog to rid his hair and eyelashes of the water when she emerged coughing and shivering.

"Oh, my God, it's freezing! You're a big fat liar." Imogen treaded water and swiped at her eyes. "Did I splash you?"

"Uh, yeah. I'm soaking wet."

"Good." She grinned. "You deserve it." She swam over to the second tube and tried to pull herself onto it awkwardly, with two failed attempts that had her bottom wiggling two feet away from his face.

"Need some help?" Ty contemplated swatting her wet, bikini-covered bottom, but figured that would send her face-first into the water. Imogen wasn't exactly a natural-born athlete.

"I got it," she said breathlessly, slipping back into the water and assessing the tube from all angles with her head tilted.

"Get in the middle," he suggested. "Then just pull yourself up."

She lifted it over her head, put her arms on either side, and tried to haul herself up. She immediately sank back into the water. "Huh," she lamented. "Guess I need better arm strength."

"Come here." Ty tugged on her tube, pulling her over to him. He leaned over. "Put your arms back up."

She did, and he caught her around the middle and lifted. "Bring your legs up," he ordered, but she overshot the mark and sent them both tumbling backward into the water.

"Oops, sorry," she said, squeezing water out of her ponytail and giving him a sheepish look.

"Not a problem unless you did it on purpose. Then I might have to punish you."

"I didn't." Which he knew, but it amused him to see her vehemently shaking her head. "I'm just a klutz."

Ty hopped back on his tube and said, "Let's try this again. Come closer so I can lift you up by your arms."

Imogen treaded water in front of him, but didn't comply. "I'm not sure I should get closer. Are you going to punish me?"

The way she said that—her eager, throaty voice immediately shifting the exchange from playful to sensual—had Ty grinding his teeth to keep from groaning out loud. "Do you need to be punished? Have you been bad? Did you knock me into the water on purpose?"

She shook her head quickly, but she didn't answer. Her mouth was open, eyes wide, her finger trailing across her bottom lip in a way that told Ty she wasn't kidding when she'd said she'd rather be in the tent. She was regretting that they'd been interrupted on the trail and was looking for him to finish the job.

Damn, she turned him on, made him hot and hard and demanding.

"I'll be the judge of that," he said. "Now get over here and lift up your arms before I have to come and get you."

There was no further protest. She swam over to him and lifted her arms up in the air, her chest rising and falling rapidly, nipples tight beads in her bikini top, goose bumps on her chest and arms, whether from cold or arousal, Ty wasn't sure. She blinked up at him, wanting him, lusting after him, wanting his body in hers the same way he wanted to take her with his cock, to pound into her again and again.

Ty reached out and lifted Imogen, pulling her up onto the tube with him, maintaining his balance with difficulty, but managing to get her settled on top of him. It was unfortunate that his ass was actually in the water and he couldn't really feel her pressing against his erection, but it would do for now.

"We're going to fall," she whispered, looking down into his eyes, her fingernails digging into his flesh as she gripped his arms, her mouth a hairbreadth from his.

"So?" he asked. "We've already fallen. And this is worth the risk of a second dunking."

"Oh, yeah?"

"Yeah." And Ty kissed her, closing his eyes as the cool, sweet taste of her lips washed over him.

He could kiss her forever, he decided, just pressing his lips against hers over and over, letting their mouths mingle together. She did things to him that no woman ever had, she made him feel hot and possessive and tender and elated. He'd never thought of himself as a romantic guy, but with Imogen he wanted to be. He wanted the words to describe to her how good he felt when she was with him.

It was a place of perfect contentment for him, lolling around on the water with Imogen in his arms, no worries about the Chase for the Cup, nothing but gratitude for his life, what he had, and where he was.

"Mmmm," she said when they broke apart. She relaxed on him, her head on his chest as they bobbed in the water.

Ty thought about finding a way to give Imogen oral sex, but decided he'd either drown in the process or knock them both into the water. So instead, he moved his hand between her legs and stroked along the front of her bikini bottoms.

"Stop that," she murmured.

"Why?" Ty used the pad of his thumb to circle around her clitoris.

"Because you're turning me on."

"And that's a bad thing?"

"It is when you can't do anything about it."

"Who says I can't do anything about it?" Ty maneuvered his fingers inside the damp bottoms and slid along her warm flesh.

"Ahhhh," was her response, which he took as a positive sign to continue.

Finding a slow, easy rhythm, he went in and out of her, feeling her body respond with a rush of moisture. It was a little bit of an awkward position for him, but he didn't care when he heard her breathing quicken and felt her hips tense.

"Oh," she said, her breath tickling his cheek. "Oh, that is rather nice."

"Yeah?" Ty played with her clitoris before slipping back inside her. Hooking his finger, he stroked deeply along the inner wall and was rewarded by her whole body jerking slightly.

"Oh!" she said again, only this time it was shock, excitement, serious hot and juicy pleasure. "Nice doesn't . . ." She sucked in a breath when he repeated the action. "Cover it. Oh, God, oh God . . ."

It looked like he'd found her G-spot again, a happy, hot discovery. Ty throbbed with desire as he stroked again and had the acute pleasure of feeling and seeing her come, her cries loud and frantic, her inner muscles convulsing around his finger. He held on until she had stilled, panting in his ear. Then he slowly slid out of her and trailed his hand up her side.

"You okay?"

She nodded, blinking at him. "That was . . ." Her raspy voice trailed off.

"Nice?" he suggested with a grin.

"Yeah."

"Good." Ty moved his legs and separated from her. "Because we're going back to the site now. We have a date with a sleeping bag."

"Nice," she said, sprawled across the inner tube like a lazy cat in the sun.

Ty laughed and rolled off into the water, welcoming the cold submersion.

CHAPTER
THIRTEEN

IMOGEN rather expected Ty to get her back to their campsite and fling her down onto the sleeping bag posthaste. Which she would not have objected to in the least.

But he was courteous enough to suggest she change out of her wet bathing suit and have some lunch. Ty also pointed out the bathroom facilities to her, such as they were.

After a precarious few minutes in the outhouse, she emerged to find Ty had spread out a lunch of sandwiches, fruit, and crackers on the picnic table.

"Wow, aren't you domestic?" Imogen took a seat on the bench and grabbed a grape.

"Note there's no red dye. I don't want you having an allergic reaction on our trip. That would seriously interfere with my plans." Ty raised his eyebrows up and down. "And my mother taught me to take care of myself. She always said she was raising future husbands, not boys."

Touched he had remembered an allergy she had only mentioned once when he'd been eating candy at Tamara's house, Imogen said, "Thank you, that was sweet. And I should thank your mother as well."

Immediately she realized how that could be misconstrued and she tried to explain. "I mean, I should thank her for ensuring you were capable of preparing decent meals, as I've now been the recipient of them twice. I wasn't at all making any reference to your potential as a husband." Imogen bit her grape and told herself to shut up.

Ty looked more amused than put out. "I kind of figured that out, but thanks for clarifying. And you already made it clear what you think of my potential as a husband when you asked Nikki why in hell she'd ever want to marry me."

She knew he was teasing her, but she still couldn't help defending herself. "I explained that to you. The girl was using absolutely the wrong set of criteria to choose a spouse and, frankly, to reach the conclusion that marriage was even what she wanted at this juncture in her life."

"I agree. But what is the right set of criteria, Emma Jean?" Ty bit into a turkey sandwich as he sat on the bench across from her. "How do you know when the time is right?"

"Prevailing opinion would have it you just know."

"I thought I knew and I was wrong." He shrugged. "Does it matter in the long run? No, I guess it doesn't. No harm came out of it. And it's funny now that I can look back and see it was more of a puppy love on my part than a true and deep love."

"What is the difference and how do you know?" That bothered Imogen, the great unknown, the wondering if there would ever be a life partner for her. She could live happily alone, she knew that, but everyone craved on some fundamental level that kind of passion and devotion. The safety that came from knowing you were truly and completely loved. But how would she know when she did have it, if she did?

"Beats the hell out of me. I don't think I've ever actually been in love the way I imagine you need to be to sustain a thirty-year marriage."

He set his sandwich down on the uncovered picnic table, which momentarily distracted her. Wasn't that table dirty? But it didn't seem to bother him, so Imogen forced herself to refocus. His wheat bread wasn't the issue here; they were talking about love.

"I've never felt that either," she told him.

They stared at each for a heartbeat, something in his brown eyes darkening and starting to smolder. There was something between them, something new and wondrous and passionate, and Imogen wondered how far it could go.

Maybe, just maybe, all the way to that sacred place they were both curious about that had thus far eluded them.

The moment stretched and she didn't know what to say, if she should rein it in, keep it light and casual, or hint, take a risk, suggest there be more than a few romps in bed together.

But then Ty's mouth split into a grin. "So we're a couple of loveless Joes, huh? At least we know how to have bang-up sex."

A little deflated, then irritated with herself for feeling that way, Imogen forced a smile. "True." What she didn't say was that they both knew at some point sex could no longer sustain a relationship, that you either had to cross over into emotional intimacy to mirror your physical intimacy, or go your separate ways. Almost no one could have a long-term sexual relationship without developing feelings for the person or developing the desire to feel more than they did. At least Imogen knew she couldn't.

She already felt more than she should.

Stuffing another grape in her mouth, she struggled to find something witty to say in return, but she was never witty. So she was chewing, wishing she could swallow her confusing emotions like fruit, when Ty reached over and ran his finger across the back of her hand.

"Do you know that when you have an orgasm, you stop breathing?" he said, his own food abandoned on the table as he stared at her with a look that she recognized.

The change of subject caught her off guard and she swallowed hard. "I'm aware of that," she said, her heart rate stepping up at the memory of his fingers inside her barely an hour earlier. "When it grabs me like that, I can't breathe."

"That silence, the way your eyes go wide and your mouth drops open, and you stop breathing for a second or two, is the hottest damn thing I've ever seen."

"Thank you," she said, not sure what else to say. While she was surprising herself by how sexually comfortable and almost coy she was with Ty, she was still no seductress. She didn't know how to play the game, only how to be honest.

"I want to see that look right now."

"Fruit and turkey don't get me that excited," she said, which was the truth. But he got her excited, and just staring at her across the table was enough to have her feeling the beginnings of a blaze stoking to life between her thighs.

The corner of his mouth went up. "I would wonder about you if they did." Ty stood up. "Come on."

"To the tent?"

"Yes, unless you want to do this on the table."

The thrill of it warred with the image of splinters in her backside. "I thought you wanted to eat first."

"Changed my mind." Ty was coming around the table, and he took the sandwich out of her hand and slapped it down on the table. "Up. Come on." He tugged her hand to get her to rise. "I'm going to make you stop breathing again."

"We talked about this, remember?" Imogen said in protest, even as she went with him. "I don't have multiple orgasms."

"That was an hour ago."

"I still think it counts . . . It's sort of like I can't have more than two in twenty-four hours, usually only one."

"We'll see."

A shiver went up her spine at that promise. "Am I going to be uncomfortable?" she asked, thinking about the hard ground and her head grinding into it.

Ty threw open the flap to the tent. "Only if having a dick buried in you makes you uncomfortable."

Alrighty, then. It was safe to say she didn't really have a problem with that, even though his words startled her. "You shock me sometimes," she told him.

Looking back at her, he paused, his eyes searching. "Am I too much for you, babe? Do I need to rein it in? Because I can do that."

She took a second, really listening to her gut. Did she want him to stop being outrageous and demanding in their sexual encounters? Uh, no. Not at all. She loved that he took charge, that he guided her and told her what he wanted. That he forced her to say what *she* wanted. There was something very sexy and primal about being taken by Ty.

"No," she told him, shaking her head. "Nothing is too much."

She knew precisely how that would sound to him, and it had the effect she wanted. His eyes narrowed, and a low groan slipped out of his mouth.

"Oh, yeah? Then in you go. Down on the sleeping bags." He gestured for her to enter the tent.

Imogen ducked and entered, getting her bearings. It didn't look glamorous or comfortable but it didn't look dirty either. And there was something cozy about the peak of the tent and the nylon walls. She dropped to her knees carefully and crawled forward on the sleeping bag. It was thicker than it looked and not as dreadful as she had anticipated. But concerns about damage to her knees disappeared when Ty moved in behind her and pulled her hips back until her backside collided with a very impressive erection.

"Hello," she said, turning to look at him over her shoulder. "I wasn't expecting that." Even though they were fully clothed, the motion of him bumping gently into her, over and over, had her thighs going damp.

"If you're on all fours in front of me, I consider that an invitation," he said, his grip on her hips tightening. "It's presenting."

"I'll be sure to remember that." So she could do it frequently. Imogen bit her lip when his hand slid across her thigh and moved down to cup her mound. Then she struggled not to moan when he undid her jeans and started tugging them off.

"They're not going to come off in this position," she said.

"You want to bet?"

Not really, because Imogen could already tell he was going to prevail in triumph over the denim. He pretty much had them down her thighs already, and when she leaned forward a little, he was able to get them down to her knees, panties included. Then his finger slipped inside her and she stiffened. The man knew dead-on right where to touch her. It was amazing. It was sexual ESP.

"Shit, I left the condoms in my backpack out there," Ty said, even as his finger continued to move. "I have to go get them."

"I'm on the pill." Imogen rolled her hips back to meet his strokes, her eyes half-closed at the delicious impact of her colliding with his finger. "As far as anything else goes, I trust you. I presume you would trust me to be truthful with you about my health as well." She panted a little, struggling to find her breath. "I mean, honestly, it's all rather bizarre. Every relationship passes out of the condom phase as a couple becomes more committed and/or trusts one another on a deeper level. Yet, unless they have actually been tested for disease during the course of the relationship, they are no more 'safe' than they were when they were still using condoms. What changes in reality? Nothing, except the skewed perception that now that they know each other, they couldn't possibly have an STD, whereas previously it was still a possibility. It's an odd alteration based purely on emotion, isn't it?"

"Very odd. And I don't have anything. I've been tested."

"But it's not like you can carry around a card indicating that you're—"

He interrupted her. "Hey, Engine?"

His finger had stilled in her, which she found disappointing. She wiggled a little to provoke a response from him but he didn't give it. "Yes?"

"Are you giving me permission to be inside you without a condom?"

Imogen processed the question and didn't hesitate in her answer. "Yes, I am."

He gave a soft, exasperated laugh. "Then quit yapping and let me fuck you."

"Hey." She reached back and smacked at his leg, which was somehow magically bare. How he'd gotten his own jeans down his thighs was a mystery to her. "I don't yap."

Ty yanked off his T-shirt. "No, you're right, you don't yap." His finger slipped into her again. "You are the smartest woman I know, with witty and interesting observations on everything around you, especially people, and I love to hear you talk, to hear your thoughts. Most of the time. Now is not one of those times, because right now I just want to grit my teeth, let my mind go blank, and sink into the sensation of your body closing around mine in a hot, wet cocoon."

She swore that with each word he spoke she got wetter and more aroused, until she was thrusting frantically backward onto his finger and gripping the sleeping bag beneath her by the time he was done talking. That had sounded hot and excited and almost, kind of, romantic. Like the Ty McCordle version of Shakespeare. "Okay," she said. "I'm done thinking."

"Good. Just feel me."

Then he removed his finger and thrust inside her, sans a condom, and Imogen's head snapped back at the acute pleasure the impact brought. "Oh, God," she said, her muscles trembling around him as she wondered for a split second if she'd actually had a mini-orgasm.

"Oh, yeah," he said, hands squeezing her thighs, his penis pulsing inside her as he paused. "Thank you, thank you for letting me go bareback."

"Bareback?" She gave a soft laugh. "I like that expression."

"I like this," he said, and started to move, a quick, hard pace that had Imogen holding on to the sleeping bag so she didn't fall.

She could honestly say that she liked it, too. It was possessive, urgent, the hot friction, the hard slap of his thighs against her like an invitation to lose herself in sex, to let it take her and sweep her under until she was screaming with pleasure. The position that had always bored her somehow took on a totally different meaning, ripped a relentless and uncontrollable response from her, a desperate need to meet his rhythm, to hold on.

"Oh, babe," he said, his voice ragged.

"Yeah?" Imogen dipped her head and let her hair slide forward over her face.

"Yeah."

He thrust so hard she actually lost her balance, then gasped when he quickly pulled out. "Oh, where are you going?"

"Too close," he said. "Lie down on your back."

Already used to his orders, she immediately did it. He always had great ideas, and she trusted this one would be no different. Once she was on her back, he stripped her jeans and panties all the way off, then did the same to her shirt. It was warm in the tent, the sun filtering down in the cracks where the window flaps were, and it felt intimate, cozy, just the two of them out in the middle of nowhere.

Imogen smiled up at him and he paused as he leaned over her. He cupped her cheek, stroking her skin, and smiled back. "Can I kiss you?"

"Of course you can. You've done everything else."

He laughed. "True enough. But looking down at you, you look so pretty, so perfect, I thought maybe I shouldn't mess up that smile."

Ty really was romantic. She could have never imagined how sexy and tender his words could possibly be, but they were. On the verge of melting like milk chocolate in the sun, she reached up and ran her fingers across his bottom lip.

"I would love a kiss."

"Then I guess I have to." Ty leaned over her, propped up on his arms, and kissed her.

She loved the way he kissed her, the way he started out slow, then got faster and more demanding, his kisses hungrier and more urgent as his tongue dipped inside her mouth. Ty pulled back and took her glasses off. He tucked them in the corner of the tent, then took her shoulders and rolled her so she was on top of him.

Sprawled across his chest, she asked, "So what do you have in mind?"

"First you're going to kiss me."

Grinning, she leaned down and moved her mouth over his, enjoying the control the angle gave her. "Yeah? And then?"

"Now you're going to sit on my face."

Subtle as usual, Ty was. "Oh, yeah?"

"Yeah." He started to push her back so she'd sit up. "And why do we keep saying 'yeah' to each other?"

"Because we don't know what else to say?" Imogen hadn't even noticed, which was interesting because usually she noticed everything.

"Yet another reason to put my tongue to better use." Now he was tugging on her hips, trying to get her to scoot forward on his chest.

Imogen was sitting up at his urging, but was looking around the tent, wondering how she could manage the position he wanted without a headboard. "I don't have anything to hold on to," she told him.

Ty took her hands and placed them on her breasts. "Hold these."

She laughed. "That's not going to give me balance."

"But it looks good." His eyebrows went up and down as he gave her a naughty look. "Rub your nipples a little."

"No. I don't think any of this is going to work, Ty." Maybe it would physically, but for some reason she felt awkward and self-conscious.

He didn't even bother to respond. He just yanked her forward until her thighs were on either side of him. Spreading her apart, he slid his tongue along her. It was an intimate position, one that surrounded his head with her body, and left her sitting up, feeling exposed and vulnerable.

One of his hands snaked up and covered hers, his thumb rubbing across her beaded nipple. "We can change positions if you really want to," he murmured between flicks of his tongue.

Imogen almost said yes. She wasn't used to being so out there in the air, so to speak. But then she hesitated. "Do you like this position?"

"I like looking up at you. I like seeing you in the power position, taking what you like. But I want you comfortable. Hell, I want you more than comfortable. I want you moaning and writhing and coming all over me."

That was a good plan. Imogen closed her eyes and took a deep breath and relaxed her shoulders. What difference did it make how her body was positioned? Would a woman who was truly confident in her sexuality hesitate to sit up when a man was offering to give her oral sex? Of course not, and Imogen wanted to be that woman. She wanted to stop thinking and just feel.

So she sat up and shut down her mind, concentrating on the sensation of Ty between her thighs, coaxing her body to desire. He was incredibly good at it, hitting her in just the right spots, with just the right pressure, kicking up her breathing into panting.

"Lift up a little," he murmured.

"Lift what up?" she asked. Was she smothering him? That wasn't a hot thought.

"Your tail."

Never having had her backside referred to as her *tail*, Imogen found that rather oddly endearing. Not wanting to deprive the man of all his oxygen, she obeyed immediately.

But it became immediately clear that air circulation hadn't been his concern when his finger slipped into her from behind and plucked her G spot. That yanked a loud moan from her. With his tongue on her and his finger stroking inside at such a sexy angle, she reached that place she always did with Ty, where she thought about nothing but their bodies and mutual pleasure. That place where just about nothing would be a bad idea, where she felt hot and desirable and wanted him, it, *everything*.

Rubbing her nipples, she dipped her head forward and bit her lip as tightness built inside her. She wasn't going to be able to maintain the position very long without pitching forward onto him, but while she was still upright, she was going to enjoy it. When he sucked her clit, she did both, groaning with ecstasy and dropping her hands down onto the sleeping bag on either side of him, needing something to hold on to, to ground her.

He started moving his finger in and out, sliding her own slickness all along between her cheeks, back and forth, the sensation erotic and exciting. Then his finger slipped inside her again, but with a whole different destination. Imogen sucked in a breath and looked down at him.

"Are you . . . ?" She couldn't say it, couldn't breathe, couldn't think. It felt good. Better than good. His finger there, and his tongue inside her . . . she was shocked, titillated, stunned at how it heightened the pleasure of what he was doing with his mouth.

He paused to ask, "Should I stop?" His breath tickled the hair above her clitoris.

She shook her head, speechless, then realized he couldn't see her. "Uh-uh," she managed.

Ty wiggled his finger at the same time his tongue went deep.

Imogen squeezed the sleeping bag and shot into an orgasm, the hard, shuddering, tight kind where she did hold her breath, and her vision went spotty. Where every muscle in her body tightened while she let the tremors rush over her and take her under.

After a minute, Ty slowly pulled back his finger and mouth and said, "Breathe, babe."

Instead, she exhaled, and tilted sideways, falling onto the sleeping bag in a heap. Then she dragged in air, shoving her hair out of her eyes, her heart racing and legs shaking. "Wow. This is the perfect time to use that catchphrase OMFG."

"What does that stand for?" Ty shifted so he was facing her, and ran his fingers down her arm.

"Oh, my fucking God. Totally blasphemous, but when you use the acronym, it softens the blow." She stared at the ceiling of the tent and tried to remember her name. "And in this case, utterly applies."

Ty laughed softly. "Good. Now on your stomach."

"I can't move."

"Yes, you can." He lightly smacked her bottom and said, "Roll over. Lie flat, and cross your ankles."

"Excuse me?" But she was already doing it, rolling in a lazy, satisfied flop onto her stomach and shifting her hands above her head. She could fall asleep at any given second.

Until he moved over her and pushed inside her.

Ty loved that first push into Imogen. She always made the same sound—a little gasp of appreciation—and that totally turned him on. As did the feel of her wet and willing body surrounding him. He couldn't get enough of her. He loved touching her body, loved making her insensible, got off on the sight of her biting her lip, her eyes half-closed, the beauty of her when she snapped her head back and had a really hard orgasm.

Now looking down at her, her body relaxed, her dark hair spilling over her shoulders, her creamy pale skin smooth beneath his fingers as he held her and thrust into her, Ty felt something big and strong and shocking rise up in him. He wanted to pleasure her, worship her, care for her, protect her. Be the one who had those denim blue eyes trained on him while she had every orgasm. He wanted to be with her.

And instead of scaring the shit out of him, the thought had him thrusting harder, faster, groans sneaking out as he started to lose control. She had very obediently crossed her ankles, which kept him in position, and she raised her hips very slightly to meet him, a hot and heady subtle invitation. He suspected he was doing things with Imogen she hadn't experienced with other men, and that only added to his own passion.

He would have never in a million years thought his sex life was in any way lacking, but his entire past paled to the satisfaction he got from burying himself in Imogen, and when she bit the tip of her index finger, he came inside her, a pulsing, hot orgasm that had him groaning loud enough to be heard back in Charlotte.

As soon as he could speak, he apologized. "Sorry, I'm sorry, I should have pulled out." It was rude and insensitive at this point in their relationship to just go for it inside her, even if he was pretty certain nothing on planet Earth could have made him stop. The position, her body, the lack of a condom . . . he only had so much control and Imogen shattered it.

"Why? I told you I'm on the pill," she said, her voice husky and muffled by the sleeping bag.

"Yeah, but most women aren't thrilled with the aftereffects of this." Ty started to pull out, but Imogen grabbed his hip.

"Don't. Not yet. I like to feel you pulsing in me."

Which was why he adored her. Ty stopped moving, wishing he could rest his weight on her, but knowing that would crush her.

"I want you to come in me," she said. "And I want you to lie down on top of me now like you really want to do."

"Really?" He ran his fingers across her back, raising goose bumps. He did want to do just that. "I shouldn't."

"'The Lady doth protest too much, methinks,'" she murmured.

"Kenny Chesney?" he joked.

"*Hamlet*. Lie on me."

"Okay. But I'm no lady."

"That is the understatement of the year. You are all man."

He liked the sound of that. Ty dropped his weight on her as gently as he could, and sighed at the feel of her warm skin beneath his. He kissed her hair and rested his head next to hers.

"I think I like camping after all," she said.

Ty laughed. "Me, too."

CHAPTER

FOURTEEN

TY was in such a good mood, he didn't even mind when he and Imogen emerged from their tent three hours later after a nap to find that raccoons had been having a party on the picnic table. Their lunch was torn into and scattered all around, most of it missing, but a few random bits of bread and fruit scraps were left behind. It even looked like one ambitious guy had gnawed on the plastic container the sandwiches had been in.

The one lone party animal left sat on the bench nibbling on a piece of cheese, staring at them with mild interest.

"Oh, my God!" Imogen said, grabbing on to Ty's arm as she maneuvered behind him. "What is that?"

"It's just a raccoon. They'll eat anything and they aren't afraid of people."

"Obviously. What do we do?"

"Nothing. They're mean as a snake and carry rabies. We're

going to ignore him and light a fire. Maybe that will send him scattering."

"He doesn't look mean."

"Trust me, you try to take that cheese away from him, he's going to spit and hiss."

"Well, it's not like I want the cheese back at this point, so why would I attempt to take it away from him?"

Ty laughed. Trust Imogen to point out the obvious and logical. "True. God, I can't believe it's dusk already. Guess it really is fall."

He started building a fire with the wood he'd gathered earlier, content and still sleepy from their post-sex nap.

Imogen perched on a rock, giving wary glances at the raccoon every now and then. "There are only a few weeks left to the season, aren't there? How do you feel about that?"

"Yep, only four races left. Not much time to make a difference. I'm in fifth place right now." Which he should be stressing more about, frankly, but for some reason he wasn't. Fifth didn't suck, and he wasn't feeling quite the competitiveness he had in previous seasons. It was a little unnerving, but at the same time, he suspected it was just that he was comfortable with his career. He had achieved a lot already and he worked damn hard. If it didn't land him in the number-one spot, that was no reason to beat himself up. There were some damn good drivers and cars out there every week.

"Wow, that's really impressive," Imogen said, sounding like she actually meant it. "What does the overall winner for the season get?"

Ty surveyed his fire pile, satisfied. He glanced back at Imogen. "Fame and fortune, babe, plain and simple." He turned full around, realizing she was shivering. "You cold?"

She nodded, her arms crossed across her chest.

"Go get your sweatshirt."

"I didn't bring one. I only brought this sweater I'm wearing. I thought it was sufficient and I was trying to pack light."

"I knew there was a catch to that tiny backpack you brought. I'll get the fire going and that will help, and the sleeping bag is plenty warm, especially with me there to heat you up." Ty gave her a wink. "But in the meantime, grab my sweatshirt. It's in my pack."

"I don't want to go through your bag."

"Why not? I can't imagine the sight of my underwear is going to upset you in any way."

"Well, no. But it seems like a privacy violation."

"I've got nothing to be private about." Not in his bag anyway. Maybe he did have one tiny little thing that he kept from most people, but it wasn't a big deal. And as much as he liked Imogen, he couldn't foresee telling her he couldn't read. She'd run for the hills and he just wasn't ready for that yet.

"Okay. Thanks." Imogen stood up and patted her front pocket. Ty knew she kept her phone in there when her purse wasn't available and she did pull it out. "Wow, I just got a message. Who knew you could get cell reception out here? I wonder if I can check my e-mail?"

"No e-mail." Ty frowned. "That's just wrong."

She nodded. "You're right. But I should check to see who called. It might be my parents or something."

"I can authorize that," he said with a smile. Hell, he'd brought his cell, too, because Toni would have a heart attack if he didn't. "Then put a sweatshirt on and come over here and share my body heat."

Imogen didn't say anything, and Ty glanced over to see her

listening to her voice mail with a weird expression on her face. "What's wrong?" he asked her when she hung up.

"Nothing." She crammed the phone back in her pocket and looked around. "What was I doing?"

"Getting a sweatshirt," he said carefully. He hesitated, thinking it was none of his business, but the red stain on her cheeks bothered him. "Who called you?"

She was inherently honest, to the point where he had heard her say something, then immediately confess it wasn't the truth. He suspected she couldn't lie to a straight question like his. He was right.

Biting her lip, she said, "Um. Evan Monroe."

That had him pausing in the act of lighting his kindling with a lighter. "Evan Monroe? Why the hell is he calling you? I didn't even know you knew him." Well, of course she must have met Evan at some point given that Evan's brother Elec was married to Tammy, and Ty had seen Imogen talking to Evan at the gym, but he wanted her to explain how she knew him.

"I met him at Tamara and Elec's wedding, very briefly. Then again in the gym." She pushed her glasses up. "He, well, has been pursuing me."

Ty supposed it wasn't anything he didn't already know, but he didn't like hearing it out loud. "What does that mean? He's harassing you?"

"No, of course not. He's merely asked me out to dinner, and this phone message was following up on that, offering specific time options."

Then she said nothing else, bending over and riffling in his backpack.

Ty felt a wave of jealousy wash over him, but he took a deep breath and tried to stay calm. "Are you going to go? Do you like him?"

"I don't know him well enough to determine one way or another if I like him. But no, I am not going to go out with him." She pulled out a sweatshirt that had his car emblazoned across the front.

It always made him feel ridiculous to wear a shirt with his own car on it in his leisure time, but his mother had given it to him, which was sweet. So he put it to use for camping and hiking, where he wasn't likely to encounter a ton of people. But for some reason, as Imogen pulled it on, he liked that sweatshirt a whole lot better than he ever had before. It swallowed her whole and she quickly cuffed the sleeves, and fussed with the hood, but seeing that car across her chest brought out those feelings again. Weird happy feelings, along with a healthy dose of possessiveness.

"So why aren't you going out with him?" It was stupid to poke at her, especially given he might not like the answer, but he couldn't seem to stop himself.

"I have altered the basis of my thesis. I was not finding it time effective, practical, or honest to pursue the dating rules myself. Instead, I'm focusing on interviewing both drivers and their wives about their courtship, whether or not stock car racing played a role in their meeting, and whether the path to marriage in any way resembled the rules laid out in the dating manual."

"I like that better," he said honestly. It had made him feel all sorts of unhappy to think that she was flirting with random men like Evan. Men he had to see at the track, who couldn't be trusted to understand just how special Imogen was. They might just see her as a different pond to dip their toe in. Nothing more than a hookup.

Ty snapped a twig in his hand. Holy shit. He had been one of those guys. Sort of. Definitely not that crude about it, but he hadn't expected that he would want a relationship with Imogen, and he did.

He really frickin' did.

"Do you think it sounds more legitimate? I'm not sure I'm satisfied with it as such either, but honestly, for someone who thrives on academia, homing in on a research topic has been a nightmare. I've had zero self-confidence and have talked myself around in circles until I can't decide if I have a legitimate thesis or a ginormous mess."

Ty barely heard her, so stunned was he by his own thoughts. "Ginormous?" He didn't think he'd ever heard that word before.

"Sorry. It's like *gigantic* and *enormous* meshed together."

"So really big?" Sort of like the heart attack he was about to have. Because he was about to lay it all on the line and make a ginormous jackass of himself.

"Exactly."

"Um, Imogen?"

"Yeah?" She blinked at him, tugging on the drawstrings of his hooded sweatshirt.

"I was thinking that, you know, I'm having a really good time with you, and well, I know that you have every right to date other guys or whatever, but just so you know, I'm not going to be dating anyone else. I'll just be dating you." Ty felt a sweat breaking out on his forehead. Oh, yeah. Serious jackass-age. "That is, if you will let me. Date you, I mean."

"Are you suggesting that we exclusively date one another from here forward in order to really get to know one another without fear or jealousy creeping into the equation?"

What she said. "Yes."

Imogen's face broke out into a shy, sweet smile that she seemed to be struggling to contain, but couldn't. "I believe that arrangement would work."

Ty grinned back, his shoulders relaxing. So they were dating. For real. "Drop the professor talk and tell me you're cool with this."

She walked over to him where he was sitting by the fire circle and looked down, taking his cheeks between her hands. "I like you. A lot," she said with more simple honesty than he thought he'd ever received in his life. "So yes, I'm cool with this."

Ty pulled her down onto his lap, wrapping his arms around her. "Good, because I like you, too." He kissed her, again feeling that ridiculous happiness rising in him. "I know my schedule is crazy, but I'll make time for you. How are your Mondays?"

"I'm busy during the day, but usually Monday nights aren't too bad. No papers to grade."

She was boldly nibbling on his bottom lip and it was causing a heat to rise in him that had nothing to do with the fire burning behind him. "There's only four more races. Then I have some downtime in November and December before we start prepping for next season."

Maybe he should have kept his month shut. Saying the only time your weekends will ever be free is two months out of twelve had to be a little off-putting.

"Can I come to another race?" she asked. "I've only been once, and I think I have a little better understanding of the sport now than when I attended because of the research I've been doing. Besides, I can pepper you with questions before and after this time."

Imogen had stopped kissing him, but she was stroking the

back of his hair, which he found incredibly pleasant. "Of course you can go. I'll get tickets for you. You can stay in my coach with me."

"Where are the upcoming races? This weekend is out. We have midterms to grade."

Ty needed to pause and think about it, which he found odd, because usually the schedule was seared into his brain, but Imogen was such a nice distraction. "Uh, Texas, Phoenix, Miami. Why don't you come to Texas? And hell, why don't you invite Tammy and Suzanne to come with you? I'm guessing Tammy would love to see Elec driving, and then you all can hang out when we're busy."

"Yeah, that would be fun. But Tamara has the kids."

"She can bring them with her. They're used to being around the track. Hunter is my godchild, you know, and I haven't seen her in a while. It would be nice to see the kids." Ty did like hanging out and playing with Tammy's kids. There was something about the way kids just bounced around and said whatever they were thinking that always appealed to him.

"Okay, I'll ask her. That way we can fly down on Friday night and it won't conflict with school for the kids or for Tamara and I."

"Sounds like a plan." Ty ran his fingers over her thigh. "And if Tammy can't make it, you'll still come?"

"Yes, I'll still come." Imogen wrapped her arms around his neck. "I will definitely come."

Ty caught the change in her voice. "Are we talking about next week or are we talking about now?"

"Both," she said with a sly smile.

"Perfect answer."

Screw the fire. Ty stood up with Imogen in his arms, amused at the squeal of surprise she gave.

They were going back to the sleeping bag.

SUZANNE stared at Imogen across the table at their favorite Mexican restaurant, suddenly envying the bliss on her friend's face. It had been a long time since Suzanne had felt that kind of moony-eyed happiness. "So I take it you had fun camping?"

Imogen sighed, her cheeks pink, eyes glassy. "Yes," she said, and burst out with a short laugh. "I really, really did. We went fishing and swimming and hiking. We had lots of great sex, and, Suz, he quoted Shakespeare for me."

Pausing with her margarita to her mouth, Suzanne felt her eyebrows head for the ceiling. "Ty quoted Shakespeare? Are you shitting me?" In all the years she'd known him, Suzanne had never once seen Ty with a book, let alone something like the Bard.

"I'm serious." Imogen pushed her glasses up on her nose and leaned onto her palm at the table, like she was too boneless to hold herself up. "Oh, it's so dangerous, but I do like him."

The old green-eyed monster rose up in Suzanne again, irritating the shit out of her. She was happy for Imogen, even if she hadn't figured Ty would be the type of guy to rev her engine. But it was clearly working for both of them, and if Suzanne had learned anything, it was that you couldn't find any rhyme or reason for attraction. Look at the fact that she herself still couldn't shake the weak-in-the-knees feeling whenever she saw Ryder and they'd been divorced for damn near two years. Not to mention he almost always pissed her off.

But there it was, and she was stuck with it, and it was really lowering to think that she could be enviousness of Imogen's happiness. The girl had been far too serious when Suzanne had met her, and if the state of her jacked-up ponytail at the moment was any indication, Ty had loosened her screws up nicely.

"That's fantastic, honey. I'm glad you're having fun and that you didn't get mauled by a bear."

Imogen laughed. "That is probably a plus. So next weekend I'm going to fly to Texas for the race. Ty says the next few weeks decide the championship. Do you want to go? Tamara said she was in, and she's bringing the kids."

Suzanne took a sip of her drink, and set it back down. "I don't think so, but thanks."

Imogen's face fell. "Why not? Do you already have plans?"

"Sort of. But even if I didn't, I wouldn't go. You're going to be staying with Ty, and Tammy and the kids will be in Elec's coach. That leaves me getting a hotel room by myself while the two of you are getting bounced. If I want to sleep alone, I can do that at home and I won't have to foot the bill for a room."

Nor did she even want to consider how long it had been since she'd had sex.

But Imogen looked downright upset at her honesty, and Suzanne felt like shit. "I'm sorry, that sounded bitchy as hell. I didn't mean it like that, Imogen. I'm really happy for you that you and Ty are hitting it off, but I just don't want to be a third wheel."

"No, I'm sorry, I didn't think about it from your perspective. I guess I was picturing you and Tamara and I spending some girl time together during the day."

"And that would be fun, it really would. I love hanging with my girls. But this way you all can go and have a romantic weekend and I'll take care of some things at home."

"Like what?" Imogen asked.

Suzanne knew Imogen was just innately curious, and normally she didn't mind it, but tonight she was feeling a little sorry for herself. She didn't really want to talk about it, but she knew Imogen would keep asking. "Well, you know how I used to be a wedding planner? I'm going back into the business, and I'm meeting with a potential client this weekend. Next weekend I'll be scouting out venues and DJs and getting myself familiar with the local wedding scene again."

"Wow. What prompted this? I thought you said you didn't really care for being a wedding planner because you always wanted to do it your way instead of the client's way."

"I did. I do." Suzanne shredded her cocktail napkin. "It's very hard to sit there and listen to some bride say she wants an elegant reception with naked monkeys as a theme. But it's sort of the only skill I have."

"But what about your board work on the children's charity? And your cakes?"

"I might have to scale back on the board, but I'll squeeze my cakes in still. I'm not giving that up." That was her pride and her passion, baking birthday cakes for terminally ill children who might not live to see their next birthdays. The more elaborate the cake, the better, and she loved seeing their eyes light up in delight.

Imogen was staring at her with those intelligent eyes, and it unnerved Suzanne. "What?" she asked, a little defensively.

"Why are you going back to something you don't enjoy at the sacrifice of what you love?" Imogen asked softly.

Suzanne glanced over at the bar. Where the hell was their waitress? She needed another drink. "I need the money. My alimony runs out at the end of this year. I should have done this a long time ago, but I was enjoying my time off. But now I'm going to be shit out of luck if I don't get off my ass and generate an income." Waving her hand at the waitress, she added, "Another reason I can't go to Texas. I can't afford the airfare or the hotel."

Boo hoo her. God, she hated sounding so damn pathetic, but it was the truth. She had been ignoring reality and now it was biting her in the butt.

"Suzanne, I had no idea. I just assumed you had a settlement or that your position on the board was paying." Imogen looked stunned. "That wasn't very long for alimony."

"Half the length of the marriage. Two years. We were married for four." And for fuck's sake, was she actually going to cry? She better well be getting her period and this was just PMS, because she had no time to get weepy. It wasn't like she and Ryder had just broken up. It was old news, and she needed to get a serious grip. "He gave me a lump sum of money, which I used to buy my condo. But I still have bills, and without the alimony, I need some kind of income."

"Well, I'm sure you're a fabulous wedding planner, despite your irritations with the clients. You have amazing taste and you're incredibly organized. I imagine some of your previous clients would be willing to give you referrals to get you started again. Who is the potential client? Is it a big wedding or something small?"

Suzanne appreciated that Imogen was just being matter-of-fact about the situation and not commenting on the demise of her marriage. "Here's the kicker." This was actually ridiculous enough to make her smile. "The bride to be is Nikki Borden."

Imogen's jaw dropped. "What? Are you *serious*? She and Ty just broke up!"

"I know. The girl wastes no time whatsoever. And she wants

a Christmas wedding, and is willing to pay out the nose to make it happen."

"Who is the groom? Is it the guy she was making out with on the hood of my car?"

"Yep. Jonas Strickland. Nice enough guy, but he clearly doesn't have the sense God gave a goat if he's saddling himself with Nikki after a week of dating. I mean, who falls in love in a week?"

"Yeah, exactly," Imogen muttered, frowning down at the table. "That's insane. Isn't it?"

"Yes, it is," Suzanne said firmly, alarmed at the look on her friend's face. She wasn't fancying herself in love with Ty, was she? Would no one ever learn?

Suzanne shook off the feeling that she was embarking on a career as the most cynical wedding planner ever, and said, "I'll give Nikki credit. She moves fast. She has her engagement ring already and she's talking about a two-hundred-guest affair. I have a feeling that she's going to leave all the details to me because of the tight time frame, and because, well, she's a dingbat, so that works for me. More money, less irritating interference."

Imogen made a sound in the back of her throat that was something between a laugh and a sob. Then she covered her face with her hands.

Suzanne sat up straighter and leaned toward her friend. What the hell was that all about? "Imogen, what's wrong? Are you okay, sweetie?"

Imogen shifted her hands to her cheeks. "How is it possible that I could feel this, whatever I'm feeling, for a guy who spent the last four months with Nikki? We are absolutely nothing alike. So which one of us is his real type, and which one of us was he/is he just biding his time with?"

Oh, Lord. Suzanne took the last remaining sip of her drink,

sucking the straw aggressively to get every last drop. "Honey, I don't think there's doubt in anyone's mind that he was just fooling around with Nikki. She was convenient, plain and simple. And you can bet your Yankee ass he never took Nikki into the woods." Though Suzanne might have paid money to witness that.

"You really think so?"

"Yes, I do. Ty likes you, for real. The man quoted Shakespeare to you!" Which Suzanne still found hard to believe. "I'm telling you, if you're interested in making up stupid shit to worry about, by all means, start comparing yourself to Nikki. But if want to be rational, accept the fact that the man is into you in the right way and just enjoy it." She rethought her wording. "And that wasn't meant to be a sexual innuendo."

Imogen gave another monstrous sigh. "I think I'm going to go home. Maybe I just need a good night's sleep. Are you ready to go?"

Suzanne had, in fact, made eye contact with the waitress already and ordered another drink, and she didn't intend to waste it. "You go ahead. I'm going to stay here and make a couple phone calls, then head out in about ten minutes."

"Are you sure?"

"Yep." Suzanne got up when Imogen did and gave her a hug. "Maybe you need to give some thought to what you really want from Ty, hon. It sounds to me like you're falling for him."

Imogen's dark blue eyes were wide and troubled. "I am."

What the hell did she say to that? There was no sense in telling Imogen to put the brakes on; that never worked. So she might as well enjoy the drive before they crashed. "Then have fun! Enjoy it, and think about what that means and where you want this to go."

"Okay, thanks. I'll talk to you tomorrow."

They hugged, then Suzanne sat back down with her newly delivered fresh margarita and pulled her cell phone out. With a sigh big enough to rival the ones Imogen had been letting loose all night, Suzanne went into her contacts list and pressed *R*. Ryder's number came up and she pressed a button to call him, hoping he wouldn't answer.

He did.

"Well, hello, darlin', how are you this evening?"

Suzanne closed her eyes for a second. God, definitely PMS, because she was damn near on the verge of tears again at the sound of his voice. It was fucking ridiculous.

"Hey," she said with a forced cheerfulness. "I'm good, how about yourself?"

"My day didn't suck too bad," he said, and there was a pause where she could tell he was drinking something. She'd bet her condo it was an ice-cold Bud in a bottle. "But there's always tomorrow."

"No joke." Fiddling with the cocktail napkin in front of her, Suzanne got to the point. "Listen, I know I asked you to host that dinner party with me to give us an opportunity to see Imogen and Ty together, but I think we need to cancel."

"Good, because I was having serious doubts about this plan."

"Me, too. Maybe we always knew on a subconscious level it wasn't a good idea."

"Oh, I knew on a conscious level it wasn't a good idea."

She rolled her eyes. "Well, I just talked to Imogen, and it turns out that she and Tammy and the kids are all going down to Texas next weekend, so it seems kind of pointless to drag everyone together for a dinner party on Monday when they're all spending the weekend together. And clearly she and Ty are digging each other if they're hanging out like this, and I don't think I should really interfere."

There was a giant pause, which irritated Suzanne.

"You don't think you should interfere? Are you feeling okay?"

Now she shredded the napkin. "I'm fine," she said through gritted teeth. There was no point in getting into an argument with Ryder.

"Does this mean I won't get my three months' worth of desserts?"

"I'll make you the pineapple upside-down cake, but that's it."

"Fair enough. My stomach thanks you. Are you going to Texas, too?"

"No. I have plans."

"A hot date?" he asked, and there was an edge to his voice.

"Yes, with a bride. I'm reviving my wedding planning business, and I have a meeting with a potential client."

Another pause. "Why are you doing that? I didn't think you enjoyed wedding planning all that much."

Dipping her finger in her margarita, not giving a shit how tacky that was, she sucked her fingertip. She so did not want to have this conversation, but it was inevitable. Might as well get it over, and do it in public, where she might actually be able to control her hormonal emotions. "It's time to go back to work."

"Why? You're plenty busy with the charity work."

Damn it, he was going to make her spell it out. "I need the income. There are only two alimony payments remaining."

"Are you serious?" Ryder sounded as shocked as she felt that it had been two whole years since their marriage had been puked out and flushed down the toilet. "If you need more time, I don't care, Suz, you know that. You want another year or two?"

Of course he would offer. And of course it would make her feel even shittier than she already did. "No, thanks, that's okay. I'll be fine. Why postpone the inevitable?"

"But—"

"Gotta go. I'll talk to you soon. Take care." Suzanne hung up and sucked in a deep breath.

Lord, she was shaking like a puppy pooping peach pits.

She was starting her life all over again for the third time at the age of thirty-three and it sucked donkey dicks.

FIFTEEN

IMOGEN was easily bouncing with as much excitement as Tamara's seven-year-old daughter Hunter when they pulled up to the entrance of the motor coach park at the track in Texas. Elec had sent a car service to collect them at the Dallas/Fort Worth Airport, and Hunter had been talking nonstop about stock car racing the entire drive. Tamara's older child, Pete, was much more subdued, reading a book on insects and occasionally glancing out the window.

Feeling a burble of excitement ready to burst forth herself, Imogen sympathized with Hunter's impatience when the girl declared, "Man, it's about time we got here!" Then the little girl added, "This ride lasted longer than Viagra."

Imogen hadn't seen that one coming.

Tamara's jaw dropped. "Hunter, we really need to talk about

your language. You should not be using words when you don't even know what they mean."

"But Suzanne—"

"I know," Tamara said grimly. "And the rule is, if Suzanne says it, you are not allowed to repeat it. End of story. Now hop out of the car. I see Elec right there waiting for us. You, too, Petey. I'll be right there."

As Hunter yanked open the door and took off running toward her stepfather, her brother following at a more leisurely pace, Tamara grimaced. "Good Lord. My seven-year-old is talking about Viagra. I think I'm going to have to have another chat with Suzanne about little ears."

From Imogen's perspective, it was actually rather amusing, but she wasn't Hunter's mother. She also knew Suzanne would never intend to be causing problems for Tamara. "You know Suzanne doesn't mean for Hunter to overhear."

"I know she doesn't. But she also has a voice that carries three rooms." Tamara hesitated with her hand on the door handle. "I feel terrible that she didn't come with us. I tried to talk her into it, but she was adamant."

"She was the same way with me. But I don't think anyone can talk Suzanne into anything."

"That's true." Tamara stepped out of the car. "Let me go get my daughter before she maims my husband."

Exiting out the other side, Imogen saw Hunter climbing up Elec's legs, her ponytail bouncing and her mouth moving a mile a minute.

Then Imogen spotted Ty heading toward the entrance, and if she could have gotten away with it, she would have crawled up *his* legs, she was so excited to see him. It had been a long ten days since their camping trip. She had been inundated with work at school and he had been equally busy both prepping and racing, plus he'd done several sponsor appearances. They had talked every day on the phone for a good hour, but aside from a quick dinner on Monday, they hadn't seen each other, and there had been no other communications. She had been hoping for random brief contact throughout the day, but she'd quickly figured out he didn't like e-mail or text messages. When she'd sent an e-mail, it had been his assistant who had responded, letting her know he almost never checked his mail, which had been monumentally embarrassing since Imogen had made an offer of fellatio in the body of the message. And whenever she texted him, he always called her back instead of just replying.

When they had talked, it had been fun and interesting, very much the type of conversations where you explored getting to know someone. They had discussed movies and books and their families and a multitude of other topics, and they had more in common than she would have ever suspected. It was also gratifying to discover that her interest in Ty didn't wane, it actually increased. It was definitely more than simply a physical attraction she felt for him.

Though the physical was quite important, she must confess. Other than a quick up-against-the-wall encounter after dinner, she hadn't touched him in five days, and when she saw him, she wanted to do nothing more than press her body up against his and kiss him like crazy.

Hunter had beaten her to the punch. When Ty had reached the child, he had tugged on her ponytail as a greeting, and she had immediately launched herself from her stepfather's arms to Ty's, and was now settled on his back with her arms around his neck.

Suddenly feeling awkward, Imogen pushed up her prescription sunglasses and adjusted her handbag on her shoulder. "Hi," she said in an act of verbal brilliance.

"Hi," he said back with a smile. "I'm glad you all made it here safely. And in case you were wondering, you look very pretty in that dress."

"Thank you." She suspected it was a stupid thing to wear a babydoll dress with ballet flats to a racetrack, but it wasn't race day and she was comfortable in it. And okay, she had wanted Ty to think she looked good after not seeing her all week.

"Hey, Imogen," Elec said, his arm wrapped around Tamara. "How are you?"

"Good, thanks, and you?"

"Fabulous now that my family's here," he said. "Thanks for suggesting this trip." He squeezed Tamara tighter and kissed her cheek.

"You're cracking my ribs," she protested, but the grin on her face said she didn't really mind.

Tamara turned to her husband, and the look they gave each other was so tender, so private, so loving, that Imogen felt a lump rise in her throat. She looked away, toward Ty, and felt that lump threaten to choke her when she saw the way he was staring at her, a smile on his face.

Who the hell was she kidding?

Imogen had spent the past two weeks interviewing drivers and their wives, and after every interview she had told herself that they had something she didn't, that there was a connection and a rightness to each of those couples that didn't exist with Ty and that she couldn't allow herself to fall for him.

But she had.

And it had been altogether too easy.

There he was, standing there in jeans and a long-sleeved shirt with a beer ball cap on his head, Hunter climbing all over his back, and giving her a secret, sensual smile. He made her feel and want more than she ever had before in her life.

"What's Viagra?" Hunter asked him, arms around his neck.

"Not anything I need," Ty told her.

Elec coughed to cover up a laugh, while Tamara looked flustered to have the subject brought up again.

"Well . . ." she said, clearly struggling with how to handle it.

Imogen decided to jump in and help her. "It's a prescription drug taken orally by men suffering from the medical condition erectile dysfunction. Unfortunately, one of the side effects of the drug is that it can last longer than is desirable, resulting in discomfort, which is why you did in fact use the word contextually correctly when referencing the ride as lasting uncomfortably long. Good job, but it is actually adult humor, and not something your friends are going to understand, though, so where's the fun in that?"

She had been banking on Hunter's eyes glazing over, and they did.

"Oh. Okay," Hunter said. She jiggled to readjust on Ty's back, and knocked his hat askew. "How's your car looking? Can I see it?"

"It's up to Elec. He's the one who's got to get you a garage pass since he's your stepdaddy. You know the rules—no kids in the garage unless they belong to a driver."

Tamara had moved from Elec to Imogen's side. "Thank you," she murmured. "I consider myself a capable mother, for the most part, but Hunter's language leaves me speechless. I don't know how to handle it, and I think you did an amazing job. You told her the truth in a way that wasn't inappropriate and you shut down the subject."

"Big words tend to bore kids," Imogen said. "And if you say something like *erectile dysfunction* fast enough, they can't process it enough to retain or repeat it."

Tamara laughed. "Let's hope that's the last of the Viagra conversations. For any of us."

The thought of Viagra led to thoughts of Ty's penis, which led to thoughts of it fully erect and buried deep inside her. Imogen shifted in her flats and crossed her arms across her chest to hide her suddenly tight nipples.

"No joke."

But Tamara was already distracted. "Petey, what's in your hand?"

Her son stood up, a fat worm dangling from his fingers. "Nothing."

"Oh, Lord." Tamara turned to her husband. "Did Evan find somewhere to stay for the weekend, or do we need to get a hotel?"

Imogen had forgotten that Elec's brother Evan shared his motor coach, which had made sense in their mutual bachelor days, but was now probably less than convenient.

"He's crashing with Ryder," Elec said. "No big deal. Unless you want a hotel, darling. It makes no difference to me."

"I want to stay in the coach!" Hunter yelled.

"The lady wants to stay in the coach," Elec said with a smile for his wife. "But it's up to you."

"That's fine. The kids can sleep in Evan's room. That's probably better than all of us sharing one hotel room anyway."

"Oh, yeah," Elec said with a look so hot that Imogen almost blushed witnessing it.

Imogen was so busy studying Tamara and Elec's marital and family dynamic with something she would categorize as jealousy, she didn't notice Ty had moved much closer to her.

"Glad I don't have a roomie," he murmured to her. Then he reached out and kissed her, Hunter still on his back. "I'm also real glad to see you, Emma Jean."

"Sick!" Hunter proclaimed, making gagging gestures with her free hand. "Let me down."

"Sure thing, monkey." Ty squatted and she scrambled off, running over to her brother to inspect the worm.

"You're good with her," Imogen told him.

He just shrugged. "I like kids. They're impulsive and honest."

"Much like you?"

"Maybe." He grinned. "Would it be impulsive to drag you away to my coach right now?"

"Inappropriate more so than impulsive."

"I'm paralyzed," he said. "I can't think of a single thing to do right now that isn't inappropriate in front of kids."

She had to really admit she loved the way he wanted her, the way he acted like it was a serious struggle to contain his desire around her. It was something entirely new for her, to have a man so passionate about her that every encounter resulted in sex. In her experience, most of her previous boyfriends had been perfectly content with once a week, and they had never allowed lust to enter their eyes in public.

Maybe she could place it in the category of "Poor Taste" and be ashamed of herself, but she liked that Ty didn't care who saw his interest.

"We could talk," she told him, feeling a smile creep over her face.

"No matter what you say, I'll take it dirty," he said. "I can't help it. Even hearing the words *erectile dysfunction* come out of your mouth gave me a boner."

"That's ridiculous."

His hand brushed across her hair. "What's ridiculous is that we're still standing here. We could have been naked by now."

Hunter suddenly wiggled in between them. "Can you take me to the garage? Elec says Mom needs to take a nap."

Imogen would bet her own mother's life that Tamara was not the least bit sleepy. She glanced over at Elec, who was trying to look innocent and failing miserably.

"Oh, really?" Ty asked Hunter, then turned to Elec. "You should be ashamed of yourself."

"Tamara said she needs to lie down. I can't argue with that. It was a long flight."

Imogen saw Tamara clear her throat, her cheeks pink.

Elec held his hands out. "I told Hunter she could watch TV for a while, but she'd rather hang out with you."

"I haven't seen Imogen in four days," Ty said pointedly. "When was the last time you *saw* Tammy?"

They stared at each other in a battle of libidos.

"Three days ago," Elec finally admitted. "But you can see Imogen whenever you want all weekend. *Our* ability to see each other is hampered."

"Fair enough," Ty said. "But you owe me."

Elec grinned. "Whatever you want."

"Is that okay?" Ty asked Imogen. "You want to go to the garage with me?"

"Sure. I'd love to." Like Elec said, they had all weekend to see each other. Even if her inner thighs wanted to be seen immediately, if not sooner.

"Alright, if your last name is Briggs, you're going with me,"

Ty said loudly. He pointed to Hunter and Pete. "That means you and you. Let's move 'em out."

"Whoop, whoop," Hunter said, doing a victory dance. She ran up and gave Elec a kiss. "Love you! See you later." She then hugged her mother's legs and said, "Have a good nap, Mom."

Tamara hugged her back and said, "Have fun, baby. Listen to Ty and don't touch anything." She touched her son's shoulder. "You, too, sweetie. Have fun. Thank you, Ty. And you, too, Imogen."

"Sure thing, Tammy. Where are the passes?" Ty asked. "Do I have to go get them? You know they'll give me crap if you're not standing right there."

Elec handed a bundle over to him.

"You were just all sorts of prepared, weren't you?" Ty asked, his eyebrows raised.

"Just efficient," Elec said.

"Uh-huh." Ty reached for Imogen's hand, but Hunter popped up between them and took his hand in her left and Imogen's in her right.

"Let's go."

Ty shot Imogen a look of frustration over Hunter's head, but Imogen just smiled. The man was a nice guy, and that did interesting and thought-provoking things to her insides. Being with him, with Tamara and her family, it all felt so right, so normal. Imogen had never thought of herself as lonely, but this was something she definitely enjoyed.

"When we're done at the garage, I'm definitely going to need a nap," Ty said, wearing a smirk as they walked.

"Then you can do that while I go interview some of the other drivers," Imogen said with a smirk of her own.

Smart-ass, he mouthed to her.

Imogen just laughed, feeling more carefree than perhaps she ever had in her entire life.

TY was proud of her. That's the thought he had as he walked the kids and Imogen around the garage, introducing her to his crew members. He felt proud and smug to have such a classy, beautiful woman there beside him, letting him claim her as his.

The first time he trotted out the term *girlfriend* when introducing her to his crew chief, she had shot him a curious look, but hell, that's what she was, right? After that damned uncomfortable conversation where he'd stumbled over the confession he didn't want to date anyone else, and she had agreed, he figured that gave him the right to tag her as his in public. And he really was damn proud that someone as intelligent and interesting as Imogen wanted to be with him. He had never realized how much he'd been spinning his wheels with women like Nikki. The most she'd ever made him feel at the track when she had visited him was a mild embarrassment every time she said something not so bright, or inadvertently offended someone.

Imogen was in a whole different ballpark. She wanted to understand everything and everyone, and she asked questions out of pure curiosity, not because she was looking for an angle or a way to get ahead. Fame and fortune meant nothing to her, he was sure of it, and every inch of her was real, untouched by plastic surgeons. Hell, she wore glasses, and how damn sexy was that?

He had it bad. There was no denying it, and while he loved Tammy's kids, he was counting the minutes until he could reasonably haul their butts back to their parents.

The need to get Imogen alone and naked was urgent, and he hadn't been boning up on Shakespeare for the past ten days for nothing. He had listened to two more plays on tape and had painful discussions on them with Toni, and he wanted to show Imogen he was capable of culture. Truth was, the plays were entertaining, it was just deciphering the language that was so difficult. But he was man enough to admit there was something cool about the dead playwright's words.

Ty watched Hunter inspecting his engine, while Imogen talked to his crew chief.

"It's just amazing how much science and engineering go into these cars," Imogen said. "I'm in awe of your experience and knowledge."

"Thanks," Sam said, looking at Imogen like he might fall in love. "We do put a lot of effort into winning."

If Ty wasn't sure that Imogen was merely curious, not at all interested in Sam, he might have felt a little bit jealous. Regardless of how married Sam was, and how much interest Imogen showed in Ty, he did still find himself edging just a bit closer to her.

"What is the process for becoming a crew chief? Do you learn via hands-on experience, or is there a formal training program?"

"A lot of the guys have mechanical engineering degrees . . ."

Ty completely tuned out what Sam was saying, focusing instead on the way the soft dress Imogen wore clung to her ass.

"Isn't that right, Ty?" Sam asked him a minute later.

"Yeah, absolutely," he said with no clue as to what he was agreeing with.

Given the look Sam gave him, he hadn't fooled his crew chief.

And he didn't care. He was in love and at the moment nothing else seemed to matter quite as much as that did.

Ty stared at Imogen, his chest tight, his mood elated, knowing he could just watch and watch her indefinitely . . . that she made him happy. God, he *was* in love with her. It was true. When you knew, you *knew*.

"We need to leave," he said suddenly, interrupting Sam mid-sentence in whatever he was saying to Imogen.

Both Sam and Imogen swung their heads to stare at him.

"Are you okay?" Imogen asked him, her eyes filled with concern.

"I'm fine. Great. I just realized there's something I need to do." What he needed to do was get her alone and tell her how he felt, because now that he knew, he felt fairly bursting with the knowledge.

"Okay. I'll catch up with you later," Sam said. "Nice to meet you, Imogen."

Imogen said her good-byes, then they were rounding up the kids and hustling them back to their parents. At least Ty was hustling. Imogen didn't seem in a hurry and the kids were downright dragging their feet, which was making him agitated.

By the time they got to his coach, he was about to crawl out of his own skin. It felt like his whole life had just shifted in an instant and he needed to share that with Imogen, the first woman he had ever truly fallen in love with, the woman he wanted to spend every moment with, the woman he wanted to wake up next to.

"What on earth is wrong with you?" she asked as he threw open the door with a fair amount of force and strode into the coach.

Ty just turned around. "Close the door behind you."

"I did." She put her hands on her hips, the gesture bunching the fabric of her soft blue dress. "Did you drink too much coffee, Ty? You're acting like you're hopped up on caffeine or amphetamines. It's a little unnerving."

He took a deep breath, then twined both of her hands through his. "I'm fine. I just wanted to be alone with you."

She smiled. "You are incorrigible and oversexed."

"Not today. I haven't had sex at all today." He leaned forward and kissed her, closing his eyes briefly.

"Very funny."

"Hey, Emma Jean?"

"Yes?"

"Do you recognize this quote? 'When I saw you I fell in love, and you smiled because you knew.'"

There was a pause, and she looked at him puzzled. "Yes. That's Shakespeare, of course. Why?"

"Because that's the way I feel. I think the first day I met you I fell just a little bit in love with you, and you knew. Something has drawn us together from the beginning, don't you think?"

"It sort of seems that way," she whispered.

"We've both been attracted to each other for months, but we didn't do anything about it, and now that we have, well, it's so good. It's better than good. It's . . . amazing."

She nodded. "It is. I'm very happy with you."

God love an honest woman who played no games. It was one more reason he adored her.

So he squeezed her hands more tightly in his, locked eyes with her, and said, "I love you."

Her eyes went wide. "What?"

"I love you. I am in love with you. I'm both of those, and I want to be with you."

The corner of her mouth lifted in a small, sweet smile. "Oh, Ty, I love you, too. I do. It's not logical to feel so much so soon, but I do. I truly love you."

Those were the sweetest, most poetic words he'd ever heard in his life.

TY loved her.

He loved her.

Her.

Imogen was stunned, thrilled, inflated with her own over-whelming feelings of love for him, and when he kissed her, she kissed him back with fervor. That was it. The big It. Love.

The very concept amazed her.

It was beautiful and overwhelming, and she poured her heart into the kiss, feeling that her words were inadequate, that she needed him to understand.

His hands raced across her breasts, then down her hips to her thighs, hiking up her babydoll dress. It didn't surprise her. Ty liked sex, and she loved that about him, too. Anticipating that he would shove her up against the nearest wall or toss her onto the couch, Imogen was startled when he dropped to his knees.

"What are you doing?" He was sliding her panties down and she already had a good idea of what he was planning, but for some reason it surprised her.

"I just want to taste you . . . I want you to hold my head while I satisfy you."

Her dress was bunched around her waist and his mouth was already on her, nipping and licking and sucking. Her hands did wind up on his head, gripping his hair tightly as the passion, the pure physical delight, intermingled with the emotion of realizing that she loved him. Ty flicked his tongue over her, in her, and she came quickly, overwhelmed by everything she was feeling.

"Oh!" she said. "Oh, my God, I only lasted about thirty seconds . . . I should be embarrassed."

He smiled as he stood up. "I'm choosing to take it as a compliment. Come to the bedroom."

They went down the narrow hall to the small room, which was like a more claustrophobic version of his bedroom at home, and Imogen marveled at the look on Ty's face. There was lust in his eyes, no question about it, but mostly, he was staring at her with so much tenderness, so much love, that she wanted to pinch herself, wanted to suck it in and hold on to it, wanted to bask in the feeling of serenity and pleasure she experienced with him.

And when he peeled her clothes off slowly and carefully, and laid her down gently on his bed, Imogen felt tears pool in her eyes. While she loved Ty's dominating tendencies, while she really, really enjoyed when he took her hard and fast, when he teased and tormented her with his dragging their pleasure out, she thought this was the perfect way to make love in this moment.

Brushing her hair off her face, he paused to drag his finger across her bottom lip. Then he eased into her until he filled her completely.

As Ty started to move slowly, pushing deeply inside her, his eyes trained on her, Imogen wrapped her legs around his waist. "I love you," she told him, in case he hadn't believed her the first time she'd said it.

Ty sighed. "Damn, I like the sound of that, Emma Jean. And I love you, too. They were right, you know. I just looked at you today, and I knew."

"It's indescribable, isn't it?"

"Yeah. It is," he said simply, holding himself over her with his forearms. "As is how good it feels to be buried inside you."

They moved together, slowly and easily, her hips rolling to

maximize his pleasure, their mouths brushing over each other, until Imogen had a slow, rolling orgasm that took her breath away. Then within seconds, Ty followed, in a quiet, raw orgasm that had tears in her eyes again as she felt him pulse and shudder deep inside her.

Life had been good before, but now that she knew this, now that she felt so connected, so complete with this man, she would never be the same again.

CHAPTER
SIXTEEN

IMOGEN was glad she was sitting next to Hunter for the race. Tamara's daughter kept her abreast of every pertinent move during the five hundred laps, pointing out maneuvers drivers made, who was a lap down, who was in the lead, and who had suffered a lousy pit stop. Trying astutely to listen and absorb everything, Imogen found she had a fair understanding of the sport by the time they were down to the final ten laps, despite the fact that she was finding concentrating difficult.

Her thoughts kept straying back to one thought—Ty loved her. She loved him. They were in love.

It was a giddy little secret that she wished she could shout out to the world. Of course, no one else would care, but she was fairly bursting with the urge to announce how she felt, and maybe mention that she was very sore in a particularly intimate spot after two days of mind-blowing sex, interrupted only by

Ty's driving responsibilities. It was a wonder the man had been able to get behind the wheel, he was so short on sleep, but he was out there, not looking the least bit like a man who had expended huge quantities of energy giving her multiples orgasms.

Watching Ty go in circles made her dizzy, and every time it appeared another car got close to him, or he squeaked out of a tight spot, she went tense from head to toe, but it was more from exhilaration than fear. It was easy to get sucked into the energy of the fans, the roar of the engines, the excitement and awe of the announcers. Wearing the Ty McCordle sweatshirt that she had somehow just forgotten to give back to Ty after their camping trip, Imogen was heartily enjoying herself playing fan girl.

And she and Hunter could sit there mildly smug as they watched the race. Ty was Hunter's godfather and Imogen was nailing him. Or was he nailing her? Truthfully, that was probably the more accurate descriptive for their relationship given that he was the one who did the inserting. While she had never considered herself a braggart, she couldn't help but feel a certain amount of petty satisfaction at the knowledge that not only did Ty love having sex with her, he flat-out loved her.

"Did you see that?" Hunter asked, tapping Imogen's leg to get her attention. The little girl was clearly glad to have a protégée to instruct. "Ty took a pass on the inside. He's in third place now."

"I didn't see anything," Imogen admitted. "But that's good. Third is good. How many laps left?"

"Nine." Hunter leaned over to her mother, wearing an Elec Monroe shirt, a Ty McCordle hat, and a Ryder Jefferson pin. The poor kid was loaded down with the effort of balancing her loyalties. "Mom, chill out. Elec's having an awesome race."

Tamara did look slightly ill. "I'm fine," she insisted. "I just shouldn't have eaten that hot dog."

Imogen was fairly certain no one should ever eat hot dogs, but she kept the opinion to herself. Tugging on the strings of her—Ty's—sweatshirt, she couldn't help standing up with the other fans as the cars roared down the track, ticking off the final laps as the drivers jostled for position. Two cars spun out in a cloud of smoke, and a half-dozen other cars narrowly missed getting sucked into the accident. In the momentary confusion, the lead cars had pulled away from the pack.

"Holy crap," Hunter proclaimed. "Look at the top five. Jimmie, Ty, Kyle, Ryder, and Elec. And Uncle Evan is sixth. Sweet."

Though she had no clue who Jimmie and Kyle were, she knew everyone else and was pleased for them. It sounded like a good thing to her, considering exactly how many cars were winging around the track.

"Very cool," she told Hunter, taking another glance at Tamara. She must not be feeling well at all if Hunter's use of the term *crap* paired with a religious sentiment hadn't triggered a reprimand from Tamara. "Are you okay?" she asked her.

"Not really," Tamara said, breathing deeply through her mouth, her chest rising and falling.

Pete was looking at his mother suspiciously. "You're going to puke, aren't you?"

"Maybe," Tamara admitted, her brow dewy with sweat. "Imogen, do you mind if I go back to the coach now? Do you know how to find your way back on your own with the kids when the race is over?"

"Yeah, I can manage. If not, I can ask directions. You go ahead and lie down. Do you have your cell phone?" Despising throwing up herself, Imogen could well imagine Tamara's urgent need to get back and do so in private.

"Yeah. Thanks." She took a shaky breath and stood up, grabbing her backpack. "You all have your passes, right? You can't get back to the coach lot without them."

"Yes." Imogen checked and saw Pete and Hunter still had theirs dangling around their necks, and hers was in her purse. "Hope you feel better."

"Thanks."

Tamara made a frantic dash down the stairs of the grandstand while Hunter smacked Imogen's leg again. "You're missing it!"

Swinging her attention back to the track, Imogen asked, "What did I miss?"

"Ty has the white flag!"

Like that meant a damn thing to her. "Is that good?" She scanned the track for the sixty car, but she couldn't see anything other than cars buzzing by in a blur.

"It means the lead car has started his final lap. Ty is in the lead."

"Well, yes, that would be good, then." Hunter had scooted forward in the seat, her little bottom bouncing up and down, and Imogen found herself leaning forward as well. "Does Ty win a lot of races?" She assumed he did, though it occurred to her she had never actually inquired as to specifics of his season. That made her a bad girlfriend. Girlfriend. She was his girlfriend. A surge of giddiness rushed through her, even as guilt made her realize maybe she should ask for better details from him. But whenever she asked him how things were going, he always gave a shrug and a Ty answer of "Alright, Emma Jean."

"He hasn't won a race in twenty-three weeks," Hunter told her.

"Oh." That didn't sound good, but again, what did she know exactly about the sport? She was trying, desperately, but she had a lot of ground to cover to understand the how, the why, and the what of stock car racing. "So this is really exciting, then."

"Yes." Hunter was up on her feet, as was the crowd, all screaming and cheering and waving their arms in the air.

Imogen surged to her feet along with everyone else when Pete gave her a grin and tugged her arm to get her up. She smiled back at him. "Think he's going to win?" she yelled to Pete over the roar.

"He just did!" Pete yelled back, pointing at the track as the crowd went wild.

The announcer came over, "That's Ty McCordle in the number sixty car for his first win in twenty-three races!"

An amazing amount of pride rushed through Imogen, and she wanted to stand on her seat and tell everyone around her, "That's my boyfriend! He's number one and I've given him oral sex."

Fortunately, she controlled the urge.

"Let's go!" Hunter demanded, grabbing Imogen's hand and tugging her toward the stairs.

"Where? What's the hurry?"

"Victory Lane."

"Victory Lane?" Imogen halted in her flats as her handbag fell off her shoulder. "I don't think we're allowed there, are we?"

"We have passes," Hunter said, holding out her badge.

"And you're Ty's girlfriend," Pete said.

She could give him a cookie for saying that unprompted. "But . . ."

"And we're related to half the top finishers," Pete added.

"Victory Lane is the most awesome-ist place ever," Hunter said. "We *have* to go or I'll die."

Imogen's logical mind couldn't come up with a legitimate

argument for not going, and all three of them wanted to, including herself, so she just shrugged. "Okay, let's go. Lead the way."

"Whoop, whoop!" was Hunter's opinion as she dragged Imogen and her brother down the stairs at a speed to rival the racing itself.

TY climbed out of his car and pumped his fist in the air. Hell, yeah. Winning had never felt so goddamn good in his life. He'd been having a good season and was in the Chase, but it had still been a long time since he'd passed under that checkered flag, and nothing beat that excitement. Add to the win the fact that his girlfriend, his first, honest-to-God, "I love this woman with all my heart" girlfriend was there to witness it.

The only thing better would be if she were standing there in Victory Lane with him, but they had never discussed anything like that, and Ty knew Tammy would never suggest it to Imogen, not wanting to interfere.

His crew congratulated him and there were handshakes and back pats all around as he offered his thanks to them, his team, and his sponsor. Slapping his sponsor ball cap on his head, he climbed onto the hood of his car and got doused with beer as confetti rained down on him.

God, there was nothing like it.

Glancing out at the crowd gathered around, he almost slipped when he caught sight of Imogen standing there watching him with a gigantic smile on her face, her hands on Hunter's shoulders. She was wearing jeans and the sweatshirt she had borrowed from him on their camping trip. With a grin so wide he about split his skin, Ty gestured for her to step forward.

She made a return gesture with her hand, eyes wide, as if she were confirming he really wanted her to come toward him.

"Yes!" he yelled. "Get over here."

There was no sign of Tammy, which struck Ty as odd, but maybe she was off planting one on Elec. Imogen shuffled the kids forward and Ty hopped down to meet them. Hunter gave him a hug and Pete a high-five.

"Awesome race!" Hunter declared.

"Thanks, punk." Ty smiled at Imogen. "Hey."

"Congratulations," she said. "It was an awesome race."

"Thank you. And I'm glad I can share it with you, Engine."

"I am, too," she said. "I'm so proud of you."

Ty stroked his hand down her cheek and looked into her beautiful blue eyes.

In them he saw everything he ever wanted—an intelligent woman who respected and loved him with her whole self. He suddenly knew that if he was being offered everything he ever wanted all in one package, he should hold on to it, right and tight. There was one way to do that, and he knew with absolute certainty that was what he wanted.

"I love you," he murmured, giving her a soft kiss.

Then, needing her to know, to understand, needing permanency, a commitment, a forever with the woman of his dreams, he backed up a step, took her hand in his, and went down on one knee. "Imogen Ann Wilson, will you marry me?"

Those beautiful eyes went huge behind her glasses. Her jaw dropped open. Her cheeks went lily white.

Ty was aware there were flashbulbs going off all around him, and he could feel the stare of the television cameras. Maybe he shouldn't have done this in such a public place, but hell, he had felt like he wanted nothing more than to make her his wife, and why should a man wait when he knew something so enormous and important?

Vaguely aware Hunter was jumping up and down yelling to his right, Ty stared up under the brim of his ball cap at the woman he loved and felt elation start to sink as she said nothing. "Well?" he finally asked her.

"Are you serious?" she asked, her voice shrill, her hand clutching the neck of her sweatshirt.

"Hell, yes, I'm serious," he said. "Do you think I would be asking in front of hundreds of people if I wasn't dead serious?" He gestured to the crowd gathered around them, all blatantly staring, capturing every minute on film and video.

Imogen glanced around and her cheeks went from stark white to beet red. "Oh, my."

"So, anyway, now that you know I'm for real . . ." Ty squeezed her hand. "You going to answer me? I asked you once if you were the marrying kind and you told me that you hadn't met any man you wanted to marry yet. I'm hoping I am that man. I know this is soon, but Emma Jean, I've waited my whole life to meet a woman like you, and I love you. Will you marry me?"

Her head started bobbing up and down before he was even finished speaking. "Yes. Yes. I will marry you." Her eyes filled with tears and she gave him a watery laugh. "I'm trying to think of a witty quote about marriage from Beatrice or Benedick, but my mind is completely blank."

Ty stood up. "As long as your mind is together enough to say yes to me, I don't give a damn about witty quotes." His heart racing, he leaned forward and gave her a slow, deep kiss, wanting to take it hotter but knowing he couldn't in this venue. "I love you," he whispered. "I'll try to be a good husband, I swear."

"I love you, too."

Then he turned to the media crowd gathered and lifted his fist again. "She said yes! I'm getting married. How's that for sweetening the day's victory?"

Knowing he was grinning like a damn fool, he put his arm around Imogen to pull her close, and basked in what was hands down the best moment of his life.

TY had asked her to marry him. He had gotten down on one knee and said lovely things that she'd been too stunned to retain in her brain, and somehow she had managed to choke out a yes. Now she was surrounded by reporters taking their picture, interviewing Ty while she stood there, still stunned, and occasionally being asked a question herself.

"Did you suspect he was going to propose?" a blonde in her early forties, with her hair pulled back in a sleek ponytail, asked with a smile.

"No. I had no idea," she said most sincerely.

Conscious of the need to be aware of both Hunter and Pete's whereabouts since they were her responsibility, and making sure she could stay standing instead of collapsing in a puddle of shock seemed to take all her collected faculties at the moment. Forget charming or witty. And she was fairly certain that her face resembled the Joker more than a newly engaged woman.

Engaged.

She was engaged.

She had known the man for only a few months, had only been dating him for weeks, and she had agreed to marry him.

Never in her entire twenty-eight years of existence had she done something so impulsive.

She kept waiting for it to feel like a gigantic mistake, but aside from the surreal aspect of the situation, she didn't feel doubt.

She just felt . . . disbelief.

Out of all those women in the world who threw themselves at race car drivers, why would he pick her?

It challenged the tenets of logic.

But then again, she believed that he loved her. She had seen it in his eyes, heard it in his voice. She trusted that, she really did, so why had her mind never leaped forward to the concept of marriage and happily ever after?

Because she had been scared to. Afraid that he would change his mind. And those kinds of doubts bothered her. It told her she wasn't as confident and secure as she would like to be, that she exhibited a vulnerability to men. To this man. Or did she? And if she did, was that a bad thing?

Sometimes, the fact that her mind didn't shut down, and analyzed from seven thousand directions over and over again, was a real pain in the ass.

She had just received a marriage proposal from the man she loved and she was dissecting it for weaknesses.

"Sorry about the media blitz," Ty whispered in her ear, his breath tickling her skin. "Didn't think that part through, babe. I just saw you and knew I wanted to marry you so I asked. I couldn't wait."

Imogen looked at Ty, at the one man who could halt her stone-cold logic and make her just *feel*. For the first time since he'd dropped to the ground, she felt a smile crack. "It's okay. I'm glad you didn't wait." She needed that, to be caught off guard, to learn to trust her first gut reaction to her emotions. There had been no hesitation on her part—he had asked and her heart had sung out a big fat *yes*.

He grinned at her. "Good. I would pay a thousand dollars to be able to kiss you with tongue right now."

She laughed. "That would get some airtime."

"No joke. I think they're done bugging you. If you want to take the kids back to the coach, I'll be there soon. Or you can just wait to the side. Where the hell is Tammy, by the way?"

"She felt sick, so she left early."

"Oh, does Elec know? I imagine he'd want to collect the kids."

"I doubt it. She looked like she was going to throw up, so it's unlikely she's had a chance to call him."

"I'll get someone on tracking him down. You want to wait here, then?"

"Sure."

Imogen gathered Hunter, who was bouncing and jumping and chattering a mile a minute, and Pete, who looked profoundly bored.

"Are we going back to the coach?" he asked. "I'm hungry."

"We're going to wait for your stepdad, and he'll take you back. I'm sure he'll feed you."

"Ice cream!" Hunter declared, her arms shooting up in the air. "So when are you and Ty getting married?"

"I don't know. We haven't talked about that yet."

"My mom and Elec got married and now he sleeps in her bed with her. I think that would suck. When I get married, my husband is going to have to have his own room."

Imogen almost laughed. "You might change your mind about that at some point. Presumably if you marry him, you'll like him enough to want to spend a lot of time with him."

"I don't know." Hunter looked doubtful. "It seems silly to me to stuff two people in one bed together."

The very thought of that, settling into sleep every night with Ty beside her, waking up to his cheerful chatter and big warm hands, made her deeply, profoundly happy. "Maybe it is silly, but when you love someone, you want to cuddle."

Hunter looked ready to refute that when she spotted her stepfather striding toward them.

"Hey, squirt, what's up?" he asked.

"Good race," she told him as he picked her up and settled her on his hip, her long legs dangling.

"Thanks, baby girl. You guys ready to go? Ty told me Mom is sick. We should head back and check up on her."

"Can we eat?" Pete asked.

"Most likely I'll let you eat at some point," Elec said, ruffling Pete's hair. "You're a bottomless pit."

"Yep." Pete grinned.

Elec looked at Imogen. "Thanks for watching them. I really appreciate it."

"No problem. We had fun watching the race."

"And I hear congratulations are in order." Elec grinned. "Ty popping the question is all anyone's talking about."

She felt her cheeks heat. "Thanks."

"We'll catch you later, then," he said, and headed off with the kids.

Imogen's phone rang and she stepped a little farther back from the media zone to answer it. It was Suzanne. "Hello?"

"What the fuck!" was her friend's reaction. "I'm watching the race on TV and then Ty drops and asks you to marry him and I'm like Oh. My. God. Did you know?"

"No! I had no clue."

"That little devil, who knew he had a romantic bone in his body. Well, are you happy? Are you shitting bricks?"

"Both." Imogen laughed.

Suzanne laughed with her. "No kidding. My God, your proposal was just witnessed by, like, a million viewers. I say you stick him for the biggest rock ever for not warning you ahead of time."

Imogen tugged on her sweatshirt strings. "A million viewers? You are exaggerating, right?" She couldn't even imagine what her face had looked like. Her hair was in a ponytail. No makeup. And she was wearing a sweatshirt, which she never did. Yikes.

"Um, no, not really. It's a popular sport. But you looked cute, I swear. Just a little stunned. But when you said yes, I think there was a collective sigh across America."

"*Stunned* is the word for it. I am still in total shock."

"Well, yeah, hello. It's really soon." Suzanne paused and her voice softened. "Are you happy? Is this what you want?"

"Yes, it is." It was. She knew that without a shadow of a doubt.

"Does he make you so happy your face could crack? Do you want to make babies with him?"

The thought of having children with Ty had never occurred to her either. Now the image of little grinning shaggy-haired kids with personalities a lot like Hunter's popped into her head and wouldn't shake loose. "Yes, and yes."

"Then congratulations, sweetheart. And guess who is going to be your wedding planner?"

Imogen laughed. "That would be awesome, Suz. I know you'll do an amazing job, and I swear I won't request naked monkeys on my cake."

"You freaking better not. Not that I would let you anyway. And no racing paraphernalia, please."

"I would love a destination wedding, actually." Though she supposed it would need to be discussed with Ty. It's not like she had any clue what his vision for a wedding was.

"Now you're talking, sister."

Her call waiting beeped and she pulled her phone back to check it. "Oh, Suz, it's my mom on the other line. Can I call you later?"

"Sure, sweetie."

"Thanks, bye." Imogen clicked over and said, "Hello," her heart pounding.

"Okay, you know I don't follow sports on television," her mother said by way of greeting. "But you know Mr. and Mrs. Hanson do and now that he's retired, he DVRs everything. He just called me to tell me that he saw you at a stock car race where some man was proposing to you. I assumed it couldn't be accurate but then he played it back for me, and Imogen Ann, I swear it looked exactly like you. In fact, it seemed like this person even used your name when he proposed, but then I thought that can't possibly be real because how is it that your mother doesn't even know you are dating someone, let alone that you were on the verge of engagement?"

You had to love the power of electronics and instant communication. Imogen bit her lip. "Well, it was me, Mom. And as I'm sure you can see from the playback, I was very surprised. I had no idea I was on the verge of engagement myself or obviously I would have mentioned that fact."

"So you are telling me that you are engaged? To a race car driver?"

"Yes." Imogen held her breath, waiting for the backlash.

But her mother, who was controlled and never particularly

excitable, actually shrieked, startling Imogen so badly she almost dropped the phone. Her mother never yelled. Never. Not in joy. Not in irritation. Not ever.

"Oh, my God!" her mother said. "Jonathon, our baby is getting married!" she called to Imogen's father. "We have a wedding to plan! And who is this man? Shame on you for not telling me about him." Before Imogen could answer, her mother continued, "Oh, no! I guess this means you'll be permanently relocating to Charlotte. Oh, Imogen, I thought you would come home."

So had she. The realization that she wouldn't stunned her a little. Was she really moving to Charlotte forever?

Obviously she was if she was going to be married to Ty.

Wow. She wasn't sure how she felt about that.

"Mom, it's not a big deal. Ty travels a lot so I'm sure I'll be able to pop up to New York frequently and visit when he's busy on the road."

"I saw his name was Ty on the television. What is that short for? Is it a family name? Are you going to hyphenate your last name, keep yours, or take his? I can't say that I really care for the sound of Imogen McCordle."

Neither did she, now that her mother mentioned it. It was not a pretty name at all, something she had never considered. Not that it mattered. His last name could be Weed and she would still marry him. But would she take his name? She supposed she could be Imogen Wilson-McCordle. That had a scholarly ring to it. "I hadn't thought about what to do to my name. Probably hyphenate."

"If you think that's best. So what is Ty short for?"

She didn't know. She had no idea. They had never discussed it. Like many other things, it seemed. "Mom, can I call you later?

Ty is finishing up with the media and I would like to get some dinner. Give my love to Dad."

"Oh." Her mother sounded nonplussed. "Yes, call me tonight or tomorrow. I want to know when you're bringing Ty home to meet us, and I want your uncle Steven to show you the ballroom at his hotel. You are getting married in Manhattan, aren't you?"

Feeling like she might actually panic, Imogen said, "Mom? Mom, I can't hear you. I think we have a bad connection. I'll call you la—"

She cut her own words off by hanging up her cell phone. Giving a sigh of relief, she tried to swallow the guilt. She hated to lie. She was terrible at it. She always confessed. But her mother had been having a severely negative effect on her anxiety levels.

Why did everyone assume once you got engaged you had to have the wedding planned three minutes later? She couldn't think that far ahead; she just wanted to bask for a day or two or six months.

Looking around for Ty, she saw he was headed her way. Her phone chimed to indicate a text message. She flipped open her phone and sighed when she read it. It was from her mother.

Your father wants to know if you're pregnant.

Nice. She clearly couldn't get engaged spontaneously without her parents assuming she was knocked up. She thrust the phone at Ty as he approached her. "Look at this. It's my mother's reaction to our news, which they saw on TV."

He barely glanced at it. "I can't see it, there's a sun glare. What's it say?"

"My dad wants to know if I'm pregnant."

Ty laughed. "Tell them not yet, anyway."

"Do you want children?" she asked him anxiously.

The smile fell off his face. "Yes. Do you?"

She nodded. "Yes."

"Whew." He tucked her hair behind her ear. "You scared me there for a minute."

She was suddenly scaring herself. There were a lot of things she and Ty hadn't discussed. Important things. Deal-breaker things.

"We have time to grab a quick bite to eat before the flight home. Damn, I wish we weren't leaving tonight. Stuffed into a commercial flight with you is not my idea of how we should be celebrating."

"Me either." Imogen really wanted to cozy up in bed with him and talk, make love, talk, make love. That would assuage the niggling little fears that were cropping up. "I do have to be back, though. Maybe we can go out to dinner tomorrow night?"

"A fancy dinner," he promised. "And I've got some ring shopping to do."

The idea of Ty picking out an engagement ring blindly brought another wave of panic. "Maybe we should do that together."

He kissed her softly. "Sure. Damn, my phone is ringing." Retrieving it from his pocket, he answered it without even looking at the screen.

After a minute Imogen surmised it was Elec. She took advantage of his conversation to answer the text to her mother.

No, I am not pregnant.

Then some little devil prompted her to add Ty's suggestion.

Yet.

She wasn't usually one to tease like that, but for some reason it felt satisfying, maybe because the inquiry as to a pregnancy had smacked to Imogen of her parents' true opinion—she *had* to get married. Otherwise it didn't make sense.

Ty hung up the phone and gave her a look of apology. "You don't mind if we take the kids back to Charlotte, do you? Elec says Tammy has food poisoning and is throwing up nonstop. She's miserable and can't fly home tonight. He wants to stay with her, obviously, but the kids need to get back and go to school tomorrow. So I said they could keep their seats on the flight back tonight, that we would take them with us and drop them off at their grandparents' for the night."

"Sure, of course. Geez, poor Tamara. Food poisoning is awful. I'm sure it will be easier for her when the kids aren't running around the coach either. Maybe she'll get some sleep."

"This is probably good," Ty said. "It will prevent me from trying to molest you on the plane."

Imogen laughed. "You were going to molest me in public?"

"Probably." Ty slipped his hand into hers. "And this will stop me from doing something totally inappropriate. Though if you use an airplane blanket, I can't be responsible for what my hand might do underneath it."

"You wouldn't dare."

"Don't tempt me."

CHAPTER SEVENTEEN

IT turned out there was no ability to do anything inappropriate on the plane. Hunter insisted on sitting next to Imogen, which left Ty and Pete across the aisle. The flight had been delayed, and they missed their connection in Atlanta. By the time they got back to Charlotte, deposited the kids at their grandparents' house, and were on their way to Imogen's apartment, it was one in the morning and Ty was exhausted. It had been an amazing day, but a long one nonetheless.

Imogen looked a little droopy herself, but as Ty walked her to the door, her suitcase in his hand, he couldn't help asking, "Can I spend the night?"

When he saw her hesitate, desire warring with fatigue in her eyes, he added, "No sex, I think we're both too dead for that. But I just want to sleep beside you tonight. I want to hold you."

It wasn't exactly tough guy, but it was the damn honest truth, and it seemed to work for her because her expression softened. "I'd love that."

God, he was gone. He was begging to cuddle. "Let me grab my overnight bag." With a burst of energy he didn't know he had left, he got his bag from the trunk and was back beside her.

Imogen let them into her apartment and flipped on a lamp in her living room. "Do you mind if we go straight to bed?"

"No, that's exactly what I had in mind. You go ahead and use the bathroom first."

"We can be in there together," she said. "I just need to brush my teeth and wash my face."

Now that held appeal. If they were going to be getting married, they should figure out how to share a bathroom. "Okay. I just want to do the same thing. I'll shower in the morning."

When they got to her bedroom, Ty kicked off his shoes and lined them up next to her dresser. He stripped down to his boxers and T-shirt, folded his clothes, and pulled out his shaving kit. As he headed to her bathroom, he saw Imogen in her bra and panties. Tempting, very tempting, but he restrained himself.

The sight of her bathroom drew him up short. He had never been in there, and while he had known Imogen was kind of a clutter bug, he had never imagined one woman could have that much shit in one tiny bathroom. There were lotions and electronics with cords and makeup scattered all over. The floor was covered in towels, panties, bras, tissues, and a couple of disposable razors that looked like they'd taken a dive off the side of the tub and been forgotten. Unable to find a surface to rest his bag, he fished out his toothbrush, then tucked it between his legs.

"Sorry, it's kind of a mess in here," she said as she bustled in behind him wearing a tight T-shirt that showed off her nipples and a giant pair of flannel pajama pants.

That was an understatement, but he just shrugged and spoke around a mouthful of toothpaste. "No big deal."

He spit, then left the bathroom to her. Bed was very appealing, even if Imogen's was a bit heavy on lace and pink. Peeling off his shirt and pulling the covers back, he sank down into bed and sighed. He was officially tired. Her face shiny from whatever girl concoction she had used on it, she slid into bed next to him. Ty reached for her, and she moved in alongside him, resting her head on his chest.

Exhausted, and not really sure what he was supposed to say to the woman he had asked to marry him, Ty was content to just lie there. Imogen wasn't.

"I hope I didn't look completely awful on TV."

"I'm sure you looked beautiful," he murmured. He was used to being on TV, so it didn't unnerve him.

There was a pause, then she said, "We should sync our calendars in e-mail. That way we can see each other's schedules at a glance."

That made him shift a little in bed. "We don't need to do that. Anything you tell me, I'll remember." He tapped his head. "It's all right here."

"It would be more practical to use a calendar feature."

"Hmm," he said noncommittally.

"Why don't you use e-mail?" she asked. "It's so convenient."

"Too busy. And I have an assistant."

"Who I'm sure was thrilled to open the e-mail from me in which I was offering you oral sex."

Ty laughed. "Really? She didn't mention that to me. But don't worry, Toni's cool. A bit of a dictator, but she keeps me where I need to be."

"That's good." Imogen ran her fingers over his chest. "What kind of wedding do you want?"

"I don't know." Truth was, he'd never thought about it one way or the other. "Whatever you want, babe."

"Maybe a destination wedding. What do you think of that?"

"I don't even know what that means."

"Where you get married on a resort, like in Hawaii or the Caribbean. You invite just a few close friends and family."

"That sounds nice." Sun, sand, he could deal with that. And considering his only months off from the season were December and January, going to the tropics was appealing. "We could go barefoot."

"Then again, that has the potential to offend a lot of people who are important to us. Maybe we should have a traditional wedding here so we could invite everyone."

"Okay."

Imogen glanced up at him anxiously. "Is that what you really want? Because planning a wedding like that is a lot of work."

"Which is why we don't need to do it all tonight," he told her, kissing her on the forehead. "Go to sleep."

She was quiet long enough that Ty let his eyes drift closed, the feel of her warm and snug up next to him lulling him toward sleep.

But then she spoke. "It would really be helpful if you answered e-mails and we synced our calendars if we're going to plan a wedding."

Ty sighed, and ran his thumbs along his eyebrows. He had to tell her, he knew he did. He was going to marry the woman, he could trust her with his secret. But the shame still bit hard. Forcing that aside, he said, "Imogen."

"You're going to tell me to shut up and go to sleep, aren't you?"

That almost made him laugh. "No. I'm going to tell you that

e-mail isn't a good form of communication for me because I'm dyslexic."

"Oh." She blinked up at him, squinting since her glasses were off. "Oh. I had no idea . . . God, I'm sorry. I'm harassing you about it."

"That's okay, you didn't know. But now you do."

She didn't just look upset, just startled. "So, it's difficult and time-consuming for you to read? Is it just regular e-mails or is it the complexity of a calendar feature that jumbles words for you?"

He should have known she would ask curious questions. It was time to be completely honest, instead of the half-truth he'd just given her. "It's both. I can't read at all, Emma Jean. I was good at faking my way through school, and I didn't figure out what was wrong with me until I was twenty or so. By then, it didn't matter. I had dropped out of high school to drive cars."

Another little secret he had failed to mention to the woman getting her master's degree.

"What?" That finally seemed to stun her enough that she sat up in bed and stared at him. "You can't read at all? Like, at all? How do you function, then?"

Ty shifted up in bed as well, a little stung by how much her wording hurt him. "I told you, I'm good at faking it. I pick up on cues from everyone around me. I have a fantastic memory. You only need to tell me once and I'll remember it. I have Toni, the only person who knows, guiding me through paperwork and anything I can't figure out. And thank God for the BlackBerry and its little pictures. Technology has been a wonderful thing . . . Now I can tell who's calling by the picture that pops up."

"But, but . . ." She squeezed her fingers into her temple. "I've seen you do stuff. Like the touch screen at the airport . . . How did you . . ."

"When those things first started popping up, I had the ticket agent help me do it. Now I do it partly from memory, partly from common sense based on the pictures. It's not that hard."

"Ty . . ." Her look was agonized. "Shakespeare?"

His heart was thumping a sickening, dull thud in his chest. He didn't like the way she was staring at him but he had to be honest. "I listened to it on audio."

Her mouth fell open. "Oh, okay, I guess that makes sense. And . . . and you're saying you dropped out of high school?"

Ty nodded.

"Why didn't you tell me? You don't have to hide anything from me." Imogen reached her hand out and touched his cheek.

Overwhelmed with emotion and relief that she hadn't called him an idiot, Ty swallowed hard. "It's not something you run around telling people. If they know, they're critical, passing judgment, or they treat you like you're a moron. If they don't know, it's a level playing field. And hell, I'm embarrassed. You're a very intelligent woman, Imogen." He used her real name intentionally instead of his nickname for her. "I didn't want a door closed in my face with you before I could even get it open all the way."

"I would never pass judgment," Imogen said, but even as the words left her mouth, she knew that wasn't entirely true. Before she had known Ty the way she did now, she might have dismissed him as a typical Southern male, too stubborn to bother to learn how to read, even when it would make his life easier. She had since learned there was so much more to him than that, and she could see why he wouldn't tell anyone. Ty had pride, tons of it, and he would see dyslexia as a weakness. Why admit a flaw when he could just work around it?

But nonetheless, it bothered her that he had hid it from her.

"Come on, it's only natural. But I'm not stupid, I just have a messed-up brain."

"I don't think your brain is messed up," she said softly, sensing how vulnerable he felt. "But I do think that maybe this is something you should have told me earlier. I mean, I asked you to read Shakespeare. You must have been sweating bullets over that."

He shrugged. "Shakespeare's easy because he's popular. It's obscure books that are hard to find on audio."

Imogen leaned against her headboard and stared at him, trying to make sense of her jumbled thoughts. It occurred to her that this was the first time he was spending the night at her apartment. They were engaged to be married and they really knew very little about each other. "What is your real name?" she asked.

"Huh?" He blinked.

"Is Ty short for something?"

"No." He shook his head. "My mother didn't believe in naming a kid something twelve letters long only to call him by a nickname. Why?"

"I'm just sitting here thinking that we don't know anything about each other at all, Ty. We don't know each other's history, or family, or favorite foods. We don't know how we lost our virginity or a million other little details."

"I could tell you how I lost my virginity. It involves Bon Jovi, a keg party, and a Mustang." He grinned. "And the car wasn't mine, it was hers. I wasn't old enough to drive."

Imogen didn't smile in return. "I'm serious," she said.

"About what?" he asked, throwing his hand out in exasperation. "Why do we have to know everything about each other right this minute? People grow to know each other, and I'm sure even married couples who have been together for twenty years don't know everything about their partner's past or likes and dislikes. What's the big deal?"

How did she say that her biggest fear was that they would get to know each other and fall right out of love? That familiarity bred contempt and he would get bored with her and she would get impatient with him?

"The big deal is that what if we don't know pivotal things about each other? Things like your dyslexia define you and yet I had no idea that it existed."

The smile fell off his face. He sat up straighter. "Dyslexia does not define me. It's just an unfortunate pain in my ass. But it doesn't change the core of who I am. I would be the same Ty Jackson McCordle with or without it."

"Your middle name is Jackson?" she asked in dismay. "I didn't know that! And of course it affects who you are. You've spent your whole life hiding from everyone the fact that you can't read. It's difficult to carry that kind of burden, always afraid of getting caught. It's no wonder you engage in reckless and impulsive behavior. You have to pass yourself off as brimming with joie de vivre so no one will guess the truth."

"Don't psychoanalyze me," Ty said, his words tight. "Maybe I just enjoy myself, did you ever think of that? Next you'll be telling me the reason you're uptight is because you're suffering from penis envy."

Imogen gasped. "Excuse me?"

"You know, Freud's theory on women. I have heard of Freud, you know, even though I'm too stupid to read."

This was spiraling way out of control. "First off, I never once called you stupid. Do not put words in my mouth. Second of all, I am not uptight."

He scoffed.

Imogen blinked at him in disbelief. "You are being entirely irrational."

"Of course I am, because you are always logical, right? Whatever."

"Don't whatever me."

"I'll whatever you whenever the fuck I feel like it."

The *f* word outside of sex always sounded so harsh. She winced. "Look, let's just both calm down and get some sleep, okay? Maybe we shouldn't have opened this can of worms tonight."

"I was just trying to be honest," he said through gritted teeth. "I thought you should know."

"I'm glad you told me," she said sincerely, feeling guilty. She did want the truth, and it couldn't have been easy for him to reveal his secret. "And I think you are a smart, amazing man, and I do love you."

His expression softened. "Thank you. I love you, too."

"And now that I know, we can talk about ways to help you. There's no reason you can't be taught to retrain your brain so you can read. You could even get your GED if you wanted to."

She hadn't meant to be anything other than helpful; after all, why couldn't he learn how to read and make life easier? But Ty not only sat straight up in bed, he pushed the covers off and climbed out, his expression stormy.

"What?" she asked, puzzled.

"I don't need to retrain my brain, thank you very fucking much. I do just fucking fine as it is. Do you know how much goddamn money I make? Do you know how hard I work day in and day out for that money? Do you know that if I wasn't a risk taker, I would never have had the balls to leave home and hit the race circuit with nothing but a hundred bucks and tenacity in my pocket?"

Uh-oh. She hadn't anticipated this sort of reaction. Trying to find words to calm him down, she opened her mouth.

But he wasn't finished.

"I am successful because of my brains and my guts, put together, and I don't need some fancy-ass degree from a bunch of sweater-vest-wearing pricks who haven't gotten laid since Bush Senior was president. So maybe being a stock car driver isn't saving the world, but it's entertaining millions of people. What impact does writing about whether dating manuals work or not have on the world either? You can read, you're brilliant, and you're wasting your time moldering in some teaching position in an academic field no one gives a shit about. Do you know who studies sociology? People who would rather observe life than live it."

Imogen felt tears sting her eyes as his last words hit her like a resounding slap. It was her worst fear verbalized. "Is that what you really think of me?" she asked in a whisper. Then she regretted even speaking. Shaking her head, she held up her hand, not wanting his answer. She'd had enough honesty for the night. "Never mind. Never mind. Just get out. Go home."

Ty was already pulling on his jeans in angry tugs. "I'm going."

"Fine."

"Is that the best you can do?" he asked, yanking his shirt on over his head. "I have a better exit. 'Well, you are a rare parrot-teacher.'"

Oh, no, he didn't. He had just compared her to a squawking parrot who was trying to instruct those around her. Imogen picked up a pillow to throw it at him.

Ty grabbed his shoes and bag off the floor and said, "That's *Shakespeare*, by the way!"

As if she didn't know. Imogen launched the pillow, hitting him in the back of the head. Now, that was sickly satisfying.

He paused at impact, but didn't turn around.

Then he was out of her bedroom, out the front door. The angry slam made her jump in bed, her heart racing.

What the hell had just happened?

WHAT the fuck had just happened?

Ty threw his car into reverse and gunned it down the street way faster than was appropriate for two in the morning in the suburbs, but he didn't give a shit. He was furious and, well, hurt, damn it.

He had trusted Imogen with his problem, and somehow he felt like she had just totally insulted him. Looking at him with pity while suggesting he take a class. Take a class. Like that was the frickin' answer to everything. It was her answer.

Okay, so he had been a little insensitive with his assessment of her career choice. But he thought it was true—she studied other people because she had spent her life being an observer, not a doer. He thought in that way, they were good for each other. He brought her new experiences, coaxed her to step outside of her boundaries. In return, she gave him logic and organization and a loyalty and love he had never before experienced.

But somehow they had wound up screaming at each other and she'd nailed him in the back of the head with a pillow. He hadn't seen that one coming, literally.

Picking up his phone—coded with pictures, thank you very goddamn much—he found Ryder and clicked Send.

"Oh, my God, do you have any idea what time it is?" Ryder said in a groggy voice after Ty dialed him three times in a row when Ryder didn't pick up. "I'm going to kill you."

"I think Imogen and I just broke up." Ty got on the highway

and shifted gears, loving the speed of his car. It wasn't the track and he couldn't break the law, but it still felt good.

"What? You just got engaged twelve hours ago!"

"Tell me about it. Can I stop by for a beer? I need to vent."

"Sure." There was some rustling. "I'm not alone, but that's okay. I can leave her sleeping and we can hang out by my flat screen in the living room."

Ryder was with a woman? He had just returned from Texas, too. The idea of whining about his chick trouble while Ryder had a warm body in his bed a dozen feet away held no appeal. "Never mind. I don't want to interrupt."

"No, it's okay."

"No, I'll just catch you tomorrow. Thanks, man." Ty hung up the phone and stared at the yellow lines in front of him. For half a second he thought about calling his mother, but he knew what she would say—that he had been a total dickhead to Imogen. Besides, he'd already gotten an earful from her on the phone earlier when she had called to cuss him out for not telling her he was going to pop the question to his girlfriend.

Lord only knew what she'd say when he told her he didn't think there was going to be a wedding after all.

That thought kicked him in the nuts, the gut, and the lungs all at once.

Holy shit.

He had lost Imogen.

He'd found the love of his life, and just like that, she was gone.

TY was gone, and Imogen cried herself to sleep.

The next morning, she woke up puffy-eyed and sick to her

stomach, running through their argument over and over again in her head. What had she done wrong? How should she have handled it differently? Those questions rolled around and around until she had lost all ability to focus on anything other than her agonizing heartbreak.

When she ran a red light on the way to school, after noticing she was wearing two different shoes, she gave it up and turned around and drove home, her hands shaking from anxiety.

Dialing Suzanne, she tried to get a grip on her emotions. How did she feel? Was she upset because she had lost Ty or upset because perhaps she'd never had him in the first place? Maybe their vision of a future had been a fantasy right from the onset of their ill-fated relationship.

"Hello, Whores R Us," Suzanne said as a greeting.

"I hope you knew it was me," Imogen said, despite the fact that she was devastated and emotionally drained. She just couldn't fathom answering her phone that way.

"Of course I did. Welcome to the twenty-first century. You have your own ringtone and your picture pops up. Like I'd say Whores R Us to just anyone other than my special friends."

Imogen winced as she made a right turn. "Right." And her overreaction just proved Ty's theory—she was uptight. She knew that, she'd always known. It was the one flaw that she feared, the one thing she had known all along would drive him away.

"What's up? Are you spending the morning in engaged bliss? I kind of thought you would need to sleep in. I figured you had a late night celebrating, wink wink."

Bursting into tears, Imogen pulled into the parking lot of the doughnut shop. "We broke up!" she wailed with a drama she hadn't shown since middle school and a poor choice involving her hair and blond highlights.

"What? You're joking!"

"No. I'm not. We . . . we said terrible things to each other, he got out of bed and left, and I hit him in the back of the head with a pillow." For some reason, the pillow seemed pivotal. It was so unlike her to resort to that kind of childish action, and she couldn't really explain it.

"You hit him with a pillow? Wow, you must have been pissed. What did he do?"

"He kept something secret from me. Something important." Imogen wasn't about to reveal what that secret was—Ty had trusted her to keep his confidence.

"Oh. That sucks. Is it a major thing?"

"Yeah, pretty major. It affects who he is. But it's not really that he kept it a secret, it was more the realization that we don't know anything about each other. How can we get married?"

"Honey, nobody ever knows someone completely. You have to just enjoy what you do know and have faith in the rest."

"Do you really think so?" Imogen stared at the doughnut shop, wishing a jelly-filled would walk itself out to her car and land in her mouth as she swiped at her eyes. Maybe she had just panicked. Maybe she had totally overreacted. "But he called me uptight and said I am an observer in life, not a participant."

"Well, that's a rude thing to say, even if it might have some truth to it."

Great. Suzanne thought she was uptight, too. "Am I really that annoying?" she asked in dismay.

"Oh, shit, come on now. I never said you were annoying, and I'm sure Ty doesn't feel that way either. The man asked you to marry him! But you have to admit, you like to people-watch, not dive into the fray yourself. It's not a flaw. It's not like you're living in a bubble. It's just your personality. If he doesn't like that, he can go fuck himself."

"I don't know what he likes. I think he loves me." She wanted to believe that, she really, really did.

"So wait for him to calm down and then go and work it out."

"But maybe this is just a way to walk away before we both regret it even more further down the road."

"So let sleeping dogs lie, then."

"But I don't know if that's what I want."

"You need to decide whether you're willing to risk being hurt, plain and simple. You can go for it and have a wonderful relationship. Or you might go for it and crash and burn brilliantly. It's up to you if you want to take that risk, up to you if it's worth it or not."

Her brain hurt. Her heart hurt. Her stomach hurt. Her vision blurred and she swallowed hard. "I don't know."

"So take some time and think about it. He's not going anywhere, honey, and his feelings for you aren't going to disappear overnight. You get your head on straight, and maybe he'll do the same."

"You think so?"

"Yeah. And if that doesn't work, throw another pillow at him."

EIGHTEEN

TWO weeks went by, and each day sucked a little bit more than the last. At the beginning, Ty could have sworn that wasn't possible, but by the time he was heading to the pits for qualifying in Miami for the final race of the season, he was amazed to find it was true. He hadn't spoken to or called Imogen since their fight. Imogen hadn't called him.

And every day the pain got a little deeper and he got a little crankier.

Especially every time someone congratulated him on his engagement.

Or asked where his beautiful fiancée was.

Generally, when anyone talked to him at all, he wasn't happy about it.

Ty wanted to be left alone, to wallow, to reflect on his own stupidity, to contemplate a course of action. It wasn't working because no one, no one, could ever seem to leave him alone.

"Ohmigawd, Ty, hi!" a chipper voice said to his left.

Glancing over, Ty tried to force a smile onto his face, no matter how much of a struggle it was. Then he saw it was Nikki and gave up the effort. "Hey. How are you?"

"I am awesome!" she declared, falling in step beside him in a sundress and high heels. She held her ring finger out for him. "Did you see my engagement ring? It cost fifty thousand dollars."

Thinking that announcing the ring price was about the most vulgar thing he'd ever heard, Ty glanced over at the rock. Damn, it was ugly. That somehow made him feel better, though he couldn't help feeling a tiny bit sorry for Strickland shelling out that kind of cash on a gaudy ring. It wasn't even a diamond, the thing was yellow.

"It's a yellow diamond," she told him.

Wow. He didn't even know they made those. "Very nice."

"I heard you got engaged, too," Nikki said, clearly not picking up on his lack on interest. "Congrats."

"Thanks."

"I can only hope that you're as happy with her as I am with my snooky-wookums."

That brought the closest thing to a smile to Ty's face in days. He just might have to call Jonas Strickland *snooky-wookums* next time he bumped into him. Making a noncommittal sound, he glanced around. He wanted to be saved from this conversation. Ridiculous nickname aside, it was not feeling so great to think that Nikki was riding off into the sunset of her happily ever after and he had screwed his up royally.

He shouldn't have called Imogen uptight. That was unfair and hurtful. Yes, she was logical. Yes, she was cautious. But she wasn't uptight. She was willing to try new things like camping and a wide variety of sexual positions.

Anyone who could have an orgasm in an inner tube was not strictly an observer in life.

He should apologize. He should call her.

Beg for forgiveness.

Because goddamn, it sucked not having his Emma Jean in his life.

"How much did the ring you got for Imogen cost?" Nikki asked, holding her hand out and admiring her bling again.

Ty stopped walking and just looked at her, appalled. "I didn't buy her a ring," he said. "She's not materialistic, and you can't put a price on our relationship. I'm going to give her my grandmother's ring." He didn't know where the idea popped into his head from, but once it was there, he liked it.

Nikki sniffed. "Well, I'm sure that will just thrill her. It's not like a boring professor has anywhere good to wear quality jewelry anyway." Then she smiled. "I'll send you an invitation to our wedding. I'm sure we'll beat you to the altar. Bye!"

As he watched her walk away, he concluded that he could take a page from Imogen's book. If he wasn't so damn impulsive, he never would have dated Nikki, and he could have filled hours of his life with something—anything—of substance.

The thought didn't improve his mood, nor did the sight of his crew chief.

"Are you ready to pull your head out of your ass?" Sam asked him, meeting him on the thoroughfare to the pits.

"I wasn't aware that's where it was," Ty lied. "No wonder I've been having neck pain."

"I'm serious," Sam said. "It's all on the line here and you've been distracted for a month." He shot Ty a long look. "I guess love will do that to a man, but I wish you had waited until December to fall for a woman."

"I'm fine." And he was a big fat fucking liar.

Especially given that ten minutes later the sight of Evan Monroe soured his mood even further. The guy wasn't doing anything, he was just waiting to run his qualifying lap like Ty, but it irritated Ty to think the guy had wanted to date Imogen. Evan was not her type.

Then again, neither was Ty.

That thought really set him on edge, and he almost groaned out loud when Evan approached him and said, "Is it true you and Imogen broke up?"

Not trusting himself to speak, he nodded.

"Man, I'm sorry. That's sucks."

"Yep."

"You must be devastated."

"I'm fine. It's not a big deal." It seemed he was getting really good at lying, because Evan's sympathetic expression disappeared.

"Really? You're not torn up?"

"No, not at all. It was a mistake in the first place." Pride was a funny thing. Ty couldn't even believe he managed to eek those words out between his lips, but for the sake of his pride, he did just that.

"Oh, okay. So you wouldn't be upset if I asked her out? I've got a thing for brunettes."

One minute Ty was standing upright, keeping his cool with Evan.

Then the next Evan was on the ground and Ty was on top of him.

He couldn't explain it. Nor could he explain his hands gripping the front of Evan's racing suit.

But everything had gone black and buzzing, and it had seemed that the only thing to do was to pound Evan into the asphalt so then maybe he wouldn't feel so damn lousy.

Even as he gripped Evan's jacket, he suspected he was wrong on that count, too.

Yep, every day had sucked just a little bit more and he just might have reached the height of suckiness.

RYDER called Suzanne, still stunned by Ty's behavior.

"Suz, turn on the sports channel," he told her.

"What? Why?"

"Ty just jumped Evan Monroe at qualifying and a camera caught it. They're rolling it over and over."

"What! That's insane. Ty never loses his temper."

That's what Ryder would have said, too. Flopping down on his couch, he kicked off his shoes. "It seems that Evan asked Ty if he would mind if Evan asked Imogen out now that they're broken up."

"Uh-oh."

"Yeah. Big fat uh-oh. I understand getting pissed, but my God, he went after him. At the track! In the last week of the season. It's a PR nightmare. The man has lost his mind."

"I'm watching it right now," Suzanne said. "You're right. He's officially one hundred percent lost his mind."

"Look, you know I've never been big on interfering in other people's lives, but Ty is a mess and I can't stand back and do nothing. We need to at least try to get him and Imogen to talk to each other and work this out. Or at least get some closure."

"I agree." Suzanne paused, then gave a small laugh. "Holy shit. We agree on something."

Ryder smiled. "It happens sometimes."

"Alright, so I think a dinner party is a bad idea. At this point, we pretty much just need to throw them in a room together and lock the door. I can't do it early in the week, I have appointments. How does Friday sound?"

"That will work. Ty is going to have a shitty week with all the backlash from this stunt. He'll need a beer by Friday."

"Keep him at your place. I'll take Imogen out and make up some stupid thing about stopping by your house for paperwork."

"Got it." Ryder hesitated. "Thanks, Suz. You're a good friend."

"Yeah, well, you don't suck either," she said.

Ryder laughed. That was Suzanne.

IMOGEN was staring at her computer, trying to find the right wording to submit her letter of withdrawal for her thesis project when there was a pounding on her front door. She debated ignoring it but then her cell phone buzzed with a text. It was from Suzanne.

I'm at the front door. Answer it.

Sighing, Imogen went to hit Save on her document then realized she hadn't actually written anything so there was no point. Trudging to her door, she glanced down at her PJ pants. Good thing it was just Suzanne. She had been having something of a drawn-out pity party for the last two weeks and dressing hadn't been a top priority on her day off.

"Hey," she said. "How are you?"

Suzanne bustled into the living room. "Where's your remote? You have to see Ty on TV."

Did she have to? "No, thanks." It was possible her wounds from their fight were finally starting to scab over, so she didn't want to tear them open to bleed again by seeing him smiling on camera at the racetrack.

"I'm not giving you a choice. You have to see this. Ty has lost his mind." Suzanne dug around on the coffee table until she found the remote and clicked the TV on. She surfed until she found the sports channel. "Come on . . . show it again."

Despite her wariness, Suzanne's agitated manner drew Imogen's attention to the screen. They were discussing football.

"Shoot, I should have recorded it."

"What?" she asked, bewildered.

"Wait! Here it is." Suzanne cranked up the volume. "Look."

The sportscaster mentioned something about hot tempers at the racetrack and then Imogen gaped at her TV. Ty was wrestling on the ground with someone. She knew it was Ty on top—she'd recognize his butt anywhere—but she couldn't tell who was on the ground. "Who is that? Why are they fighting?"

"That's Evan Monroe. Ryder told me that Evan found out from Elec that you and Ty broke up, so he asked Ty if he minded if he asked you out. Obviously, Ty minded."

"You can't be serious."

"Oh, I am. He threw him down and had to be hauled off. It's all they're talking about in stock car racing. Ty's going to get penalized some serious points for doing this. He probably just lost the championship."

"Oh, my God, that's awful!" Imogen stared at the image of the man she loved gripping Evan's shirt. "Why would he do something so incredibly stupid and macho and . . . *stupid*?"

"Because," Suzanne said triumphantly, "he is in love with you. This is jealousy, honey. The man is so cut up from your fight that he just threw his own season down the toilet."

Imogen felt her cheeks start to burn at the very thought she had Ty behaving irrationally. "That's insane. It's irresponsible. It's—"

"Hot. That's what it is," Suzanne said. "Just admit it. The fact that he's torn up and wanting to beat up guys over you has you just a little damp in the panties. I know that's how I would feel."

Imogen shook her head rapidly. She shouldn't think that was hot. It was macho and ludicrous and . . . hot. "Okay, I admit it! I want him to be upset. I want him to be jealous." She flung herself down on her sofa. "I want him to want me. This has been just horrific."

"So remember what we talked about? Go see him."

"I can't!" she wailed.

"Why not?"

Because the thought of him telling her she was uptight rolled over and over in her head like a video recording of all her worst fears. "I don't know."

Suzanne huffed in impatience. "The man just might need a friend this week as all hell breaks loose over him and his career. Maybe you should be that friend."

The thought that Ty would be hurting hurt her. Imogen suddenly knew what she needed to do. "I will. I am. I'm going to." She jumped off the couch. "Can I talk to you later? I have something I need to do."

"Hopefully it's to take a shower," Suzanne commented. "Your hair could use some help."

"Later. I have to do something else first." She knew exactly what she needed to do.

Imogen wanted to spend her life with Ty.

But before she told him that, she had a few projects to take care of.

SATURDAY blew. Sunday blew harder. Monday sucked less in comparison. Tuesday would have been a shitty day in a better week, but under the circumstances, Ty thought it wasn't half-bad. Wednesday and Thursday were a numb blur, and Friday brought relief that maybe the worst of it was over.

So maybe knocking Evan Monroe to the ground hadn't been one of his better ideas. He could admit that. He had even apologized to Evan.

But he'd had his ass chewed from one end to the other by everyone from his car owner, Carl Hinder, to his sponsor rep, to Toni, to Ryder and his own mother. He'd been issued a penalty and a fine. The money he didn't care about, but the penalty of losing points had knocked him out of running for the championship. That honor had gone to a driver who wasn't even on the Hinder Motors team, which had really upset Carl.

Ty pulled into Ryder's condo parking lot and rubbed his eyes. It had been stupid. He knew that. But what could he say? Love made a man crazy, and he was crazy in love.

Now that the week was behind him and the season officially over, he was planning to have a beer with Ryder, then he was going over to Imogen's unannounced and probably unwanted. He was going to apologize for his harsh words, then he was going to pretty much beg that she take him back.

It wasn't going to be sophisticated. It wasn't going to be attractive.

But he was a man on the edge and he wanted his woman back, no matter what it took.

He was going to throw some more Shakespeare at her. Hell, he'd quote the Bard until the cows came home if she wanted him to, and he was going to tell her that he had signed up for a private tutor to assist him with his reading skills, or lack thereof.

As he walked to Ryder's front door, he rubbed at the pain in his chest. He was getting old. He constantly had a burning sensation in his chest, like acid reflux or something, and he would kill for an antacid. He knocked on the front door but Ryder didn't answer, even though Ty could hear him talking to someone inside the condo. It was a woman, and Ty heaved a sigh. Just what he didn't want—having to make small talk with Ryder's flavor of the week.

Opening the door, he stepped inside and saw it was actually Suzanne who Ryder was talking to, which brought him some relief. He could handle Suz hanging around, since he'd known her for ten years. Plus he could potentially pump her for information about Imogen.

Suzanne and Ryder were arguing.

"He was supposed to be here!" Suzanne said in an irritated stage whisper.

"Well, what am I supposed to do about it?" Ryder asked. "I asked him over, but I can't make him show up on time."

"She's getting antsy! She said she has plans. Which scares me because she's been shut up in her apartment all week. I'm afraid she's going to do something drastic."

"Like what?"

"Dye her hair blond or something scary like that."

"Oh, damn, that would be bad."

Ty started down the hall. "Who is dying her hair blond?"

Suzanne squawked and put her hand to her heart. "Jesus, you scared me." Then she frowned. "It's about time you got here. I've had a hell of a time keeping Imogen here for no apparent reason whatsoever."

"Imogen is here?" Ty's heart rate kicked up a notch, and even as his palms grew sweaty, he was relieved. He wanted to fix this, the sooner, the better.

"Well, duh. Of course she is. That's why Ryder invited you over, so we could force you two to be in the same room and work this out because you're driving us insane."

"Shouldn't we act like it's a coincidence that they're both here?" Ryder asked.

"Wait a minute." Ty just realized what Suzanne had said now that he knew who they were talking about. "Imogen is going to dye her hair blond?"

"Probably."

"*No*. No, no, no. You can't let her do that. She looks perfect the way she is." The very thought of her ruining that lush brown hair with bleach made him downright sick to his stomach.

"So go in there and tell her. She's in Ryder's living room listening to her iPod—"

Ty stopped listening to her as he moved toward the living room, trying to figure out what he should say. The words were jumbling in his head, how he wanted to tell her he was sorry, that he loved her, that he wanted to spend his life making her happy. He paused for a moment in front of her just to drink in the sight of her sitting on the couch.

Earplugs in, she wasn't aware of him yet, and she was wearing a black sweater and jeans, a lot like the ones she'd had on that night out on Tammy's porch. Her glasses were sliding down her nose, but her hair was neat and tidy in a ponytail.

It was then he realized that he'd left the ring in the car because he hadn't known she was going to be there. Debating whether to forge ahead or to go out and get it, he was standing there in indecision when she looked up.

"Oh! Ty." She yanked the buds out of her ears. "What . . . what are you doing here?"

Standing there like an idiot at the moment. Not sure of her mood, whether she was still furious with him, or if she was having second thoughts like he was, he tread lightly. "I was on my way to your place, actually, but I stopped off to have a beer with Ryder first. Good thing I did, since you're here."

"Suzanne and I were having coffee and she needed to get some paperwork from him." She glanced down the hall. "I think they're arguing so I put on my headphones."

So Imogen hadn't known they'd been set up either. "Can . . . can I talk to you, Emma Jean? Somewhere private?"

He'd been afraid she would say no, but she just nodded. "I think that's a good idea."

"You want to sit in my car with me?"

She nodded. "Okay."

Standing up, she grabbed her purse and followed him. Once they were both in his car, staring at each other, Ty lost all his nervousness, all the reserve. This was his Emma Jean, and they were supposed to be together.

"Goddamn, I'm so sorry," he said. "I said terrible things and I have no excuse. I was overly sensitive about my dyslexia, and I turned it around and criticized you and that was so wrong of me. I'm really sorry . . . Can you ever forgive me, Engine? I'm just miserable without you."

Tears rose in Imogen's eyes. "Oh, Ty, of course I can. I'm sorry, too. I was totally insensitive. I was just so scared thinking about how illogical it was to have fallen in love so quickly, two totally opposite personalities. But I should have just trusted my feelings, trusted you."

Oh, thank God. Relief washed over him, just about making him dizzy. He leaned closer to her, wanting to touch her, taste her, but she pulled a CD out of her purse and shoved it at him.

"What's this?" He took it from her and saw there was no label, not that he could read it if there were, but it was clearly something she had burned herself.

"It's a compilation I put together. You just put it in your computer and you can listen to it."

"Compilation of what?" he asked, puzzled.

"Kenny Chesney and the intro to my book."

That made him smile. "Kenny Chesney, huh?"

"Yeah, singing about how he won't be eating or sleeping until she's back in his arms. That's how I've felt these last few weeks . . . I've missed you so much." Her voice cracked, and Ty reached over and brushed his hand over her cheek.

"I've missed you, too, babe. God, so much. And what's this about your book? What book?"

"I formally withdrew my thesis. It wasn't working and I need to reassess and regroup. But I have so many fabulous interviews with drivers and their wives about falling in love and their marriages, so I'm putting them all together in one volume. Sort of a true love on the stock car circuit kind of book. I'm hoping a publisher will want to buy it."

"Wow, that's a great idea. I'm so proud of you for putting all that hard work to good use. I think people would love reading those stories. Everyone loves hearing about a happy ending."

"Thanks." She smiled softly. "And I recorded myself reading the intro so you can hear it privately, without asking Toni to do it."

That gave him pause. "Why? What's in the intro?"

"It's my story of how I fell in love with the driver of the number sixty car when I was least expecting it."

Ty's throat tightened up. "I hope you mention how that driver fell right back in love with you. And by the way, I got myself a tutor. I'm going to learn to read. Or try to, anyways. No guarantee I'll be successful at it."

"That's fantastic," she said. "I'm proud of you, and I think you'll be pleased with how even a little bit of progress will make your life easier. And hey, you're tenacious, remember?"

"And you're adorable and brilliant and honest and loyal and loving and sexy as hell, and I am the luckiest man alive."

Imogen laughed. "Either that or you're delusional."

"Nope." He leaned over and kissed her, savoring the taste of her lips. He had missed her so damn much, and now that he had her back, he was never going to let her go. Pulling back, he popped open the glove box and pulled out the case holding his grandmother's ring.

Imogen sighed as she watched Ty fussing around in the glove box. She didn't know what he was doing, nor did she care. They were back together, and all was right with the world. Then she suddenly realized what he had in his hand, and she did care.

"Oh, Ty," she said, tears flooding her eyes.

"Will you marry me?" he asked, holding up a white gold princess cut diamond with a crusted band. "It's not some fifty-thousand-dollar yellow diamond or anything, but this was my grandmother's and it meant a lot to her. If it's too old-fashioned, we can get another one, but I wanted to have something in my hand when I—"

Imogen put her hand over his mouth. "Shh. It's perfect. I love it," she managed to choke out. "And yes, I will marry you."

He grinned and gave her a kiss that made her hair and her toes curl and everything in between go hot and damp.

"So I think we should go camping for our honeymoon," she whispered between kisses, burying her hands into his hair.

"Hell, we should just honeymoon in the car. This is where all our deep conversations take place."

Imogen laughed. "We've never had sex in the car, though."

Ty glanced into the backseat. "Let's go for it."

"We're in the parking lot of Ryder's condo complex."

"Details." Ty kissed the corner of her mouth, her jaw, her ear. "Okay, fine, we'll go to my place as soon as I finish kissing you."

"So you agree that we should honeymoon at Lake Norman?"

"I don't care where we get married or where we have our honeymoon or where we live. The only thing I care about is that we have Shakespeare involved."

"Well, he can't be there since he's dead," Imogen said, closing her eyes and enjoying the feel of his lips on her neck.

"True, but we can have his words and I have the perfect ones. Maybe we can put them on the invitations or something."

"What words?" Imogen asked, her nipples tightening and desire pooling between her thighs. She had missed him so much.

Ty pulled back and met her gaze, his rich brown eyes dark with emotion. When he spoke, it was in a soft, husky voice.

"'No sooner met but they looked; no sooner looked but they

loved; no sooner loved but they sighed; no sooner sighed but they asked one another the reason; no sooner knew the reason but they sought the remedy; and in these degrees have they made a pair of stairs to marriage . . .' "

Oh, my.

Imogen tried to remember to breathe and told the man she loved, "Get in the backseat."

His eyebrow shot up. "For real?"

"Oh, yes." She kicked off her flats and ditched her purse on the floor. "I am very serious."

Ty grinned. "That's kind of impulsive."

"Yes, it is." And she was okay with that.

"Alright, then."

Ty climbed into the backseat, Imogen followed, and they spent a hard and fast five minutes taking the edge off how much they had missed each other. Once they caught their breath, Imogen still on his lap, her jeans around her knees, Ty holding on to her waist, he said, "I don't think we can put *that* on the invitations."

Imogen laughed. "Probably not. Let's stick with Will."

"I'm sticking with you."

That worked for her.